Henry opened the front door to examine the clearing around the cabin. "Quick!" he whispered. "Come look at this!"

It was a lynx, still as a statue, staring at the cabin with ears cocked, their tufts plainly visible in the morning light through the trees.

Jordan stepped up behind them and peered over their shoulders. "Been here before, always in the morning," he said. "Go ahead. Move and see if it runs."

Fowler waved his hand. The lynx didn't react. He took a step forward; still no motion. Henry chuckled and said, "Bold little bastard."

"Walk right up to it," Jordan encouraged.

"Not me," Fowler said. "It may claw our shins off."

"Either of you have the guts to go right on over?" Jordan asked. Henry glanced at Fowler. They grinned nervously, shaking their heads.

"Fine," Jordan said. He pushed between them and walked up to the cat. Fowler expected the animal to puff up, scowl and run. But still its gaze was fixed on the cabin.

"Touch him," Jordan said. "Not just Henry. You too, Larry."

Fowler put his hand beside Henry's on the cat's fur. He withdrew it suddenly.

"Goddamn thing's frozen," Henry said. "Stiff as a board."

"Minimum temperature last night, twenty-nine degrees Fahrenheit," Jordan said. "Couldn't freeze a wild animal, not when it's moving or holed away in its den. Animals have ways to stay warm."

Henry looked at his fingers and held his hand out to Fowler. The tips were covered with white.

"What is it?"

"Skin, I think," Henry said. "Cat just froze a layer to powder."

PSYCHLONE

GREG BEAR

A TOM DOHERTY ASSOCIATES BOOK

PSYCHLONE

Copyright © 1979 by Greg Bear

First TOR printing: July 1988

A TOR Book

Published by Tom Doherty Associates, Inc.
49 West 24 Street
New York, N.Y. 10010

Cover art by Greg Bear

ISBN: 0-812-53165-5
CAN. ED.: 0-512-53166-3

Printed in the United States of America

0 9 8 7 6 5 4 3 2 1

This book is for Barbara, Cathey and David.
On the literary side, of course, it's for
James Blish

8:16 a.m., August 6th, 1945

PROLOGUE

FINAL MESSAGE FROM THE U.S.S. *MATHESON*, RECEIVED 1630 hours May 24, 1964:

"Mayday, repeat, Mayday. Situation is getting worse. They are all over the decks now. Blue fire crawling over my radio and the ports. Jesus, Mary Mother of God, I can hear the captain and the mate. They are killing each other. The sickness is in me but I'm alone. All I see are the faces. Our position is West 183 degrees 14 minutes 23 seconds, North 35 degrees 14 minutes 20 seconds. The faces aren't all there. Not all there. The ones who tried to warn us—" (Interruption due to static.)

"The wind must be heeling the ship over. Mayday, Mayday. [Position repeated.] Everyone has gone mad. I can't stay at the key. God, God, God . . ."

From The Los Angeles *Times*, March 17, 1977:
PAPEETE, Tahiti (AP)—Police are investigating the death at sea of five members of an English family whose boat was found drifting erratically near Anaa island in the Tuamotu group, 240 miles east of Tahiti. The yacht *Enchanted*, rented from owners in Tahiti, was spotted by a

patrol boat, which towed it into port on March 15. Police report that Mr. and Mrs. Wayne Hamish and three of their children, names unknown, were found dead in the cabin, bound hand and foot with their throats cut. They had been severely beaten. One officer reported that the yacht was "covered with bloody handwriting."

The surviving children—the oldest is eighteen—were suffering from exposure and shock. Police indicate they are not suspects at this time, but no other suspects are being sought.

BOOK ONE

CHAPTER ONE

EVENING WAS COMING WITH AUTUMN LEISURE TO THE WHITE Mountains. Clouds hooked onto the distant peaks and fanned to the East in layered saucers. Their tops were gray-violet, but a single billow of white still rose above Earth's shadow. The air was cool, and gray shadows fell across the sinuous road. A light mist slipped between the trees and collided silently with the truck's windshield.

"You'll enjoy my dad," Henry Taggart said. "He's cut loose quite a few ties since Mom died."

"How do you mean?" Larry Fowler asked. His foot pressed hard against the bare floorboard as they banked into a curve.

"He's not crazy," Taggart said. He shot Fowler a worried glance. "I don't want you to get that impression."

"You mean he acts crazy?"

"No, his . . . philosophy is a bit strong for most people. He's been looking hard at death and making over his thoughts. Some of his talk gets pretty mystical."

Fowler nodded. He had known Henry Taggart for thirteen years, since high school. Taggart's father had always seemed a pragmatist. "He sold real estate, didn't he?"

5

"Best in his city for six years running," Taggart said. "I used to think that was a meaningless accomplishment. I respect him for it now."

"You've mellowed a lot."

"Me? How about yourself?"

"Both of us." They had been heavily involved in the counterculture of the late sixties, up and down the scales of drug experimentation, subdued political radicalism, acid-rock music. Fowler had been drafted in 1970 and had served in Vietnam. Taggart had escaped the draft by giving up his student exemption for a three-month period when no one was inducted. They had gone their own ways since, communicating three or four times a year, finding pleasure in each other's company, but never the strong ties that had united them in youth. Even now, however, they would react in the same way to a given stimulus, or think up the same joke or pun and say it simultaneously, as though there were an invisible link between them.

Taggart had gone on to business school after college and now managed a chain of bookstores in Los Angeles and San Diego. Fowler had followed up on electronics training in the Army and gone into computer design. That they had succeeded was evident by their dress. Taggart looked affluently woodsy—upper-class Sierra Club—in a fake-fur-collar mackinaw and twin-zipper European blue jeans. Fowler was wearing a rust leisure suit and a pair of Taggart's hiking boots, a spare set unused until now.

"The world has us by the nose, I think," Fowler said. "Oh, for the good old adolescent funk."

Taggart smiled and offered him a cigarette, which he declined. The truck's headlights suddenly shot out above a broad green valley and Taggart pulled over to a clearing by the highway. They got out and looked at the last of the daylight.

"Dad's cabin is on that low hill," Taggart said, pointing. Fowler saw a faint black speck in the general gray-green.

"No lights," he said.

"He should have them on soon," Taggart said. He sounded apprehensive.

"Where will the river be?"

"When the floodgates are opened next month, two little creeks will dribble around either side of the hill. The cabin's already been cleared by inspectors—no drainage or erosion problems. So he's planning to build a little log bridge to the road and stick it out."

Tiny lights came on far below.

"There. He burns every light in the cabin after dark."

"Lonely?"

"No," Taggart said. "You'll see."

Fifteen minutes later, the truck's oversized tires grumbled in the cabin's gravel driveway. Taggart shut off the engine and the headlights.

"Need help with the luggage?" he asked as Fowler hauled two suitcases and a cardboard box over the liftgate.

"Sure," he said. "The equipment is in the big metal one. I'll get these."

"What's in the box?"

Fowler grinned sheepishly. "I figured what with living in the woods and everything, your father wouldn't have this kind of stuff around."

"What kind of stuff?" Taggart asked. He pried open one corner of the box. "My God, it's full of Twinkies!"

"Not just Twinkies," Fowler said. "Marshmallows, candy bars, Cracker Jacks, you name it it's in there."

"I didn't know you were a junk-food freak."

"It hit me in Vietnam," Fowler said. "That was what I really missed about stateside." They carried the luggage to the front porch. The door opened before Henry knocked.

Jordan Taggart had aged a lot since Fowler last saw him. His nose was visibly hooked and his wrinkles had deepened into roadmap seams, showing all the directions his life had taken in sixty-eight years. Jordan looked them over carefully, squinting.

"Larry Fowler," he said, holding out his hand. His grip was still firm and dry. "Come in, come in. It's chilly this evening."

"So we noticed," Henry said. "It didn't take much talk to get Larry up here, Dad. Seems like he needed a vacation."

Fowler looked from father to son. They resembled each other more now than they had two years before. Henry would look more like Jordan the older he became, even to losing the same amount of hair in the same places.

"I've kept it neat," Jordan said, shutting the door behind them and waving an arm at the comfortable furnishings. "It's warm, has room for my books, and the weather is generally peaceful around here. Winters are mild."

"Larry seems willing to help us, Dad."

Jordan shook his head. "I hope you haven't told him what I said."

"No, sir."

"Better he hear it from my own mouth. Better to judge me crazy directly."

"Here's the equipment, as much as I could muster," Larry said. "And some things you didn't mention specifically."

"Microwave detectors? I read about those."

"Yes," Fowler said, "and electronic thermometers with a chart recorder. Cameras with infrared film."

"What do you think we're up to?" Jordan asked.

Fowler shrugged. "Henry says you've been thinking a lot about death recently. Philosophizing." He sat on the oak-frame couch and looked at the book shelves above the fireplace. "You're looking for ghosts, I'd say."

"Still whip-smart," Jordan said. "I remembered you as smart. But you're not exactly correct this time."

"No ghosts?"

"I'm not looking for anything in particular, Larry. You're in electronics now, aren't you?"

Fowler nodded.

"Borrow all this equipment from your company?"

"Yes."

"I'm not looking for something. I've already seen. Now I want to know what it is I've seen. You're well-versed in science, aren't you?"

"Not where ghosts are concerned."

"Not ghosts, I think," Jordan reiterated.

"I'm up on electronics and I read a lot of journals otherwise. I can hold my own."

"Got a bunch of *Scientific Americans* myself. Henry gave me a subscription three years ago."

Henry sat in a recliner near the fireplace and pushed the chair back until he sighed with comfort. "You've held dinner, I hope, Dad?"

Jordan nodded, his face brightening. "If you can put up with corned beef and steamed vegetables."

Fowler wasn't enthusiastic, but hungry enough to accept the prospect. Jordan left the living room and began rattling pots in the kitchen.

"Well?" Henry asked.

Fowler shrugged. "I'm open-minded. I don't think the equipment will do him any good. Other investigators have used similar stuff. What *is* he after?"

"I don't know," Henry said. "I've only stayed the night here twice. How open-minded are you?"

"Not a believer, if that's what you mean."

Jordan laid the food out on the dining-room table and brought out cans of beer. He preferred to eat in silence, apparently, and they did. The woods were preternaturally quiet, relieved only by the occasional sough of a dove. Henry finished his helping and slipped his fork onto the plate with a clink, leaning back.

"Larry's our man, Dad," he said. Jordan looked briefly at Fowler as he chewed.

"So he may be. I'm not the one, that's for sure. My brain doesn't have the cutting edge necessary for this."

Fowler examined the titles on the shelves behind him: *Cosmic Consciousness*, *The Vampire in Europe*, a three-volume set called *Materials Toward a History of Witchcraft*, scattered paperbacks with a sensational appearance and a long row of occult novels. He smiled. "Ghost stories bore me."

"Then we'll spare you campfire terrors tonight," Jordan said. "Gentlemen, I sleep and wake by the sun. I've held dinner only for you, and bad as it is for an old man to snooze on a full belly, I feel so inclined. You may sit up and talk if you wish. Good night."

When Jordan was in his bedroom with the door closed, Fowler leaned over the table and asked, "What in hell is going on?"

"Stay the night at least. You'll know as much as I do, which right now is nothing. He's not senile, Larry. I know him pretty well—we've gotten reacquainted in the last few years. He's just as skeptical as you and I."

"But these books—"

"I know, some are ridiculous. Not all, however. There's genuine scholarship on that shelf."

"Mixed with a healthy dose of bullshit. All this Frank Edwards crap, Jeane Dixon, strictly *National Perspirer* stuff. Are you two trying to set me up for a night in a haunted cabin?"

"The cabin is two years old. I doubt if anything larger than a skunk has died in its vicinity since it was built. It's not haunted."

"Ah, but it rests on an old Indian mound, and—"

"Pocahontas won't disturb your sleep, either."

"Then the ancient wolf-spirit?"

"I don't know about that one. Dad's only described a few incidents, and I haven't seen anything."

"Jesus, I'm an engineer, Henry! You should have called in Hans Holzer."

"You'll spend a night in the peaceful woods and breathe clean air for a while. If nothing happens, it's a vacation, right? Or is your mind completely closed after all?"

Fowler gave him a pained look and backed his chair away from the table. "I deal with reliable things, things I understand. Death isn't my cup of tea."

"What about Vietnam?"

"I never got into direct combat. I saw a couple of idiots blown up playing chicken with a fragmentation grenade. They didn't leave enough to suggest a ghost. That taught me what death was—final and unpleasant. A big cosmic accident, and no bookkeeper to keep track of us. Where's the box?"

"In the kitchen," Henry said. Fowler found it next to the refrigerator and dug out a cupcake. While he chewed on it, he opened the equipment case and began pulling out components.

"But I came up here, and I'll follow through. Sit down and I'll explain what all this is. If I remember rightly, following old horror movies, one or more of us will be incapacitated by dawn."

Henry shook his head. "Okay. Explain."

"This is the microwave detector. Just a little radio receiver, actually, hooked to a meter and also—through this cord—to the chart recorder. I'll set it beside the couch, next to the door. Two digital thermometers, one for inside and one for out, also hooked up. I didn't bother with a tape recorder. Now the camera is a regular camera, but it has an automatic film advance and I can adjust the focus and exposure by this little remote panel here. I built it myself—used to be a model-boat control box. There's

infrared film in it now, and some regular stuff in the case
if we need it. Okay?''

Henry nodded.

''Let's get everything in its place and the drama can
begin.''

After rigging the equipment and starting the roll of chart
paper moving on the machine, they sat up talking about
their work until eleven. The fresh air began to affect
Fowler. They unrolled sleeping bags, and Henry insisted
Fowler take the couch. As his head hit the pillow, he took
a last look around the room—noticed the kitchen and
porch lights were still on—and slept.

The old man was up and about with the first rays of
light. Fowler rolled over and tried to cover his ears, but
after a half-hour gave it up and sat in the bag, listening to
morning birds. ''Nothing happened,'' he said as Henry
opened his eyes.

''Quiet night, gentlemen?'' Jordan asked, bringing in
three cups of hot coffee on a tray.

''I feel like a fool,'' Fowler said sleepily. ''I was expecting a giant to step in and ask for Hungry Jack biscuits.
Now all I get is *to-wheet, to-whoo* and a fine cuppa.''

Henry dressed and opened the front door to examine the
clearing around the cabin. His gaze had swept through
about forty degrees before he stopped and tensed. ''Quick!''
he whispered. ''Come look at this!'' Fowler put down his
cup and joined him in the doorway. Henry's finger pointed
to an animal standing on the drive.

It was a lynx, still as a statue, staring at the cabin with
ears cocked, their tufts plainly visible in the morning light
through the trees. Henry turned his head slowly and smiled
at Fowler. ''Worth it just to come here and see that, isn't
it?'' he asked in an undertone.

Fowler nodded. ''It looks like it's jacklighted.''

''Oh, it'll take off if we move.''

Jordan stepped up behind them and peered over their shoulders. "Been here before, always in the morning," he said. "Go ahead. Move and see if it runs."

"What?" Henry asked, fascinated by the animal.

"Move. Try and scare it."

Fowler waved his hand. The lynx didn't react. He took a step forward; still no motion. Henry chuckled and said, "Bold little bastard."

"Walk right up to it," Jordan encouraged.

"Not me," Fowler said. "It may claw our shins off. Maybe it's rabid."

"Summer's the season for rabies, not winter," Jordan said. "It isn't rabid."

They both jumped up and down and waved their arms. The animal could have been stuffed for all the reaction it showed, but there was a sense of vitality in the tension of the legs and the glitter of its eyes that assured them it was alive.

"Either of you have the guts to go right on over?" Jordan asked. Henry glanced at Fowler. They grinned nervously, shaking their heads. "Dad, it *is* acting a little weird."

"Fine," Jordan said. He pushed between them and walked up the drive to the cat. Fowler expected the animal to puff up, scowl and run. But the elder Taggart stood beside it, and still its gaze was fixed on the cabin. "Come on out," he said. "First lesson."

They walked cautiously across the gravel. Henry bent down beside the animal. "Must be dead," he said. "Or paralyzed. Too sick to move."

"Touch him," Jordan said. "Not just Henry. You, too, Larry."

Fowler put his hand beside Henry's on the cat's fur. He withdrew it suddenly.

"Goddamn thing's frozen," Henry said. "Stiff as a board."

"Minimum temperature last night, twenty-nine degrees Fahrenheit," Jordan said. "At least, that's what your graph shows. Couldn't freeze a wild animal like this cat, not when it's moving or holed away in its den. Animals have ways to stay warm."

As they watched, frost started to form on the cat's fur. The eyes clouded over with rime. Henry looked at his fingers and held his hand out to Fowler. The tips were covered with white.

"What is it?" Fowler asked.

Henry rubbed his palm against the fingers. White flecks drifted down. "Skin, I think," he said. "Cat just froze a layer to powder."

CHAPTER TWO

KEVIN LAND WAS FORTY-SEVEN YEARS OLD AND HAD LIVED IN Lorobu, New Mexico, most of his life. Half of that time, he guessed, he had been drunk. He was aware how disgusting he was. His clothes were dirty, his face unshaven, his eyes waxy yellow: He spent most of his time indoors, in the cheap shack that Jim Townsend rented to him for twenty dollars a month. The rest of his money went for booze and the tiny amount of food he judged was necessary to keep him alive. He was sick most of the time with something or other. He was never sure what, but probably it had to do with his liver. He had nightmares of taking out his own liver and whipping it as it lay on the ripped easy chair. "Take that, you son of a bitch," he would shout melodramatically in the dreams. As a teenager he had read a book about Greek gods—he had read quite a few books as a kid—and now he looked upon himself as Prometheus, and booze was his eagle, eating his liver each day.

All because he had brought fire down to earth. He couldn't remember doing it, but he must have. It fit the story.

Kevin Land was in his shack when the wind started to

rise. It came from a clear, cold late-morning sky. He heard
it dimly and worried when it began to shake the shack.

"Life and death," he muttered, pulling the blanket up
over his head. "Matter of."

Jim Townsend was eating a lunch of turkey and dressing
left over from Thanksgiving, two days before. He was
carving the last of the bird and handing it around to his
wife and younger son. The meat was like gold. He was out
of work. Barrett's service station, where he had been a
mechanic for thirteen years, had closed down after John
Barrett died of a stroke. Barrett's son had sold the property
to another oil company and, preparatory to rebuilding the
office and garage and installing a whole new crew from
out of town, the oil company had fired Townsend. His
family's only income now was from the six pieces of
property they owned around town. It had always been
Townsend's wish to rent the properties to needy people at
bare minimum rates, as long as he was making a good
living and his family got along comfortably. Soon that
would have to change.

Lorobu serviced several mines operating in the area, and
every winter did a spotty business with tourists. But mining operations had been halted recently because of conser-
vationist lobbies in Washington and Sacramento, and the
local businesses reported sharply reduced tourist spending
for the past year. Lorobu was not in an up period, Townsend
knew, and the properties weren't going to rent for much
more than he was charging now.

It was a bleak prospect. He worried most when he
looked at his wife, Georgette, who was still bright and
perky and loyal after twenty-five years of marriage. His
younger son, Tim, was eleven and doing well in school.
The boy seemed interested in working with his hands—he
was a whiz at plastic model kits—but Townsend didn't
want him to follow in his father's footsteps. Tim was too

bright and capable to spend the rest of his life repairing cars. Their older son, Rick, had married a Mormon girl and moved to Salt Lake City. They seldom heard from him. That hurt Georgette, but she didn't blame the Mormons as much as Jim did. Their middle child, a girl, had been killed in a motorcycle accident two years before. Townsend knew she had been reckless. He had loved her most of all, but his memories of her seemed to stop at her twelfth birthday.

He cut the turkey leg and apportioned it between his plate and Tim's.

"It's blowing harder, Dad," Tim said. Townsend broke his reverie and looked out the window at the scrub lot next to their house. The dry weeds were rustling and the tree beside Norman Blake's workshed was twisting this way and that, like a dancer warming up.

Michael Barrett had just finished making love to his girl friend, twenty-year-old Cynthia Furness, who was a hellion in bed but sometimes a pain outside of it. She was a Jesus freak. Michael never could put the two sides of her together and had finally given up, telling her one night, philosophically, "I guess it's just like being hungry. When you're hungry, you eat, Jesus or no, and when you're horny you screw." Cynthia wouldn't be very pretty in ten or fifteen years—she was already a touch too plump—so he had no plans for marrying her. She probably thought he did. He probably should, they'd been getting it on together long enough. But Michael had been feeling very well off since his father had died, leaving thirty-five years of savings—over fifty thousand dollars. He was sure marriage didn't fit into his plans. He wanted to move to Los Angeles and get into real estate.

Cynthia lay on the other side of the bed, breathing hard, hair disarrayed, eyes closed and mouth open. Very sensual, Michael thought; he might screw her again if he had the strength. But for the moment he was dog-weary and contented. He put his arm around her and pulled her close.

She made an animal sound deep in her throat and snuggled closer to him. She was a funny girl. She thought his Right Guard smelled sexy. She liked the way he kept his hair fluffy-clean. And last Christmas, she had given him a white leather-bound Red Letter Edition King James Bible. She had plans for him. The rising wind made her feel very cozy, lying next to him. The house heater clicked on.

Norman Blake was Lorobu's sheriff. He was on the highway between Montoya and Lorobu when the wind came up. His car swerved and he brought it back in line, swearing, looking up through the windshield at the pristine sky. His radio crackled and went dead. His neck hairs stood up and he pulled the car to the side of the empty highway.

"What the fuck is going on?" he asked himself. He tried the radio several times, but it was gone. The wind and the radio at the same time. Blake wasn't much on meteorology, but he thought maybe it had something to do with the sun. Was that eleven-year cycle kicking up again?

He cautiously swung back onto the road, balancing his wheel against the wind, and continued on to Lorobu.

In the evening, the wind died and the temperature plummeted to forty-five degrees. Blake ate his dinner at the Lorobu Inn, maintaining his loyalty to the owner, even though the food was better at the new Holiday Inn on the east side of town. When he left the restaurant and walked to his car, his neck hairs tingled again and he scrunched his head closer to his shoulders, as if to avoid a blow. The town was dead quiet. He looked up at the still, starbright night sky and lowered his eyebrows, squinting to see something indefinite.

Then he shook his head, opened the car door, and got in. He sat at the wheel for several minutes, ostensibly to let his food digest before he put in his last few hours cruising the small business district. But something was on his mind.

He couldn't shake the picture from his head. Thirty-five years ago, when he was twenty-one years old, he had served in the Navy on the small island of Tinian in the Marianas. He was seeing Tinian now as he closed his eyes, and almost feeling the warm heat. What was so important about Tinian that it should come back to haunt him? He saw a pilot waving at him from the window of a bomber. That must have been before they sealed off the runway, because after that he couldn't have gotten within a thousand yards of any planes. He couldn't remember the pilot, but the face was very clear.

He backed the car out of the parking lot and drove slowly through what he affectionately called "downtown" Lorobu. It was six-thirty and everything was closed and locked, security lights on, streetlights okay, none shot out by the young hooligans who occasionally drove through. When Blake had been a kid, he had taken out his aggressions shooting at jackrabbits, not streetlights. But then, he hadn't had his first car until he was seventeen, just a year before he enlisted.

That was the year he had met Molly. Back then, she had been young and gangly, not very striking, but after coming home in '45 and getting married, she had filled out and become positively beautiful—"my own Miss America," he had called her. Such foresight, he thought, would have made him rich if he had applied it to stocks and bonds.

They'd moved to Lorobu in 1950 and he had worked in the sheriff's office ever since.

It had been a good job, a good life. It still was, although Molly had become more than pleasingly plump after hitting forty. She was no beauty now, but she had kept her sense of humor. That was more important anyway, he told himself. He was going on seventeen stone himself.

"Seventeen stone," he murmured, turning the corner onto Kelso street. "Damned Crabber is going to make a limey of me yet." Fenton Crabber owned the Alamogordo Bar and Grill, where Blake went on weekends for a couple of beers and a game of darts. Crabber had been in the RAF, and they liked to lie about their war records.

Barrett's service station, dark now, stood on the corner of Kelso and Gila Lane. He got out of his car at the curb and walked up to the office to peer inside, making sure no vandals had broken in. The window glass was okay everywhere. Even the pumps were intact. He wondered when the Standard Oil people were going to come in and claim their land. Damned shame, Barrett dying and leaving everything to Michael. Michael wasn't a bad boy, but he had big dreams, and Blake knew instinctively he wasn't smart enough to follow through. He would spend it all on women and dumb business schemes and come back to Lorobu someday, poor, maybe a rummy like Kevin Land.

As if in answer to the thought, he saw Land coming down Gila Lane, walking steadily and in a straight line. Blake took a last look at the station and strolled across the service lanes to see how Land was doing.

"Hey, Kevin!" he called. Land turned and goggled at Blake. "How's things?" Blake asked, approaching quickly, then slowing as he saw the expression on the man's face.

"Carrying the fire," Land said.

"What?"

Land pointed to his right hand, hidden in the pocket of his dirt-mottled jacket.

"Sure," Blake said. Land was drunk as usual. "Getting late, Kevin. You'd better get home soon." Blake was still trying to find out who sold Land liquor. There were only three liquor stores in town, and he knew all the owners personally. One of them was probably feeling obliged to do Land a favor and keep him stewed. When Blake found out who, he would read the riot act to him—or her, if it was Miss Louise—and maybe Land would have a chance to dry out.

Land turned stiffly and continued walking.

Blake's car radio crackled back to life as he was crossing Main on the last part of his route. Jason Franz, the senior deputy, told Blake there had been a complaint from Park's Hardware and Sundries.

"Had a hard time getting you," Franz said.

"Radio was on the blink. Must have been jolted back. What happened?" Park's store was at the end of his route.

"Clerk there—I think it was Beverly—says Kevin Land just walked in and tore up her paperback stand. She's leaving it alone for you to look at."

"Bloody hell," Blake said. "I just passed Land. I'll pick him up and go have a look."

"First time," Franz said, and signed off. Indeed, Blake thought. Land had never pulled a stunt like that before. He was a damned decent fellow for a drunk. Probably would have been a bright guy if the booze hadn't grabbed him.

The car spun around on the empty street and Blake backtracked, stopping near Barrett's station to remember which direction Land had gone off in. Down Gila Lane, not swerving, if he was truly drunk. To deviate would be disastrous. That was how some drunks thought. When they drove—those who did drive, the idiots—they would swerve a bit, and then, to compensate and show they weren't filled to the gills, they'd change lanes, sometimes right into another car. There had been a messy accident on 60 near Vaughn like that just yesterday.

The breeze was starting again, mild this time, when he spotted Land standing where Gila Lane ended at a road block and scrub country. He aimed the car headlights on the man's back and stopped twenty paces from him. Being cautious, even with old customers, was why he had never been wounded on duty. "Kevin," he said, stepping from

the car. Land turned and faced him, quick on his feet, not
even lurching.

"What's up, fellow?" Blake asked. "Feeling rough
tonight? Beverly at the Park store says you damaged some
merchandise."

"Justice," Land said thickly. "Life and death. Matter
of. Lieutenant William Skorvin. You saw him."

"What?" Blake asked, stopping.

Land took his right hand from his jacket pocket and
aimed it up at the sky.

"Jesus, Kevin, what did you do? Dip your hand in
phosphorus?"

Land shook his head. Blake stepped closer. His neck
hairs were at full rise this time, but he had to take Land in.
It was his job.

CHAPTER THREE

JORDAN TAGGART TOOK A ROLL OF CANVAS AND PICKED UP the frozen lynx carefully. "Hold this end," he told Fowler. Together they carried it to the woodpile behind the cabin and laid it gently against a log.

"Now watch," Jordan said, rolling back the tarp. The morning sun fell bright on the woodpile and the cat. Fowler and the Taggarts sat on the back porch of the cabin, saying nothing, keeping their eyes on the reclining animal.

The animal slumped. "There," Jordan said.

"It's thawing," Fowler said, a touch of irritation in his voice. That was believable enough—to freeze and thaw.

Then it stood up, all its fur on end, hissed, yowled, and ran into the trees.

Jordan smiled and shook his head. He stretched out his arms and said, "See? Not a crazy old man after all." He opened the porch door and entered the cabin.

Fowler was stunned. "That's impossible," he said.

"We saw it."

Henry walked around the back. Fowler stared at the woodpile for several minutes. Then he went to check the equipment set up the night before and see if there had been any change.

The chart recorder was working properly. Everything seemed normal, except for a small peak in microwave activity at about four in the morning. He decided to place the detector's extension just outside the front door.

After examining all the connections, he put a new roll of paper into the recorder and marked the time with a red felt pen. "All set for another day," he told Henry. Henry nodded.

"What do you think it was?" he asked.

"A frozen kitty," Larry said grimly.

"How did it stay alive?"

"Sperm do it. Goldfish. Freeze anything fast enough and it might live. Dump a baby into ice-cold water and he might not even drown. His face hits the water—zang! Down goes his breath rate, his heartbeat slows, he goes into suspended animation. His blood system drains circulation from the extremities and concentrates it in the head and chest cavities, where it counts. Drag him up in less than forty minutes and there's a good chance he'll survive."

"What froze it?"

Fowler shot Henry a dirty look and tapped the recorder. "Tell your father we're ready. Any time he thinks it's best to start the recorder—"

"Around sundown," Henry said. "That's when it usually begins."

"What happened the nights you stayed here?"

"I didn't see anything," Henry said. "But I heard something."

"What?"

"It sounded like a woman was being murdered right outside the living-room window. Nothing but screams and sounds—I don't know how to describe them."

"What kind of sounds?" Fowler prompted.

"Thunks. Knife-hits. Ripping sounds. I became sick and didn't hear any more. I was in the bathroom."

"Jesus. Both of you are nuts."

Henry smiled. "I won't doubt you."

"If it isn't a ghost, what is it?"

"Sure you're just not trying to humor us?"

"I'm a diehard skeptic."

"And the cat doesn't change that?"

"What in hell does a frozen cat have to do with supernatural phenomena? It's weird, but it doesn't make me a believer. Now answer my question."

Henry shrugged. "We posit no hypotheses. Newton said that about something—"

"Action at a distance, I think. So we wait and see?"

"I suppose seeing is the only way."

Jordan brought in brunch and they ate sparingly.

They played chess and read until nightfall.

Then, at a nod from the elder Taggart, Fowler crossed out his previous mark and put in a new one—*6:14:30 sec.*—and started the machine.

CHAPTER FOUR

FOWLER WAS DIPPING INTO THE FIRST VOLUME OF THE WITCH-craft set, skipping over the extensive Latin passages, when Jordan came out of the bedroom in his blue pajamas. Henry was asleep on the couch.

"Nothing yet?" Jordan asked. Fowler shook his head, no.

Jordan put his hands in his pajama pockets and looked up at the ceiling, his jaw clenched. "I've been feeling things," he said. "Haven't told Henry about them." He looked down at Fowler. "Don't know that I should tell you."

"What sort of things?" Fowler asked, more out of politeness than curiosity.

"I feel like an ant in a nest," Jordan said. "And this . . . whatever we're looking for . . . it's like another kind of bug. And . . . I don't know . . . there's a stick coming down, stirring everything up. Us, the other bug, just a big stick coming down. To stir everything up. A very big stick." He paused, still looking at Fowler. "Does that make any sense?"

"I don't know," Fowler said. "It might."

"Doesn't come every night," Jordan said, turning around and walking back to the bedroom. Fowler closed the book. He reached over to the recorder and made another mark, writing *9:45:24 sec.* on the moving graph paper.

At ten the fire had died down and the living room was getting cold. He put a blanket over Henry and checked the readings on the thermometers. The outside temperature was steady at forty-five degrees Fahrenheit. Inside the cabin it was sixty-three. No increase in the level of background microwave radiation.

A mosquito had gotten into the cabin somehow and was flying around in front of him. He swatted at it and sat down after selecting another book from the shelf.

The mosquito repeated its attack several minutes later. He tried to focus on it, reached out with an open palm, and closed his fingers, tightening them and gritting his teeth. "Got you, you bastard," he muttered. He brought his hand down and opened it. No sign of squashed insect.

At ten-thirty, Henry came awake and looked around, blurry-eyed, finally fixing on Fowler in the chair. "Anything?"

Fowler shook his head. "I'm getting lots of relaxation." He held up the paperback. "Ghost stories don't bother me any more. Used to scare the shit out of me when I was a kid. Guess I'm immune now." He unwrapped a bar of chocolate and took a bite.

"Overdosed," Henry offered. "Want some coffee?"

An hour later, Fowler was skimming through a Frank Edwards book, alternately shaking his head and laughing. "Must take lots of split crockery to make a living off books like these," he said. Henry turned away from the front window and let the curtain fall back.

"You believe in God?" he asked.

"Something far away and unconcerned with us, maybe. A personal God, I doubt it."

"My father says he believes in God, but that God

doesn't mess around in this universe much, like you say. Division of labor and all that. He read about demiurges.''

"So we should pray to the subcontractor."

"Something like that."

Fowler checked the microwave reading and saw it had risen slightly. "I should have asked you earlier—do you have any relay stations in the area—you know, TV or phone company towers?"

Henry shook his head. "I've never seen any."

"Well, there's a small increase in the microwave background. Could be the radar of a plane flying over, could be a relay station."

"Or . . . ?"

"Or maybe we're getting hotter. All warm objects radiate microwaves. Feeling toasty?"

"Not me," Henry said. "Dad doesn't even have a microwave oven."

After disposing of some coffee byproducts in the bathroom, Fowler opened the front door and looked out at the quiet, calm night. "Want to take a short walk?" he asked. Henry made sleepy noises. "Just out to the main road. I want to stretch my legs and clear the cobwebs."

"No, thank you," Henry said. "I wouldn't recommend it."

"Because of spooks?"

Henry smiled enigmatically. "Call it a hunch. Besides, someone might have opened the door to their microwave oven and be out there roasting porcupines."

"A weak attempt at humor," Fowler criticized pompously, "indicating fraying nerves and too much coffee."

"I'll watch from the window."

"And sing funeral dirges for me."

"If need be."

Fowler picked up his coat and closed the door behind him.

After walking around the cabin and stopping by the

woodpile, he took the gravel-covered path to the main road. Getting out of the smoke-stuffy interior cleared his head. With his hands in his jacket pockets, breathing the clean, cold air deep, he felt at peace, happy that humans could be silly sometimes—else why would he have come to the wild, rejuvenating woods?—and contented with his lot in life.

He looked back in the direction of the cabin and thought of what Henry had meant to him in the past, and how they enjoyed companionship now but seldom sought each other's company. For a moment he could imagine himself sixteen, seventeen, finishing high school, worrying about college, living with his parents. He shook his head and smiled. Living one life was like changing souls every decade, entering the realm of a new person. Henry had done the same thing, and now they were bound together only by memories. They'd have to forge new ties to feel the same way they'd felt as kids. Marriage, Fowler supposed, was similar, which might explain why he and Marissa had broken up.

He shivered and decided to return. The gravel crunched under his boots, the only sound in the stillness. Then, off in the trees, a bird he'd never heard before mourned softly. He stopped and smiled at the strangeness of the sound.

A bit of glow fell to the ground in front of him, twitching on the gravel. Bending over, he saw that it was a deerfly lit up like an ember, but frosty green instead of orange. He squatted, fascinated. Where had it come from? It was obviously dying.

The wings darkened and curled. The body shrank. Suddenly the glow vanished, leaving only a dark husk wafting back and forth on the gravel.

Then another fell. A constellation of mosquitoes seemed to materialize and fall around his feet. A moth two inches wide, red as a burning coal, swung about and dropped on his boot. He kicked reflexively and the insect fluttered onto the gravel. "Henry!" he shouted. Someone else had to see this.

His eyes began to sting. Looking at the drive, Fowler felt a shifting somewhere beyond his line of sight, a reorganization. The gravel took on new meaning. In the aimless mix of small rocks he found geometric patterns, then pictures—and finally forms that moved. He swayed, looking down at the grainy image of a wild boar. The moth glowed red again, providing a staring eye for the animal. The thing's head swung up, vague tusks connecting with his boot, and he felt a sudden spasm in one calf muscle. His legs wanted to pitch him down to the gravel. No, he thought, not just down but *through* it. All around him, insects fell from the sky in shimmering bead-curtains. "Henry!" he screamed. "Mr. Taggart!"

The cabin door opened. (But it was over the rise and out of sight. . . .) He was on one knee, supported by a hand on the gravel, and the gravel was pulsing, ready to suck him down. Henry ran toward him, arms outstretched. In one hand he carried a meat cleaver.

Fowler tried to stand but the half-seen boar lunged again and his other leg crumpled. He fell back on his butt. Beneath him the gravel parted, waving out like water in slow motion. Everything seemed to take an endless time. Henry stood by him, meat cleaver raised at the sky. There was something darker than the night hanging over them, a rainbow of hues beyond the black, like the mysteries on an exotic butterfly's wing. Henry sliced at the hypercolored rainbow. Cold air fell on Fowler in a shower of distinct but dry drops.

And then it was over. He was standing by the intersection of the drive and the road, sweating ice-cold under his arms, feeling his stomach and guts tied in knots. Perhaps for the first time, he screamed, then caught himself.

It was a dream. He'd fallen asleep standing up. That had to be it. Back to the cabin. Not running. Then, running.

CHAPTER FIVE

CYNTHIA FURNESS LOOKED AT HERSELF IN THE BATHROOM mirror and liked what she saw. Then she scowled and shut her eyes. All these impure thoughts. She was so pretty, though. And Michael wasn't around enough. So impure to think of pleasuring herself.

She put on her bra and stopped, turning off the bathroom light and the blower to listen for Michael making dinner in the kitchen. Then the dark became pleasant by itself. She reached down and touched her pubic hairs lightly. Less guilt not to see herself.

Michael had taught her how to do this, had done it for her the first time.

She closed her eyes and it was no different, just as dark, but she couldn't even see the crack of light under the door.

Then she jumped, almost screaming. Her eyes flew open. There was something with her in the bathroom. Her hand fumbled over the switch. She couldn't find it. But her fright was already subsiding.

She could see it in the mirror. Her breath slowed.

It was a long ways away.

"Sweet Jesus," she said. "Come for me. It's life in death."

In the kitchen, Michael was listening to the six o'clock news from Albuquerque, which was half over. He wanted to hear the sports scores. He didn't like the announcer much, but he put up with him for the list of teams and figures. He was thinking about buying a football franchise some day. Maybe he would become New Mexico's next sports tycoon.

The television set dimmed. Michael swore and dropped the tenderizing hammer on the steaks he was preparing. He tried to bring the set back to life, but it was gone. Then the kitchen light went out. He jumped and swore again. Through the window, he could see that every light in the neighborhood was off. "Goddamned road crews," he said. Then he wondered whether road crews would be working this late at night. Didn't the town have old emergency generators, from when they had made their own power? He waited in the dark for a minute, hoping everything would come back.

There was a footstep behind him. He turned and saw someone standing in the kitchen doorway—just the hip of someone actually, blocking out the Everlight digital display on the living-room clock, but leaving one number visible—6.

"Cynthia," he said, swallowing. "All the power's out." Goosebumps ran up his arms. "Don't creep up on me," he said. The 6 went out.

He stood still in the dark, bare feet on the kitchen floor, suddenly aware he was naked except for his BVDs. He started to raise his hands, to fend something off. One hand touched a breast. It *was* Cynthia. His breath whooshed out.

"Jesus, Michael," she sighed, coming into his arms, feeling for his crotch. "Again. I need it real bad."

"Shit," Michael said. "Can't cook anything now."

"Up against the kitchen table," she said. "Hard."

She'd never been like this before. She grabbed him tight and bit his shoulder as he entered her, grunting through her teeth. Her hand touched a carving knife and she opened her eyes.

Someone was watching them. A crowd.

"Stop squeezing so hard," she told him. "Michael. . . ." They came apart. She could see right through him, bones and everything. She rolled off the table and landed hard on the kitchen floor. The knife in her left hand rose.

CHAPTER SIX

OFFICER LAWRENCE PEREZ PRESTON—NICKNAMED "SERGEANT Preston of the Mexies"—entered the west end of Lorobu on Highway 54 at five minutes after twelve. The restaurant at the Lorobu Inn stayed open round the clock to catch the scant truckers' business, and he was looking forward to coffee and doughnuts fresher and warmer than the remains in Thermos and Baggie. He pulled off the road next to the inn and cut his lights, noticing for the first time that the town was completely dark.

He got out of the patrol car and walked up the steps to the restaurant door. At least the few regulars would be huddling around the candles inside, warming coffee over the gas stove and passing out Coleman lanterns for those going home. That was the way it had been six months ago when a flash flood had brought down the main power lines into the town.

Preston's beat was one-fourth of the state of New Mexico, covering US 54 from Carrizozo north to Vaughn, then taking US 60 to Encino, then branching back to 54 and patrolling north to Lorobu. After Lorobu he would retrace his route to Interstate 40 and take 84 to his home in Las

Vegas, New Mexico (not to be confused with——), and a
warm bed, where he would snuggle in his electric blanket,
or—if he was lucky—Lucy's arms, or Marguerita's.

It was lonely work, but he generally liked being alone.
He tried the screen door and then the glass door. Both
opened freely and a bell tinkled.

The restaurant interior was dark. No candles, no lanterns, and silence. "Evie?" he called. "Barney?"

He shined his flashlight along the counter and rows of
booths. Their red vinyl, barely held together by brass
studs, was the brightest color in the room. Along the
walls, paintings of coyotes and jackrabbits alternated with
standard pastel desert scenes, cards in the corners of the
frames announcing prices and the artist's address.

"Anybody here?"

The counters were clean. There were four pieces of pie
in the mirrored display case over the soda and coffee
machines. He could take a piece and lay down change . . .
but he shook his head and closed the glass door. The back
of his neck tightened and he flinched, then looked up.
Preston was not one to believe in a patrolman's ESP, but
something was spooking him, and he didn't like being
spooked. He crossed himself quickly and returned to the
car. Occasionally, on the whim of the owner, the Alamogordo Bar and Grill was open late. He backed the car
out of the lot and drove through the dark, empty street,
flashing his spot back and forth across the houses and
storefronts.

He was halfway through Lorobu, nearing the turnoff for
Crabber's bar, when he saw a light in the back of Park's
Hardware and Sundries. It was a weird sort of glow, not
like a candle or a Coleman, perhaps a fluorescent lantern
with a battery pack, or one of those chemical light tubes he
had seen in Albuquerque. He stopped the car and turned
on his rotating yellow and blue lights, in case some truck
driver came barreling through without noticing the town.

There was a tricky intersection just before the Holiday Inn. With all the lights out, someone could get hurt.

The door to the hardware store was open. The light had gone out or been moved, however, and now the store was dark. He waved the beam of his flashlight back and forth in slow arcs. Everything seemed to be in order. Then the light fell on the floor and he saw paperback books scattered all over. The wire display rack was resting across the yellow wood magazine stand, a few books still leaning in the wire bins. There were bits of paper scattered, but not a whole lot of them—as if one book had been picked out and torn to shreds. He retrieved a corner of a mangled cover. *"Hiro—"* he read. "By John—"

He kneeled and rummaged his hand through the piles of books, frowning, feeling he was missing something important. "Anybody here?" he asked.

He returned to the patrol car and proceeded down Main Street, lights flashing. He resorted to the loud-hailer but nobody came out. "Jesus God," he said under his breath as he approached the end of Lorobu. Then all the town's lights came on and he jerked in his seat, hand automatically reaching for his pistol.

"Now they'll show," he reassured himself, but he was still doubtful. He finished his drive to the edge of the town, slowing to read the notice on the Holiday Inn sign.

Relax! it said in bright-red plastic letters, like a theater marquee. *You've made it this far.*

CHAPTER SEVEN

PRESTON PULLED THE PATROL CAR OVER A MILE EAST OF Lorobu and lit a cigarette to calm his nerves. He hadn't felt that scared since Korea. It was like a drive-in movie. He had half-expected to see trucks filled with seed-pods drive by.

"Where is everybody?" he asked himself.

Every light in the town seemed to be on. It looked like stage lighting, a bit too bright for reality.

Perhaps all the townsfolk had gathered together in a meeting place—the church or an Elks' Club hall—until power was restored. Lorobu didn't have to worry about looters much. He nodded. They were all together.

All eight hundred of them? No; he hadn't looked into every house, just a few. It was just chance that the ones he saw were empty.

He threw the cigarette onto the roadway, half-smoked, looked at it guiltily for a moment—there was a Smoky-the-Bear sticker on his dash—and swung the car around. No matter how much he rationalized, it was hard to drive back into the town.

Nobody had come out with the lights. He cruised slowly

37

down the center of town, stopping at every intersection, hoping to see a face, someone he could question: What had happened to Lorobu? Logically, nothing had happened—the buildings were intact, no fire, no flood.

His shoulders itched again. He saw a streetsign on the corner ahead—Gila Lane—and looked between the rows of homes and the old warehouses which had once serviced trains. His foot hit the brakes and the car skidded to a stop. A sheriff's car was parked at the end of Gila Lane, lights so dim he could barely see them. He picked up his mike and pressed the button on the loud-hailer.

"Norm, you near your car? This is Perry Preston, Highway Patrol." There was no answer. He knew Blake would never leave the car with its lights on, not unless he planned to return quickly.

Preston turned onto Gila Lane and approached the end of the street. His spinning lights cut arcs of yellow and blue along the houses and old buildings. He stopped behind the car and shifted into neutral.

"Norman?" he called out. With his hand near his pistol, he opened the door and stepped out, automatically hunched to let the door protect him. It smelled like an ambush. At the very least, there was something unpleasant near.

Preston straightened and drew his gun. He walked toward Blake's car slowly, peering into the shadows behind the old warehouses, trying to outguess whoever—whatever—was waiting for him.

He stopped and his breath left him. Blake was lying a few yards in front of his car. Blood puddled under his middle.

"Norman!" Preston groaned. He knelt by the sheriff and noticed instinctively the man's holster was empty. Then he saw the revolver lying near the barricade at the end of the lane. He aimed his pistol in that direction. Something was slumped behind the road reflectors.

"Get up and walk over here, hands in the open," he said, voice quavering.

"Won't hear you at all," Blake said weakly.

Preston bent over and saw the sheriff's eyes flick open.

"His hand," Blake said.

"Hold still, Norm. I'm calling an ambulance."

"I been here a long time, don't have much blood or spit left. Listen, then call the ambulance. It was Land. He . . . his hand was burning, like a torch. He tried to touch my face and he got my gun with his other hand. Shot me in the stomach and leg, I think . . . three shots. But I turned the gun on him and damn near blew his head off. He flew back over the posts. I been lying here, listening."

Everything was silent except for Blake's voice.

"What you listening for?" Preston asked.

"It's gone now. It was here. People screaming. A tornado. Bunch of damned . . ." His throat crackled and he tried to wet his lips and tongue. "Souls. Not God. On Tinian . . . some guy I didn't know. Couldn't help himself."

"Don't say anything, Norm. I'm getting an ambulance."

"From where?" Blake rasped, his voice echoing. "Perry, you stupid Mex, everybody's dead. Clinic's dead. Everybody. I heard them."

Preston returned to his car and called for emergency vehicles. "Get the State Police out here. Sheriff is down, I don't see anything moving in this fucking town. I don't want to be here alone!"

He took out a first-aid kit from its attachment under the dash and squatted by Blake again, shaking his head, trying to figure out what to do first. Nothing. Blake was hurt bad, in the gut. There was so much blood all around him. Then he saw that Blake's chest was motionless.

He tried to administer CPR, but when his palms pressed the lower sternum, blood welled out of the holes in Blake's shirt. There was nothing he could do. The sheriff was dead. Preston wiped his eyes clear and sobbed, standing

up. He lurched over to the barricade and looked down on
Kevin Land, avoiding the head, which was half gone.

Blake had mentioned the man's hand. It was dark behind the barricade, but he could see the arm and hand
clearly enough. The fingers were gone and the palm was a
charred stump.

"Dad*dyyy!*"

He twisted around and looked up Gila Lane. A boy was
walking down Main.

"Hold it, son!" Preston shouted. He ran toward the
boy, who had stopped in the middle of the street.

"Have you seen my dad?" the boy asked as Preston
came near him, out of breath.

"Where are your folks, son?"

The boy was crying. "I don't know."

Then Preston saw that the boy's hands were covered
with blood.

"What's your name?"

"Where's my *father*?"

"Your name—I have to know your name to find him."

"Everybody's gone, mister." The boy trembled.

"You from this town? Lorobu?"

"I'm Tim," the boy said. "Tim Townsend."

"I know your dad, Tim. I've been in his garage. What's
happened to you?"

"I want to find them."

"Sure." He heard a rumbling noise and looked up, eyes
widening. Four headlamps bore down on them, air brakes
screaming. He grabbed the boy and ran out of the way.
The semi was jackknifing on the road. Its rear wheels
jumped the curb and two tires blew, lurching the trailer
over until it threatened to topple. But it leaned, steadied,
and fell back with a thump.

"God damn, right in the middle of the road!" the driver
shouted from the cab. "What in God's name were you two
doing?" He leaped from the cab and rounded the truck to

confront them. Then he saw Preston's uniform. The driver looked around, nostrils flaring, his paunch rising and falling under a half-tucked-in T-shirt. "What kind of asshole carnival is going on around here?" He looked at the boy's bloody arms and his paunch froze. Then he backed away.

"Something's wrong here," he said.

"Stay and help us," Preston said. "I've got the State Police coming in."

"Something's *very* wrong."

"Stay here and help! We need somebody else!"

But the trucker was in his cab, revving the diesel and pouring black smoke over the road. He pulled the trailer around and the truck roared west, rear duals flopping and smoking.

"Help me!" Preston shouted.

They stood by the side of the road, Preston clutching the boy's bloody fist. "Shit," he said.

CHAPTER EIGHT

"ONE FROZEN CAT AND A NIGHTMARE," FOWLER SAID, STANDING by the truck. "Sum total."

"Sorry," Henry said, helping him heave the last of the equipment into the rear. They brought up the tailgate and lowered the rear window.

"No, that's quite all right. The nightmare was enough for me."

"If."

"If what?"

Henry smiled and shook his head. "Go back and tend your machines. I'm staying with Dad for a few more days."

"You mean, I take the truck? How will you get back?"

"Drop it off in town and pick up your car. I'll have Sam Cooper drive the truck up here loaded with groceries and take him back myself. I've got to make some arrangements in town, but I don't want to leave now. In a few days. We'll be fine."

"Your dad wasn't too impressed."

"Well, shit, Larry, you practically had a nervous breakdown, but you won't admit there's anything funny going on up here.''

''The cat almost qualifies.''

''But you can explain it?''

''I don't want to try,'' Fowler said. ''You don't need me up here. You need . . . I don't know who. I'm an engineer. I deal with repeatable phenomena. Anything else and I'm way out of my depth.''

''The microwaves jumped when you were outside having your dream. That's your equipment; the needle registered a whopping increase.''

''Other things could cause that.''

''Other what sort of things?''

''Henry, I'm not even personally qualified. This sort of thing disturbs me in a way I don't need right now. My real world is shaky enough without having my metaphysics challenged.''

''Sounds like a copout to me,'' Henry said.

Fowler took a deep breath. ''Judge me that way if you want. Maybe I am a coward—''

''I didn't say you were. Well, not a physical coward, anyway. But you're leaving us to face something just as real as any problems you have back home. Just because we can't define it clearly doesn't mean it isn't real.''

''Even if this is more than dreams and flukes, I'm not the one. I just don't qualify.''

''You're leaving your junk food behind?''

''Fortify yourself if you need it. I'd even leave the equipment here, but I'm responsible for it. I'll send you the names of a few rental places if you still want to follow up. Myself, I think we drew a blank.''

''Larry—''

''And please don't try to convince me otherwise. I feel pretty rotten right now as it is. Let me think it over.''

''We won't be giving up. Hell, we can't. Dad has most of his money sunk into this property and he doesn't feel like selling—wouldn't feel right selling to someone who didn't know. If you do change your mind, or just want to come up and see the cabin again—"

Fowler raised one eyebrow doubtfully.

"—or whatever, Dad and I want you to have a key. Come right in, whether we're here or not."

Fowler opened the front door and threw his coat onto the seat. "I do thank you for inviting me. I've needed the fresh air for a long time. No hard feelings one way or the other?"

Henry shook his head.

"I'll try to find out if any planes went over last night, or if there are TV towers in the area. If not, maybe you have something. But get somebody who knows his business to come in and check it out, okay?"

"Sure," Henry said. "Good-bye, Larry."

"Come down to LA sometime, I'll show you the town."

"I was born there," Henry said. "I'll show *you* the town."

"Fair enough." They looked at each other for a moment, then shook hands. "Take care," Fowler said. He backed the truck down the gravel road, wincing at the sound the tires made, then honked before edging out on the asphalt. He honked again and waved, but Henry was beyond the crest of the hill.

He felt like a complete bastard.

CHAPTER NINE

THE CLEAN WHITE LIGHTS OF THE DRAFTING ROOMS, THE SMELL of paper and developer and toner and blueprint machines, the hot dusty smell of the electronic equipment—Fowler was back in his sea, and glad to be there. His vacation had ended the day before, giving him four days to sort things out after returning from the mountains.

He greeted the chief engineer and a secretary cheerily before entering his office. The hotplate and glass coffee pot waited, pleasantly clean and uncommitted, and he laid a box of doughnuts down beside them. His day always began in an orderly fashion—coffee and two doughnuts, an hour looking over the designs and revisions on his board, fifteen minutes catching up on office memos, and then two hours of work before breaking for lunch.

Fowler had always found work cathartic. Whatever problems he might have on the outside, he could drop them at the employee gate and come to work clean, ready to concentrate. That had saved him many times from long days of waiting (for his wife to call, her attorney to call, the kids to call or all three) and involvement. Involvement had never been his strong point. Best to put up appearances and hide behind them

Now that he had no wife, and effectively had no kids, he was saved from waiting for them *not* to call. It was an interesting distinction. And he had warned Dorothy several times that calling him at work was forbidden. Dorothy took him at his word.

He rigged the coffee pot and opened the box of doughnuts to see what he had picked up at the Winchell's. As he ate a cream-filled orange glaze, he leafed through the stack of mail on his desk.

"Larry, development needs the designs for those new demonstrator peripherals toot sweet. The salesmen are screaming for them. How soon?"

He looked up from the letters and blinked at Regis Hinkel, the vice president of marketing. "Albert tells me they're being held up because the computer fouled up on the feedthroughs. We won't get them here for another day or two."

"Christ. We have to get on the stick or we're going to drop next month's promotion. Castle hates to drop."

"I'm on it, Regis," Fowler said, looking down at the spike-full of notes next to the fluorescent lamp base. "We *do* have these ready." He referred to a roll of designs leaning against a file cabinet. "Development wanted these two weeks ago. Why haven't they picked them up?"

"Beats me. I'll tell them."

"Oh—Candice didn't bring this morning's paper. Could you remind her?"

"Certainly. Have you heard?"

"I doubt it. I've been away. Heard what?"

"Looks like we won't have to service one of our accounts."

"Why?"

"New Mexico," Hinkel said. "Whole town's gone.

Somebody in the FBI just decided to pull the cover off. Happened less than a week ago. We had a few sales to businesses there.''

''Which town is that?''

''Laramie or Malaru. Something like that.''

''You're kidding.''

''Scout's honor.''

''Disappeared?''

''I'll get the paper. Hold on.''

He returned several minutes later with the front-page section and spread it on Fowler's desk.

The headlines read:

NEW MEXICO TOWN WIPED OUT

Lorobu, Population 813, Ghost Town Overnight

ALBUQUERQUE, New Mexico (UPI)—FBI Director Douglas Davis announced today that eight hundred and thirteen people were murdered in Lorobu, apparently on the night of November 26th, by unknown assailants. The bodies were discovered by a New Mexico Highway Patrolman, whose name has not been released, and by members of the New Mexico State Police. Neither of these agencies has released any information on the calamity. Director Davis called a special news conference late Monday evening.

There are three survivors: Cynthia Furness, 24, a postal clerk; Beverly Winegrade, 19, employed in a local hardware store; and Timothy Townsend, 11. Reporters were not allowed to question the survivors, who are being kept under close guard at Pasteur Community Hospital in Albuquerque. Although no one connected with the case has given details, Times reporter Austin Heiser flew over the town in a light plane two days before the FBI announcement. He reported that, "Lorobu was completely deserted. I saw no sign of life whatsoever. I didn't see any bodies." Heiser was researching another story in the area at the time.

Fowler turned to the third page to read Davis's statement. He scanned the page, then glanced at the second page and caught a name in one of the News Brief articles.

"Isn't that incredible?" Hinkel said. "Really nuts."

"Oh, my God," Fowler said, sucking in his breath.

"What?"

The name that had caught his eye was Henry Taggart. The article was short and terse. Jordan Taggart had murdered his son with a butcher knife and then committed suicide by hanging himself from a tree limb. The bodies had been discovered by Sam Cooper, a delivery man.

Fowler leaned back in his chair and let the paper slip to his lap. One section fell on the floor.

"Hey, what's the matter?"

"I don't know," Fowler said.

"You look like hell. Should I get you a cup of coffee?"

"Everybody's dead," he said slowly.

"Yeah, it's awful—did you know someone there?"

"No."

"You look like you lost—"

"Another story. A friend, two friends, murdered."

"Jesus H. Christ," Hinkel said.

"I was with them five days ago."

"Can I read it?"

"No," Fowler said irrationally, folding the paper and standing up. "It isn't true, what they say here. It couldn't have happened that way."

He left the office. Hinkel stood by the desk, flipping the paper between his fingers, frowning.

Fowler didn't know where he was going. He was out in the overcast but still shirtsleeve Sunset Boulevard weather, on the corner of Highland, before he realized he was wandering. He needed a plan, some way to get through the day. He found a pay phone booth and stood in it for several minutes before deciding to call Dorothy. Her number was usually quick to mind, but for the life of him he couldn't think of it now. He fumbled through his wallet, then searched the mangled and scribbled-on phone directory. There were four Dorothy McKinleys, but he remembered her address.

The phone rang six times before she answered, sounding peeved.

"Dot, this is Larry."

"I was in the bathtub."

"Henry is dead."

"Henry who? Your friend Henry?"

"Henry and his dad, his father. It's in the paper."

"I don't take the paper. You just saw him. How did it happen?"

"Paper says his father killed him and then killed himself."

"Oh, Larry, that's *awful* . . ."

"It couldn't have happened that way. I've got to find out what happened."

"Are you at work?"

"No," Fowler said. "I'm in a phone booth, corner of . . . Sunset and some other street, can't see it."

"Did you tell anybody at work you were leaving? It's still the morning—"

"No," he said.

"Listen, Larry, I know you're upset—"

"Shit, Dot, I'm scared! It couldn't have happened the way the paper said. I don't know how it could have happened, except there was something peculiar going on."

"What?"

"I don't know. I can't tell you over the phone." He heard a doorbell on her end.

"Larry, there's someone at the door. I've got to get a robe on and answer it. First you tell the people at work that you've had bad news, have to have a day off. Okay?"

"Yes."

"Then you come over here and tell me about it."

"Of course."

"See you soon. Drive careful."

She hung up and he waited on the phone, too numb to put it back on the cradle. Then he shook his head and left the phone booth, looking this way and that to see which lot he'd parked his car in. The company had reserved spaces in two lots.

He wouldn't tell the people at work. He would come back in the afternoon and explain he had had some crucial business to take care of. Right now he couldn't think straight, and he didn't want to make a scene in the office.

He was standing by his car and could hardly remember walking there. His hand drew the keys from his pocket, coming first on the key to the cabin. He moved it aside and took the door key between his fingers.

He had often wondered how he would feel when someone close to him died. Now it was here and he knew. For a moment it seemed ridiculous that he should believe a simple newspaper account. He hadn't *seen* the Taggarts dead. But he was confident in his sources of information. The chain of reporting in a case like this was too tight. They were dead. Father had killed son. That was it.

That was not it. Death was theoretical, or had been. None of Fowler's close relatives had died, only distant cousins and great-uncles he had never met. He had grown up, gotten married and had two children without having to face the issue. And Vietnam didn't count—none of his buddies had died. He opened the door and climbed into the Datsun 280Z. The motor started with an irritated cough. He closed his eyes before backing out.

And saw the burning moth, the gravel boar, the jabbing, indistinct tusks.

Dorothy lived in a bungalow off Coldwater Canyon Road. He drove into a narrow, tree-hung passage leading to the twin garages at the rear of the Greene and Greene home. She met him on the back porch, a tumbler of Scotch in one hand, and her glass of Martini and Rossi in the other. She was wearing a shift with curved stems and stylized flowers flanking the side seams. Her hair was tied up in a bun and she looked upper-middle domestic.

"No dings?" she asked.

"Z is clean," he said. She walked ahead of him through the service porch into the kitchen dining area. She had spread a lunch of fruit and cheese, with a concession of sliced cotto salami for his carnivorous appetite.

"Who was at the door?" he asked.

"My other lover. No—sorry. Wrong moment for that kind of crap. It was Tommy, the gardener."

Fowler nodded. He liked Tom DeCleese. DeCleese had been doing work for the McKinleys ever since Dorothy's father had been a boy. Now her father was dead, her mother was living in New York—"suffering from terminal bitchiness," Dorothy had once said in a charitable mood. DeCleese still charged the rates he had charged in 1960.

"Tell me about it," she said.

Death and dying. He had been so bored by Kubler-Ross. So far removed from reality.

"I don't know where to begin."

"When you came back you were tight as a clam. Something had to have happened. I've been curious, and now you should tell me."

As he sipped at his Scotch, he told her about the trip to the cabin and everything up to the frozen lynx. She nodded at the right points and offered to refill his glass. He declined.

"And you're frightened now," she said.

"Goddamnit, Dot," he burst out. "I'm—"

"Sorry, sorry. I'm not very good at this sort of thing. I don't believe in death very much, or won't until Mom dies, perhaps. Father's death was *de rigueur*. I mean, he admired John Barrymore so much, how could he go any other way?"

"And when it's time for you?"

"Punch my ticket and move to the back of the bus, which is cryptic Dot language for I don't know. You're sure Taggart wasn't going off the deep end—sorry—sure he wasn't crazy before you arrived? He was—ah—exhibiting novelistic behavior with all the talk about ghosts or whatever."

"He never said it was a ghost."

"What 'it'?"

"Dot, this is off the issue. I don't know anything about what happened except what was in the paper. I'm sure that isn't the complete story. I have to find out more."

"Then call Bishop, or Lone Pine—whatever the town was."

"Bishop."

"Call the police there. The coroner. Find out."

He shook his head. "How would they know?"

"Larry, they investigated."

"I have to do better than that."

Dorothy leaned back and shook her head. "I've only seen you with that expression once before. You had to find out what school she was sending the kids to.'' They never mentioned his wife's name unless it was absolutely necessary. ''That was a real fiasco.''

''It was my duty as a father. I didn't like doing it.''

''You got in trouble for doing it. Every six months you can see them for a while, right?''

''I had to.''

''So now,'' she pursued, ''this is your duty as a friend?''

''As a coward,'' he said. ''I don't believe Jordan Taggart was nuts. It isn't possible.''

''What's the alternative?''

He wasn't willing to face that, either. For a moment he was more willing to accept Taggart's insanity than the alternative. ''For crying out loud,'' he said. ''I don't know. I have to find out.''

''Larry, your vacation is up. You can't go back now.''

''I can arrange for another week's sick leave. Say it's an emergency.'' He suddenly felt queasy. The thought of losing the office and his work was unnerving. His work—and Dorothy—were all he had going for him now. ''I can't keep thinking of myself as a coward.''

''There was really something up there?'' she asked.

''No. I don't think so.''

''Then what will you find? The same thing the police could tell you here, on the phone. Call. Don't be silly about this—''

''I'm not being silly,'' he said ominously.

''Okay, okay,'' Dorothy said. ''But you're upsetting me now. I've always thought you were stable, maybe a little too stable, but reliable. Someone who wouldn't do strange things. God knows I've—we've had enough of that sort of person.''

''You think I'm acting unstable?''

''I make no accusations,'' she said. ''Only suggestions.''

''I backed down out there. Maybe there was something there. Whatever, I backed away from it.''

"We're both immune to spirits and spooks, aren't we?" she said. It was their private joke, in reference to their avowed, deep-seated agnosticism. "Matter is all."

"I have to go back."

"So be it, then. But make sure everything is set here, first."

"I will." His armpits were damp. She was right.

The thought of going back was terrifying.

CHAPTER TEN

Timothy Townsend turned twelve on December second. He put together a spaceship model kit given to him by the hospital staff, and looked out the window at the hospital parking lot, the church across the street and the airplanes leaving the airport.

There was still blood on his hands, but only he could see it. He had learned that the doctors didn't want him to see it, so he didn't. It was better not to talk about certain things.

He had been allowed to see Cynthia Furness in her room, once. It had been bad. She was still unconscious, and her hand was in bandages, but he could see it glowing through the dressings. He had screamed and they had taken him back to his room. In her sleep, Cynthia had moaned and turned her head a little.

So he didn't tell them about that any more. He didn't like the hospital, but his future was even more bleak. Rick, his brother, was going to pick him up in a few

weeks and take him to Salt Lake City to live. Tim didn't
like Rick very much. They used to get along fine, but now
Rick was different. He had changed since being married.
His hair was short, he wore funny clothes, and he talked to
Tim in a funny way. But the only choice was to go to
Rick's house or stay in the hospital. Neither prospect
sounded good.

Tim knew he had problems to solve—personal problems. His nightmares were bad. Sometimes he would dream
he was back in the house when everything happened.
Other times he would dream his mother and father and
somebody else were coming to visit him. They were very
unhappy. The third person was a man in a uniform. Tim
was pretty good at recognizing uniforms, but this fellow's
was a puzzle.

It was better not to think much at all. So he put together
the spaceship model, careful that no glue slopped over—
only little kids slopped glue, and it was time to grow
up—and glad that they had finally let him use enamels and
thinner. For a while he had used a plastic paint that a nurse
had brought in. She was an artist as well as a nurse and
she said that paint was called "acrylic" and wouldn't hurt
him, wouldn't catch on fire or anything. But it scraped off
with just fingernails. The enamel was better. Permanent.

When he was done with it, the nurse put a tack in the
ceiling and hung it from a thread. The doctor who talked
to him that afternoon congratulated him. "It's a good
job," he said. His name was Jason, a neat name, and he
was black-haired and dark-skinned, a Mex probably, but
he was okay. Sometimes Tim's father complained—had
complained—about Mexes, but he had once called Juan
Oliveros the best mechanic in Lorobu, and Juan was—had
been—a Mex.

He hadn't told them that he wanted to see if the enamel
thinner took the blood off his hands. He tried and it didn't.

Tim ate dinner, feigning an appetite, and the orderly

who picked up his tray said, "You'll be out of here real soon. Cynthia and Beverly are coming along fine, too."

But he was lying. Cynthia was still in a coma. Another doctor had said that in the hall when Tim had gone to the bathroom. Cynthia was sleeping and she didn't even need to. Her hand was doing fine, though. She didn't have any fingers left, he could tell that because of the shape of the bandage, but it wasn't going to kill her.

Tim wondered if Michael Barrett came to visit her, and if the fellow in the funny uniform was with him.

He wrote a name down on the cardboard model box, using the citrus-smelling glue tube. The glue made the name shiny and transparent, just like his night visitors. Dream visitors, he corrected himself. He was asleep—must have been asleep—when he saw them. The name was *Corporal S.K. Percher*.

CHAPTER ELEVEN

THE FIRST SNOW OF WINTER FORCED LARRY FOWLER TO SPEND the night in Lone Pine. He bought a local newspaper looking for more details on the killings, but the story had blown over quickly. Father-son murder-suicides were odd, but not odd enough to excite comment.

Most of the news stories concerned Lorobu. There were conjectures about "killer" satellites, hidden caches of nerve gas, germ warfare and even UFO attacks. Several religious groups used the story to further their own ends. One evangelist in North Carolina announced that Lorobu was merely the beginning of God's wrath, brought down on the United States because of loosening laws against homosexuals.

Fowler paid no attention. For the moment he simply wasn't interested. His heart was like a shriveled walnut. He watched the drifting flakes of snow through the venetian blinds in the motel room. Something occurred to him and he picked up the paper to re-read a notice he had barely glanced at before.

The dam Henry had mentioned would be diverting water soon—December tenth, weather permitting. The forecast was for weather warm enough not to freeze the water in the spillways. The cabin would be surrounded by two streams soon.

He had less than a week. It wasn't much time.

He spent the night polishing and testing the equipment. In the morning, he loaded it back into the Z, bought chains at an exorbitant price from a garage near the motel, and headed north on US 395.

By early afternoon the storm was too thick and he had to stay over in Independence. While there, he made a phone call to Bishop but hung up before it was completed. It would be no good trying to convince the sheriff's department or State Police that his cause was noble. Better to just hope the roads were clear and make it to the cabin before a big snow closed everything.

The next morning was sunny and warm and his fears abated with the melting snow. He drove into Bishop at eleven and filled his car with gas, asking for directions to the local library. Then he stopped for lunch at Jack's Barbecue, keeping his eye on the fluffy clouds whisking over the town.

He spent an hour in the library, reading week-old newspaper accounts and thumbing through the occult shelves briefly. There was nothing there to help him, he was certain; the two experiences he had had at the cabin didn't seem to fit standard categories.

"This is crazy," he muttered as he climbed back into the Z, clutching three Xeroxes of short news stories. There wasn't much more to learn about the killings, apparently—murder-suicide clear and simple.

The car had been giving him some trouble going up the long grades, overheating twice between Independence and Bishop. In Bishop everything showed normal, and in the service station there was no sign of coolant spillage. The Z was almost new—he had only put five thousand miles on it—so he decided there was something wrong with the temperature gauge.

Just to be sure, he double-checked the hoses and radiator in another garage before leaving Bishop and heading into the White Mountains.

The roadsides were dotted with patches of melting snow. He had to watch for game on the highway—deer mostly, but once a lynx.

It was four-thirty when he reached the rest stop above the valley. He pulled out and stood by the guard rails, his hair blowing in the rising cold wind.

Fifteen minutes later he turned onto the drive and heard the unpleasant grind of the gravel beneath his tires. He turned off the ignition and sat in the car, looking at the cabin, suddenly uncertain.

If the cabin was sealed for evidence, he would have to break in. That was illegal. On the other hand, if the case had already been decided and no further evidence was necessary, why would they seal it? The state would probably seal it, he told himself, until the will was put through probate, if there were any heirs. Fowler didn't relish the idea of breaking the law. Still, he had come this far, knowing (at least subconsciously) what he would face when he arrived. The only alternative was to turn around and go home, feeling foolish and carrying a guilty little hairball around for the rest of his life. He tapped the steering wheel, then pounded it and swore.

The equipment was in two aluminum camera cases. He swung them out of the back and put one under each arm, then reached into the car and pulled out his suitcase. Waddling slightly, he approached the front porch. Night was coming fast and the cold bit through his windbreaker.

A latch had been screwed onto the door and frame, and a steel cable with a lock and a tag hung from the latch eye. He put the cases down and read the tag, then tugged on the cable. Sealed by the State of California.

He returned to the car to get a pack of tools and spent the next ten minutes removing the latch. This far out in the country, such a seal was bound to be ineffective. He made sure he didn't damage the fitting, so he could re-seal the cabin after he left.

"Optimistic, aren't you?" he said grimly. The key slid into the lock and he pushed the suitcase and equipment across the threshhold with a foot while reaching for the light switch. "Open for business," he said aloud, closing the door behind him, "with advertising." Anyone who was curious would see the lights in the cabin, just as he had seen them a week and a half ago.

It was a chance he'd have to take.

Next, to get it out of his mind, he searched for the bloodstains. There'd been no description of where the killing had taken place. If it had been in the cabin, he wanted to know about it and, if possible, avoid the area completely. The police usually cleaned up after shooting photographs and collecting evidence—didn't they? He had never read much about such things.

There were no bloodstains in any of the rooms. The killings must have taken place outside.

He pulled the shades on the living-room windows—no sense in being blatant—and took a few sticks of wood from the hopper to stock the fireplace.

There was nothing to do now but wait. He hummed an ominous "do-*dooo*" as he started the fire, then shook his head. No sense trying to cut the gloom. Be grateful for small favors. The larder was full, the cabin looked like Jordan had just left for a walk, and it hadn't snowed enough to block the roads.

He wondered if he should try to call out. He tested the phone and it hadn't been shut off yet. It was a cinch the phone company didn't expect any outgoing calls from the cabin. He wanted to tell Dorothy he had made it safely.

But that would take courage. Suddenly he wanted to be very cautious about advertising his presence in the cabin—to anyone.

CHAPTER TWELVE

TIM TOWNSEND WOKE UP FROM A PLEASANT DREAM ABOUT fishing with his parents at Tahoe—pleasant, but peculiar, because the man in the odd uniform was in the boat with them. He listened for a moment, trying to decide what had awakened him.

He shut his eyes. Then he sat up as someone ran by his door. There were voices outside—nurses and orderlies, whispering anxiously. Something was going on.

He climbed out of bed and bumped his shin on the night table. The room was still unfamiliar. Following the gleam of the door crack, he walked across the cold tile and stood by the door, leaning forward to catch any outside noises.

"She's not in her room," a man said. "Nancy checked there a half-hour ago and everything was fine."

Tim turned the doorknob slowly and peered through. Two nurses walked past quickly, one with a green sweater thrown over her whites. An intern followed shortly thereafter, then a security guard. Tim opened the door farther and stepped into the corridor.

"Hey kid!"

He spun around and saw another nurse, a man, at the end of the hall. He started to go back into his room.

"Hey! Hold it! Kid, did you see a woman go past here in a nightgown?" The nurse approached Tim with a clipboard in one hand. He looked at the board and frowned. "Say, you're Tim Townsend, aren't you?"

Tim nodded.

"It was Beverly Winegrade, Tim. Remember her?"

"Yes."

"Did you see her?"

"No. What's going on?"

"She's not in her room. She was supposed to be sedated."

"Maybe she's sleepwalking," Tim suggested. The nurse shrugged and patted his shoulder.

"Back to bed," he ordered. "We'll find her."

Tim turned to the dark room and wondered how he'd made it across a few moments earlier. Even with the door wide open, there were shadowy areas he didn't like. He thought he'd left the nightlight on, but it was off now. The nurse was at the other end of the hall, and besides, Tim didn't want to look like a sissy. He walked across the floor slowly, his stomach doing funny flipflops. When he was by the edge of the bed, his ankles tingled and he *knew* something was under it, reaching out to get him. He jumped up and pulled the sheets over his head, wrapping himself until only his nose and mouth were exposed. Then he arranged the blankets so there wouldn't be any "leaks," places where something could seep in, and felt better.

He was almost asleep when a woman screamed. He jerked up and strangled himself. The covers tightened around his neck as he tried to unwind them. Then he was free. Someone had closed his door, but he heard voices outside anyway. A woman was sobbing.

"My God, she *killed* her! She got the one in coma—"

Another voice, whispering harshly: "Where did she get

the scalpel? All the equipment rooms are supposed to be locked this time of night.''

The voices trailed off down the hall. Tim didn't need any more information. It was obvious what had happened. "Keep her away from the kid," he mouthed through his rewound sheets. "Keep her away from me."

Now he was the last one. Beverly Winegrade—the blond clerk he had had a crush on several months ago—had killed Cynthia. Next she would try to get him, and if she didn't succeed, she would kill herself. That was the way it had been before.

He was the last one to hold out against the insistent voices behind the smiling images of his parents and the man in the uniform.

Maybe Cynthia would join them.

Welcome

And Beverly, eventually. Then they would all come for him. And behind them, controlling them like puppets, would be the voices, screaming in a language he didn't understand.

CHAPTER THIRTEEN

FOWLER SLEPT SOUNDLY ON THE COUCH. THE MORNING WAS normal. Ice frosted the front window but no snow had fallen. As he watched, the sun began to warm the glass and melt the crystals. He raised the curtain, stirred the ashes in the fire to make sure they were out, and fixed a cup of coffee.

For the moment he had banished all introspection to a tiny corner for future reference. If he was going to stay at all, he had to accept the situation and whatever came of it. It was difficult.

Subduing the rational had never been easy for Fowler. His problems with love and emotional commitment had shown that. When questions arose that had no clean and bounded answers, like why he should love a particular woman, he fumbled and backed down. Begging the issue wasn't enough—getting away from it completely was the only solution. Even with Dorothy he was more inclined to be glib and clever than to express simple affection. That she put up with such a mask was over half the reason they had lasted together more than a year. Fowler loved her—he was finally willing to admit that much—but was still frightened by the thought.

So it was with the cabin. Whatever had happened here did not have a rational explanation. Jordan Taggart had not been going insane—Henry would have known that, and had not dragged Fowler into the mountains just to humor his father. Something had happened from outside.

The usual crazy-but-acceptable alternatives had occurred to him and been dismissed. There had been no cultists rigging a human sacrifice, or drug-maddened bikers, or any of the other manifold paranoias which hung on the edge of the middle-class mentality.

Something else.

Something he couldn't accept, but couldn't put aside, because the only other alternative was even more bizarre. That left him facing the irrational, but postponing the confrontation until it was unavoidable.

The gravel. Another rain of insects. Perhaps the sound of a woman being murdered, or the things Jordan had seen which Fowler hadn't been told about.

He walked across the gravel drive to the road without incident, noting the yellow-ribboned surveyor's stakes on the gulley around the cabin's rise. He crossed the road and stood for a moment by a meadow of dry grass, then doubled back and found a trail through the pines.

There was nothing unusual about the forest. The path was rough and circuitous, an old horse trail long since ignored and divided by the asphalt road. It took him several dozen yards along the road. The area hadn't been visited by tourists for at least five or six years. Perhaps Jordan had hacked the trail into the shape it was in for his own purposes.

Fowler walked back to the drive and stood in front of the cabin, scrunching his feet into the gravel. With a misplaced sense of boldness, he bent down and cleared a heap of the rocks away until the dark loam beneath was visible. He hefted a handful and squeezed it between his fingers. There were no ants or other ground life, but then it was getting cold. Even now the outside thermometer read forty-eight.

He stamped his boots off by the door and sat in the living room for a few minutes, deciding how to occupy his time. The box of junk food was untouched in the kitchen; he removed a package of Twinkies and took Jordan's portable radio, setting both on the kitchen table. As he chewed, he tried to find listenable stations. The radio had dust all over it, and no wonder—the reception was awful. Only on the shortwave did he find any periodically clear signals, but even those were liable to fade out.

Where do they get their energy?

The question came unbidden. He knew the reasoning behind it, but it still surprised him. "Who?" he asked himself out loud. "Ghosts, of course," he answered. If he was going to face the supernatural, he had to fit it into his system. He shook his head and grimaced. He'd have to find something more worthwhile to occupy his time, or the questions would get more and more theoretical, making less and less sense.

His suitcase held two popular novels of the literary variety—John Fowles and Graham Greene—and a number of trade journals he hadn't read in the office. Now was the best time to catch up on them. But he didn't want to.

The indecision was almost painful. He blew it away by sitting in a chair, picking out a magazine on software advances and forcing himself to read. By noon he was fed up. He ate lunch—supplemented by a candy bar—and checked his equipment for the third time. Everything was working and all the indications were normal. The outside temperature was sixty degrees.

At two o'clock the temperature was sixty-three. For this time of year, it was warm.

At three o'clock he awoke from a nap and looked

around, slightly dazed. Then he remembered where he was. His skin was covered with goosebumps. He put on a coat and looked at the thermometers again. Inside the cabin the air was forty-eight degrees. Outside it was forty. As he watched, the mercury fell to thirty-nine.

He walked to the road and looked toward the south end of the valley. Fog was spilling over the hills like grayish smoke into a bowl.

Brow wrinkled, he returned to the cabin and built a fire.

CHAPTER FOURTEEN

"MILLICENT? THIS IS ARNOLD TRUMBAUER. IS YOUR HUSBAND home?"

"Arnie, you calling all the way from New Mexico?" Millicent Jacobs straightened her graying hair, as she always did when receiving long-distance phone calls, just as if it was a personal visit. Her husband, Franklin, had noticed this and told her she'd do very well when television phones were installed.

"Yes. I have to talk to Franklin. It's very important."

"Certainly. He's out writing in his shed, but if it's important, I'll go get him."

"Please. You know I wouldn't interrupt him for something minor."

She put the phone down on the table and walked through the living room, pulling aside the lace curtains over the side windows on the off chance Franklin was in the garden. Sometimes the writing didn't go well and he'd spend a few minutes gardening to clear away the cobwebs. The writing was going well, apparently. Not even the tools were out.

Franklin Jacobs was a portly, pepper-haired man of

sixty, with wide, accusing eyes and a rounded face which seemed incongruous whenever he spoke. His voice, Millicent said, would have been more appropriate coming from Charlton Heston. His office, in the small rear servants' quarters, was cluttered with stacks of paper and shelves of books. He was tapping away steadily on an old Royal upright, eyebrows meeting above his beaky nose, two index fingers amazingly fast on the keys.

"Frank? Arnie's on the phone."

Jacobs stopped, sighed and turned toward her slightly without taking his eyes off the page. "What is it?"

"Important, he says."

His shoulders slumped and he left the desk reluctantly, weaving a path through stacks of old magazines. His foot caught a shoebox full of correspondence and kicked it into the door, scattering letters.

"I'll get these," Millicent said, stooping to gather them. "Go talk to Arnie."

Jacobs patted his wife on the fanny as he went by. "You've got to clean this out sometime soon," she said, ignoring his pass.

"Yes, yes." He climbed up the steps and took the call on the kitchen extension. "So what is it, you interrupt my masterwork, Arnold?"

"Something you want to know. Very unusual."

"Yes?"

"You know Mr. Tivvor, Mr. Frenk, Miss Unamuno, Mr. Kermit Smith, and Mr. Daniel Jones."

"Yes?"

"Franklin, they're the best psychics in this town. All topnotch."

"I know, I have letters from most of them. All corroborated. Good people. So?"

"They're in the hospital now."

"What? Accident?"

"I don't know. They came down sick just a couple of

days ago . . . no, not all. Miss Unamuno became ill last night. But she's the least strong, I think, the least capable psychically.''

"And?" Jacobs tapped his black-leather shoe on the kitchen linoleum.

"Before I give you my guess, maybe you can suggest something.''

"I don't know. What should I suggest?''

"Please don't be obtuse.''

"I don't know, Arnie. What?''

"I've only talked to Mr. Frenk. He's a good friend.''

"I know. And what did Mr. Frenk have to say?''

"It started with the Lorobu trouble.''

"And you think . . . ?''

"I don't want to even guess what happened in Lorobu. You've read about it, of course.''

"Yes, yes. I've read.''

"The whole world is crazy these days, but this is something else. Anyway, they're all in hospitals in Albuquerque, except for Mr. Jones, who is in Las Vegas—the New Mexico Las Vegas. I think the two things are connected.''

"Lorobu and everybody getting sick.''

"Yes. I think maybe what happened in Lorobu is important to us, what we're studying.''

"Perhaps. You want me to come out there?''

"Yes.''

"I will. Get affidavits from all the people you mentioned, if that's possible. I'd like to meet them, too. Can that be arranged?''

"Yes. I don't think there's anything physically wrong with them.''

"And make reservations for me at a good hotel. I'll fly out there tomorrow morning. Okay?''

"Fine. I'll get everything ready here, though I don't know about the affidavits—''

"As many as you can. Is that all, Arnold?''

"Yes."

"Then good-bye." He hung up the phone and turned to face his wife, who was standing by the washing machine.

"I'll be going to New Mexico tomorrow."

"You mentioned that town . . ." Millicent said.

"Yes," he said, staring at her fiercely.

CHAPTER FIFTEEN

NOT EVEN THE FIRE WAS KEEPING FOWLER WARM. HE LET HIS breath exhale in a thin, pale cloud—not four feet from the crackling blaze—and subdued the chattering of his teeth. In ghost stories, the house or haunted area usually had a central spot or shaft which was cold. But no matter where he went in the cabin, the temperature was bone-chilling. When he put on a jacket and went outside, walking up and down the drive and behind the house, the air was like a touch of dry ice. Inside and out, the temperature was the same. Was the entire valley freezing?

"Of course," he said. "It's winter. I'm imagining it all." He squinted hard at the fire. It seemed to be darkening. The lamp on the table next to the recliner was also dimming. "Smoke," he said. Yet the updraft in the fireplace was strong and the flue was open. It wasn't smoke. "My eyes, then." He rubbed them experimentally.

For an exercise, he mentally began to convert units of heat into units of mechanical work. He paced the room as he thought. The obvious didn't strike him until the fire was almost black. The rest of the cabin was suffused with a reddish haze, and all direct-lighting sources were hidden as if behind polarizing filters. He pulled back the window curtains and looked outside. The fog was impenetrable.

He began to rattle off old school equations. "One calorie is the heat required to raise one gram of water one degree Celsius." His chemistry teacher in high school, Mrs. Perry, had been an elderly, dedicated taskmaster with a strong belief in rote learning and laboratory experience. Fowler had pickled up much of his scientific attitude from her, even though he had never made higher than a C in her class. "One calorie is equal to four point one eight times ten to the seventh ergs. The work required to lift one kilogram one meter is nine point eight one times ten to the seventh ergs." Or, he amended for simplicity, about ten joules, each joule equal to 10^7 ergs.

He removed a piece of scrap paper from Jordan Taggart's desk drawer and fumbled for a pencil, stopping to rub his gloved hands to keep them warm. The temperature was now below freezing, inside and out. The fire was almost invisible. His eyes stung, and he could barely see to write.

"Got to keep thinking," he told himself. "Keep figuring." The remaining pink, marshmallow-covered cupcake on the desk was almost too hard to bite into. Still, he pried a chunk away with his teeth and chewed hard until the marshmallow and cake thawed. His calculations were aimed at something, but he wasn't willing to admit what the point was. "Specific heat of air—what? About a fourth. Fifty meters around the cabin"—about the size of the rise—"and five meters up . . . say a square fifty meters on a side." He penciled the figures and squinted at them. The volume of air in such a region would be twelve thousand five hundred cubic meters, each cubic meter containing a thousand liters, each liter weighing . . . how much does air weigh? He whapped his arms together and stamped his feet. About a gram a liter, he recalled, maybe a little more—say one point two grams a liter.

That was about fifteen thousand kilograms of air.

Fifteen thousand kilograms of air dropping to thirty degrees Fahrenheit—"Wait, convert to Celsius." He computed quickly in his head and wished he had brought a pocket calculator with him. He searched the desk quickly, hoping Jordan might have owned one. No luck.

"Dropping from fifteen and a half degrees Celsius to minus one point one degrees . . . sixteen point six drop, in less than three hours." The pencil raced, scratched the paper, and he threw it down, finishing the calculation in his head. "That's about sixty million calories lost." The air was almost black. "Stop it!"

It was an incredible amount of potential energy going somewhere: at least two hundred and fifty million joules, just in a fifty-meter square around the cabin. Of course, that wasn't taking into account the second law of thermodynamics, but—

He realized what he was aiming at.

If whatever was outside, draining the heat, was only capable of using a thousandth of that energy, it could lift a good-sized car forty or fifty feet in the air. Even a truck. His figures were rough, but he was in the right area.

"Stop it, please," he groaned. Then again, whatever it was, perhaps it was acting like a battery, storing power and releasing it. So far, it had done nothing overt.

He clenched his fists and backed away from the desk, feeling as if he had been tricked. It was all nonsense. He was babbling, shooting in the dark, fantasizing.

The air cleared and the room lights came back on.

The fire was out. Across the ashes, white frost was forming.

Fowler looked at his watch. The liquid crystal display was blinking erratically, but as it warmed, the numbers returned. Fifteen minutes had passed since the lights began to dim. It was now six o'clock.

He was past being rational. There was nothing to do but admit his ignorance. Something abnormal *was* in and around the cabin. Whatever it was, he could now guess where it got its energy—from the air, perhaps the ground as well. Direct conversion of heat to other forms.

He walked into the bathroom and looked at himself in the mirror. Frost dripped and melted from the strands of lank hair hanging across his forehead. He brushed melting crystals from his eyebrows. His lips were blue. "But I'm alive," he said. "And it didn't freeze me like the cat."

He heard a tinkling sound and returned to the living room, his knees shaking. Outside, wind was blowing the fog away in gluey wisps. The forest seemed to be filled with hundreds of tiny wind chimes. He opened the door slowly and listened. It was a sad, dead sound, the embodiment of winter. It made him want to cry. Then he did cry. Jordan and Henry were dead. It had killed them by getting into their minds, driving them mad. Now it was after him.

CHAPTER SIXTEEN

ARNOLD TRUMBAUER PICKED JACOBS UP AT THE AIRPORT AND drove him through late-morning traffic. Trumbauer was a thin, stoop-shouldered man with silvery-gray hair arranged in a fancy pomp. Jacobs had often suspected him of being homosexual, not that it mattered much. Inside, where it counted, everyone was the same. (But in his youth, as a sailor and general roughneck, Jacobs would have sooner punched Trumbauer in the mouth than take a ride through town with him.) "We're not going to the hospital," Trumbauer said.

"Oh?"

"Miss Unamuno was released late last night. She works in a turquoise shop in the tourist area of town. I'm going there now."

"I read in the paper that two of the Lorobu survivors died yesterday. One killed the other, then killed herself."

Trumbauer nodded.

"Any notion what's going on?" Jacobs asked.

"Very confusing. I talked with Miss Unamuno last night. Her first name is Janet but she prefers Miss Unamuno. She's been making up a list for us."

The architecture of the shopping area was patent Mexican, with touches of rustic old-West. The air was warm, as it had been in Arizona, where his garden was at this very minute surviving without him (vanity of vanities). Trumbauer parked the car and Jacobs stood under the sun patiently while he pointed out a few shoddy attractions.

"And where is Miss Unamuno?" he finally asked, dark eyes boring into Trumbauer.

"This way. Was your flight pleasant?"

"No." He shook his head. "I hate flying."

"That's right. You once crashed in a PBY."

Jacobs had never told the man, or anyone else in his acquaintance, about the unpleasant episode, but it didn't surprise him that Trumbauer knew.

"How did *you* manage to stay healthy?" he asked.

Trumbauer shook his head. "My guide. Her name is Proserpina, you know. She was an oracle in another life."

"Delphic?"

"Heavens, no. Much earlier than that. She might have been the Witch of Endor, for all I know—but she never gives out more than hints. She told me to pull in my antennae, as it were. I did, but I could still feel the . . . backwash, if you see what I mean. Then I knew the others would be in trouble. Proserpina is really first-rate. I wish others could afford guides half as good."

The turquoise shop was in a small, well-kept room off an alley, across from a bookstore which specialized in Western Americana. The lighting was fluorescent and the walls were painted a cool, pale blue. It was pleasant, Jacobs thought, but antiseptic and not to the advantage of turquoise. A man was standing behind a glass display case—about thirty years old, blond-haired and balding in the same late-collegiate fashion Jacobs had found so amusing in the Smothers brothers. "May I help you?"

"We're here to see Miss Unamuno," Trumbauer said. "Is she—"

"She's in the back room now. She wasn't feeling too well, just got out of the hospital." The man was wearing jeans and a plaid shirt and looked uncomfortable in them, as if he would prefer double-knit suits of beige or slate-gray. Jewelers are a breed unique, Jacobs told himself, looking around nonchalantly. Most of the stones were fake— dyed in purple automobile coolant and sealed with wax. The authentic stones were pale and common. He couldn't see a really desirable piece in the store.

"It's important. We're friends," Trumbauer persisted.

The man nodded and walked through the rear door. A few moments later a pale young woman with red hair and wary eyes emerged. She was wearing a simple green shift and no makeup, though her skin was ghostly. The room lighting drained her color even more. "Hello, Arnold," she said tonelessly, looking at Jacobs. "Is this—"

"Franklin Jacobs," he said, offering her his hand. She looked at it but didn't bother to reciprocate. "Mr. Trumbauer tells me you've had an unusual experience."

"Unusual?" She smiled weakly. "Happens quite a lot, actually. But never this bad."

"I've been told," Jacobs began, staring significantly at Trumbauer, "that this might have a connection with Lorobu."

The woman's features tightened and her hand began to shake on the counter. "I'm going to lunch in a few minutes. Tom doesn't like this kind of talk in the store, so if you'll wait for me outside . . ."

"Of course. We're buying," Jacobs said.

Outside, Trumbauer shook his head and sighed. "From what I've heard—the grapevine, as it were—the poor woman's guide is a true foulup. Rumor has it he was a Roman consul in another life."

"No plumbers?" Jacobs asked. "Only witches and royalty?"

Trumbauer smiled tolerantly. "Consuls were politicians,

Frank. Plumbers are usually smart enough to get off this mortal coil and leave everyone to their own troubles. Guides are the misfits of the beyond, wouldn't you say?''

"I wouldn't know," Jacobs said. "It's always been my fortune to be psychically blind."

"It *is* a burden," Trumbauer admitted. Miss Unamuno walked through the door, having difficulty with the heavy glass until Jacobs helped.

"Thank you," she said. "I know a place around here that doesn't serve Mexican food or hamburgers. Sound good?"

They agreed, and she walked between them under the covered walkway.

The restaurant was small and dark. Jacobs disliked small, dark eating places—he had learned to examine his food closely in the Navy—but Miss Unamuno seemed happier where her paleness wasn't so obvious.

After they ordered, she pulled a piece of paper from her purse and spread it out on the white tablecloth. "I wrote these down in the hospital," she said. "I don't know if they have any connection with Lorobu or not." She shuddered involuntarily. "Mr. Jacobs—"

"Frank."

"These—receptions. They caused me a great deal of distress. I've never felt so sickened by a contact. There was nothing but pain and burning and . . . incompleteness. I don't know how else to describe it."

Jacobs looked at the list by the candle lantern. "These were the people who talked to you?"

"They weren't the only ones talking. They were just the only ones I could understand. It was cacophony. I'm not even sure whether the background noise was people speaking. Or just animals, or demons . . ." She stopped as if to gauge his reaction. "Do you believe in demons, Mr. Jacobs?"

"I believe in the forces which create them."

"That's an ambiguous response."

"Miss Unamuno, I have never met a demon. Other people tell me they have, and that demons are real. When I meet one, I'll judge." He lowered his voice. "However, I've seen things attributed to demons. My attitudes are too complex to explain here." He reached into his coat pocket for a pencil, then hesitated. "Do you mind if I copy these down? And ask more questions?"

She shook her head. "If anything can be done to ease their misery, I'm only too glad to help."

"Just the names. Is that all you received?"

"And some visual impressions. I believe one of them was a pilot or something. He appeared in an airplane cockpit. Another was on a ship. Not actually, while they communicated with me—if you can call it that—but by way of biographical shorthand. Like we use names."

"Lieutenant William Skorvin, United States Navy," he read from the top of the list. "Corporal S.K. Percher, U.S. Army Air Force." He wrote the names carefully on his paper. "I'm surprised there were no serial numbers," he said.

"There were," she said, "but I was too sick to write them down."

"What made you sick?" Jacobs asked.

"Like I said, they were in misery. A big bundle of . . . agony, suffering. These people, these names, they were caught, I think. Like bits picked up by a cyclone."

Jacobs wrote her description down, then noticed he had misspelled a word. He brought the eraser down and hesitated. He had written *psychlone*.

CHAPTER SEVENTEEN

"YOU'RE GOING TO LIKE IT IN SALT LAKE CITY," RICHARD Townsend said, bending over his younger brother. "Suzanne and I have a real nice home up there. You can meet your nephew—you're an uncle, know that?"

Tim nodded. "Will I have a room to myself?"

"Yes, I think so. They've got good schools in Utah, lots of pretty country. I can take you out hunting, fishing—"

"Don't want to kill anything," Tim said.

"Huh?" Rick stood up straight and frowned. "No, no," he said thoughtfully, "of course not. I mean animals, Tim, fish, not people."

Tim saw the nurse who had just entered the room give Rick a disapproving look and shake her head. "Mr. Townsend," she said, handing him papers, "here are the hospital release forms. A lot of newsmen have been trying to speak to Tim. We don't recommend they be allowed to do so for a long time."

Tim was about to say, "But I *want* to tell someone—" but he kept his mouth shut. He wanted to talk to someone besides doctors. He already knew they didn't understand.

Rick gathered up the luggage and a cardboard box full

of spaceship and airplane models. He opened the lid on the box and peeped in, then smiled. "Got a real fine hobby store near us, too."

"Let's go," Tim said. He looked up at the nurse and said, "Thank you."

She smiled and tousled his hair. "No problem, Tim," she said. But he could tell she was relieved. At least *he* wouldn't go around acting crazy and killing people, she was thinking. Cynthia Furness and Beverly Winegrade, dead. Tim Townsend, alive. He could tell. All the doctors and nurses were afraid of him. Even the FBI agent didn't treat him like a little boy, but like someone in a movie—somebody infected, or perhaps possessed. They would all be glad to see him go.

And just as obviously, they hadn't told Rick about their fear. Something like that couldn't be talked about easily, not by professionals. Since nobody knew what had happened in Lorobu, they couldn't assume Tim was dangerous.

They didn't even know whether he had killed anybody. Neither did he. There was a lot he didn't remember. Not *couldn't* remember, didn't. Someday.

Rick's car was an old 1965 Ford Fairlane, well-kept but hardly a limousine. Their father had once said Rick was doing well by himself, should be able to afford a new car, but there had never been much explanation for such talk. The luggage was loaded into the trunk. Rick opened the front door for him. "All set?" he asked before turning the key. Tim nodded.

"Off to a new life," Rick said. "You'll like it."

Rick looked a lot older than Tim remembered, but that was natural. Everybody had died, after all—*except myself,* Tim amended—and that was quite a burden for someone as young as Rick to bear up under.

The long drive began. "Suzanne's a real nice cook," Rick said. "Almost as good as Mom."

Tim looked over and saw Rick's face all screwed up, like he was about to cry, but that passed.

Tim hadn't cried yet. After all, he saw his parents almost every night. Now Cynthia and Beverly were with them. All the ones who knew him. Partly they wanted something he didn't understand, or refused to understand, and partly they were afraid. But that wasn't the exact word. They were more than just afraid.

That was why Tim had to grow up very fast, and why eventually he would have to tell somebody. Something had to be done. If they wanted him, then probably they'd want others, too.

CHAPTER EIGHTEEN

HE WOUND BACK THE CHART RECORDER STRIP AND FOLLOWED the wavy line of the microwave detector. It was smooth and continuous, with the usual random jags, until the time of the freeze. Then it jumped to a plateau for at least twenty minutes. Fowler wanted to calculate the approximate size of a black body—an ideal heat source—large enough to account for such a microwave increase, but he didn't have the texts and his memory was incomplete.

Besides, it was obvious that whatever caused the increase was not physically normal. It was immaterial, apparently capable of extending its influence through solid matter, and capable of affecting the human mind. His mind, the minds of Jordan and Henry Taggart.

"Where did you come from?" he asked the cabin softly. He looked around and shivered, still chilled. "I certainly don't want to hurt you."

He listened to himself and shook his head vigorously. Now he had gone full circle. Nothing but a cold snap and he was going off the deep end—

"No!" he shouted. "Not just a cold snap. Dropped sixteen degrees, inside and out. Nothing could do that, especially not a cold snap." He sat in the lazy boy and pulled his knees up to his chin. He was not trapped, he could get out and drive the Z back to civilization. It was a real temptation now. Instead, he stood up, put more wood on the wet ashes in the fireplace, and poured lighter fluid on woodchips around the base. In a few minutes he had a good blaze and he warmed himself in front of it.

In the kitchen, he brought out a can of beans and franks and set them in a pot on the stove. Such was the ignominy of life, he thought—this would all end with his being arrested for freeloading and breaking-and-entering.

While he ate the beans, he picked up the phone, heard the dial tone, and tentatively punched out Dorothy's number in Los Angeles. The call went through without interference. After three rings, Dorothy answered the phone, breathless and a little piqued.

"Dot, this is Larry."

"I was in the bathtub," she said. Suddenly he was laughing, choking on his beans and spraying a bite of frankfurter across his shirt. She started laughing, too, and the hysteria went on for half a minute before he controlled himself.

"What was that all about?" Dot asked. "I said I was in the bathtub, I'm standing here dripping all over the God-damned rug, and it's cold. Are you all right?"

"I'm fine. But don't tell me about it being cold. I just met the ghost. He runs an ice factory."

"Ghost? *He?*"

"No, not exactly. Something, I don't know what."

"You mean you can't describe it?"

"Not can't, just don't want to until I get my thoughts straightened out."

"Jesus, Larry, this is unreal. You're not kidding, are you?"

All hilarity went out of him suddenly. "No. Dot, I called to tell you I'm okay. And I'm going to call every night about this time—about seven—to check in. Is that okay with you? I'm going to call collect so I won't rip off the phone company.''

"The phone's still open up there," she said.

"Dot the obvious. Yes, still open. And as I said, I'm fine, just a bit confused. I'm going to stick it out."

"A night in the haunted house? Do you have a talking mule with you, too?" She didn't sound flippant; she sounded worried.

"No, no, I'm fine."

"You told me that, but are you sane? Getting your vitamins? Going to bed early?"

"Enough, Dot."

"Jesus, Larry, you're telling me you saw something, but you aren't telling me what! I'll go bananas!"

"I didn't actually see anything. Here's what happened, judge for yourself. The temperature dropped sixteen degrees Celsius in about as many minutes. The fireplace froze and I got frost all over my moustache. It was cold inside and out. Then it warmed up, went away."

"How long are you going to stay, Larry?"

"A couple more days, I think. No one's bothered me yet. This is about the only time that's happened. But if I don't call, you contact the authorities and tell them to come arrest me."

"What if they just pull the plug on your phone?"

"Good thought. Okay, give me four hours' leeway. I can get into Bishop and call from there if I have to."

"Is this going to be dangerous, do you think?"

"I don't know."

"What am I saying—you think it killed Jordan and Henry, don't you? Could it get you, too?"

"I'm alone. Maybe not. Maybe it takes two. But don't worry about me unless I don't call. Okay?"

"Larry, somebody already asked about you and I told them where you were."

"What? That's a stupid-ass thing to do—"

"No, I don't think so. It was a reporter from Sacramento, said he was investigating the Taggart thing and wanted to talk to you about it. He sounded sincere, so I said you were already investigating. He may be at the cabin tomorrow. I thought you might need help."

"I should be angry, Dot, but I'm not. Maybe you did the smart thing. I'll look for him."

"But Jesus, Larry, that could put two of you in the cabin—could it get you then?"

"What it?"

"Don't toy with me. The icebox monster."

He chuckled. "Good description. I don't know. We'll just have to find out, won't we?"

Dorothy was silent on the other end.

"I'll be okay," Fowler said softly.

"Castle called. He wants to know where you are."

"Don't tell him!"

"Larry, they're worried. You don't have much time. They're—"

"I'll handle it. I have a couple more days. I'll call them if I need to stay longer."

"I don't believe this is happening. I don't believe you're off chasing ghosts, for Christ's sake."

"Not ghosts," Fowler said. "Dot, I have to do it."

"Even if you lose your job?"

He sighed. "Maybe even then. I owe it to Henry."

"Yeah."

"I love and cherish. I'll be back."

"Soon. I miss you."

There was the usual awkwardness getting off the line. Then he was alone again. He wiped his shirt off slowly with the napkin. "First resolution," he said, "is not to talk about *it* as if it were an intelligent being. I'm not giving you any breaks, you hear?" he shouted.

The silence was worse than any answer could have

been. He finished the beans and straightened up the kitchen sullenly, wondering who the reporter would be, how he would look upon Fowler's Folly. If anything more happened, it might be good to have another witness besides himself and the chart recorder.

He picked up a copy of *Scientific American* and began to read. Four hours later, getting ready for bed, he said, "And yea verily, the rest of the night was peaceful, unto morning, and the poor man slept soundly."

And he did.

CHAPTER NINETEEN

"SHE WAS DESCRIBING AN EVENT OF INCREDIBLE PSYCHIC power," Jacobs said, putting his legs up on the bed as he sat in the hotel room chair. He leaned his head back on his arms and sighed. "Arnold, you know as well as I that psychic events are subtle, weak. Yet this goes outside all bounds. And it may involve the dead."

Trumbauer shook his head adamantly. "The dead do not wield great power."

"Not the newly dead, no. Nor those of normal character."

"Franklin, you're talking nonsense. The dead protect us, warn us. They're our friends, usually more than they are in life."

"If they bother to stick around at all."

"I see this picture, two crazy old men sitting in a hotel room, talking ridiculous talk. This is what people I know would think. Franklin, what can we do?"

"I'm only a writer. For a long time, I thought that by keeping my work popular, I could help bring on the age of spiritual awakening. I haven't been very successful. But now we may have an awakening forced upon us. Whatever this event was, it killed many people. An entire town.

Important people are bound to be looking into it. And so must we, because we may know something they don't.''

"What?"

"The names.''

"What will we do with them?''

"The Army and Navy may help us. If these are real people, deceased or not, there should be records. I'll call in the morning. If they have some connection with Lorobu, we'll go there and find out. There must be records in the town.''

"What now?''

"I rest,'' Jacobs said. "And call my wife. See how my garden is doing. Also, tomorrow we'll talk with the others, if they'll let us.''

Trumbauer shook his head pessimistically. "I don't know. Today I talked with Frenk and Tivvor. They said no more. No more bother about it all. They want to think it's over.''

"Do they believe that?''

"No. Frenk cried. He was ashamed of himself—I know him well—and this is just beyond him. He says another such thing will kill him. And he's terrified about that sort of death.''

"Why?''

"If this psychlone, as you call it, is evil, it may not just let people die.''

Jacobs blew out his lips.

Trumbauer folded his hands and bent his head. "You've never been receptive to the idea of evil beings.''

"Maybe I'm learning, Arnie.''

"It may take those it kills along with it. Perhaps that's how so many names are connected with it.''

"A giant string of spiritual flypaper, winding across the land,'' Jacobs said.

"You're being ornery now.''

"No. It's a ridiculous image, but I won't say it's un-true.'' He held up his hand as Trumbauer started to say more, then reached for the room phone. As he called his wife, Trumbauer lay back on the far bed and closed his eyes to meditate.

The morning was clear and cold. Jacobs made his calls to Washington early, found a cooperative clerk, and was promised a return call or letter if he couldn't be reached by phone. Then they went to pick up Miss Unamuno. It was her day off, and she had agreed to accompany them to Lorobu—or as close as she could go.

Trumbauer's station wagon was well-equipped with water bottles and cans of gas, food rations, and other safety paraphernalia which Jacobs looked over with an approving but humored grin. "So much for seeing into the future."

"The Boy Scout motto outweighs all spiritual faith, is that what you're accusing me of?" Trumbauer asked. "I never said I had rapport with my car. It could crap out without anyone predicting, and where would I be?"

"Mr. Trumbauer is a very smart man," Miss Unamuno said defensively, not catching the bantering tone.

"I know, dear, I know. But we are each, in our own way, old fools, so allow us our mock battles."

She flushed, embarrassed, and Jacobs patted her cheek lightly. "I love making young women blush," he said. "But don't tell my wife."

"First," Trumbauer said, "we go to the hospital and see if any of the others will talk to us. Then to Lorobu."

The hospital was a disappointment. Half of the remaining psychics had been discharged, and the other half refused visitors. In the reception area, Trumbauer rubbed his chin and looked at Jacobs. "I'm afraid I was right. It was such a shock they don't want to be reminded. I imagine quite a few are looking around for new guides, as it were."

"Miss Unamuno, here, is our bravest, apparently," Jacobs said. "We'll just have to rely on her."

"As far as she goes," she said grimly. "I'm not too happy about it."

"On to Lorobu, then," Jacobs said. "How long a drive is it?"

"We'll be there by four or four-thirty," Trumbauer said. "But I don't know how much good it will do us. They have it sealed off to outsiders."

CHAPTER TWENTY

FOWLER STOOD BY THE Z, LOOKING UNDER THE OPEN HOOD. He checked the hoses, the belts, and tapped the coolant reservoir. Then he brought the long hood down and got to his knees in the gravel to see how the tires were doing. He crept around the side.

His eyes focused on the paint below the door.

"Jesus H. Christ." The paint and metal along the body's base were pitted and scratched, in some areas almost sandblasted in appearance. He felt the surface with his hand. Above a palm-span, the paint was fine.

He got to his feet and looked around helplessly. It wasn't wind damage, it wasn't road damage—he would have noticed while unloading the equipment—and that meant it wasn't covered by his insurance.

It had happened some time after he parked the Z in the cabin driveway.

He wasn't feeling very well anyway, and the discovery irritated him more than it should have. He returned to the cabin and felt his forehead. He was warm. Jordan Taggart's medicine chest yielded aspirin and a thermometer. He took his temperature—edging 100—and popped two pills, swal-

lowing a glass of water after. The bitter aspirin taste made
him wince. He decided to take a shower before he got any
sicker—much preferring to be clean while he was ill—and
pulled back the shower curtain as he undid the top buttons
on his shirt.

The shower tub was covered with something. He bent
down to get a look and recoiled at the smell, like ammonia
mixed with animal dung. The bottom of the tub was
marred with thousands of crayonlike strokes of color, each
stroke growing fuzz and sending out sympathetic circles of
mould. He backed away and took a deep breath from the
hall, then stood over the tub, looking at the patterns. He'd
taken a shower yesterday afternoon. It wasn't possible all
this could have grown since.

He went to the kitchen and came back with a bottle of
disinfectant, a can of cleanser and a scrub brush. He
poured the disinfectant freely around the tub and then
added cleanser, scrubbing the enamel vigorously. The pine
smell effectively masked the corruption, and soon the tub
was white and stainless. The stuff seemed to liquefy as it
came away, and all of it went smoothly down the drain,
just like ordinary dirt.

He then showered and washed his hair.

When he finished drying himself, he took his temperature again—101. Time to get to bed. He was feeling
wobbly, though not queasy yet—perhaps it was just a
cold. After last night he wouldn't be surprised. That kind
of a chill could bring anything on.

After mixing frozen orange juice and eating a piece of
processed cheese, he lay back on the couch and propped a
copy of *Computer Age* on his stomach. "I'm no fit
ghost-sitter now," he told himself a half-hour later, trying
to squeeze back a growing headache.

Everything demanded a nap. He rolled over and shut his
eyes. Then opened them. What if the reporter arrived? All
in good time. Give him the disease, too. Infections for

the nosy. On cue, his began to drip and he stuffed a Kleenex into the lower nostril.

He was dreaming about a trip to Disneyland—he hadn't been there for six years at least—when the cabin door rattled. One leg went over the side of the couch and he lurched unsteadily to his feet. He felt weak. The aspirin had had little effect.

"Hello," he said, swinging the door open. "Pleased to meet you." He craned his neck. The porch was empty. He looked down and saw a few chunks of gravel on the doormat. Making it back to the couch was difficult. He lay on his back, feet flopped over the far arm, trying to make sense of his feverish impressions. "I'm still dreaming," he said. "Christ, what a headache."

The door rattled again. Something tinked against the window glass above the couch. Fowler opened his eyes and sat up on one elbow, parting the curtains. Something gray passed out of view, perhaps a squirrel jumping down from the eaves. "Go away."

More liquids was the prescription, always more fluids. In the kitchen, he poured another glass of orange juice and wondered how a bourbon slug would taste added to it. "I'm not *that* sick," he decided.

He leaned against the refrigerator as he drank the glass down. The acid juice tickled his throat. He sincerely despised all the debilitating symptoms of colds, all the tiny pains and dull aches and vacant drynesses behind the nose, and overwhelming wetness under the nose . . . There were no vitamin C tablets in the cabin or he would be dosing himself without caring whether Linus Pauling was right. If there was the barest chance the ascorbic acid made viruses feel half as irritated as they were making him feel, megavitamin therapy was justified. "Death and destruction to all the little buggers." He returned to the couch and tried to concentrate on a million tiny metal spears, each one going deep into a virus, rupturing its little protein wall, spiking its delivery tube, splintering its insidious genetic material.

Again the door rattled. He decided it was the wind.

Again the window glass tinked. He didn't hear it.

He was deep asleep, his face flushed and beads of sweat breaking out on his forehead, across his chest, and staining the underarms of his shirt.

Something brought him sharply upright on the couch a long dream-passage later. He blinked and rubbed his eyes, clearing away the swimming images. There was a knock on the door. He stood up, preparing to be unsteady. But his footing was strong, his fever was gone and he was no longer weak.

He checked himself over quickly, wiping his nose—which was dry—swallowing without pain in his throat, focusing his eyes without an answering jab in the front of his head. He was well.

"Yes?" He swung the door open. A tall, black-haired man in a fawn-colored business suit, very natty, smiled at him.

"Mr. Fowler? Lawrence Fowler?"

"Larry, yes. And you're—"

"Samuel Prohaska. I'm a reporter for CBS in Sacramento, local news. I called your wife—"

"Not yet, you haven't."

"Well, your friend in Los Angeles, and she indicated you were up here—are up here—with the same doubts I have about the case."

"I don't know if they're the same. You didn't tell the police, did you?"

"No, sir. Nor did I tell my boss. I'm technically on vacation. But I met Henry Taggart when I was covering a book convention in San Francisco."

"Come on in. I'm just getting over something—a cold, I think. I caught it this afternoon and now it's gone."

"What?" Prohaska smiled, confused.

"And my Z has been sandblasted in the driveway, so I can suggest you park your car off the gravel if you value the finish."

Prohaska closed the door behind himself and looked at Fowler doubtfully. Fowler brushed back his hair, straightened his sweater, and returned the look.

"Sam—if I can call you that—are you willing to stick around through tonight? You may find out what really caused it all. Have the time?"

Prohaska nodded.

"I don't think you have any idea what it was."

"Probably not," the reporter admitted.

"Good. Now be skeptical. I'm going to tell you what's happened to me so far, and I want a sane opinion."

Prohaska sat down on the couch.

"First, something to drink? Plenty of orange juice—vitamin C, you know. I'm beginning to think Linus Pauling is right."

CHAPTER TWENTY-ONE

TIM STARED BLANKLY OUT THE WINDOW. IT WAS A NICE HOUSE, with a large room for him. Suzanne, Rick's wife, was nice to him, all blond-haired and slender and dressed in business outfits because she worked as a secretary in the church. Very pleasant.

Tim knew he had to get out of there or they would all be dead soon. Even as he built his models or walked with Rick through the new school he would be attending, Tim knew he was a time bomb. Sooner or later, the image of the Lorobu people—and the others—would appear and the blood on his hands would glow, and he would be consumed.

That night, while Tim lay in bed upstairs, a government psychologist visited the house and told the Townsends about the boy's condition. Rick sat in the easy chair, chin in hand. Suzanne perched on the edge of the couch, her face drawn from a long day at work. The thin, birdlike psychologist walked back and forth on the living-room carpet, his knees making faint cracks, as he described Tim's trauma and what they would have to do to alleviate it. Suzanne glanced up at the ceiling. She wanted to ask if Tim should be sleeping so near the baby, but it was too frightening an idea to voice.

Rick didn't half understand what the man was saying. He distrusted psychologists. Suzanne had once had a nervous breakdown and the psychologists had done her no good at all.

"I don't think you'll have to worry about violent behavior," the man concluded. "Not against you or your child, anyway. Again, I commend you for taking Tim in—"

"He's my brother," Rick said.

"Yes, and he's a very frightened young boy. Remember that."

"It's going to be hard to forget," Rick said.

"He has a lot of trauma to overcome, but with your help, I think he can do it. Do you, yourselves, have any problems I might be able to help you with before I go?"

Rick shook his head.

Tim was sitting up in bed, watching the window. The air in his room was cold. The voices were coming again. The hurt ones, the angry ones, the ones half there. One voice emerged that he could understand—Georgette, his mother. She faded and another replaced her. Tim tried to rub his stained hands on the counterpane. "Go away," he said. "Please go away."

He scrunched his eyes shut. The faces of people from Lorobu flashed in his head like images on a pack of shuffled cards. He twisted his head back and forth, trying to drive out the vision.

He couldn't. Behind the faces, rapidly fading, there arose redness, then a purple smoke, something like water . . . and for the first time, he saw *them*. . . .

Eyeless, mouths open.

He screamed. They remained, calling for him, hungry and in pain. His voice was raw and failing by the time Rick and Suzanne and the psychologist came into the room.

As Tim writhed on the bed, Rick shouted at the psychologist who stood in the door, doing nothing. There was nothing any of them could do, and Tim knew that.

BOOK TWO

CHAPTER TWENTY-TWO

CELEBRATING COMPANY, FOWLER BROUGHT OUT JORDAN TAG-gart's last steak, fried it with onions, and served it with boiled potatoes and two cans of beer. The reporter ate appreciatively and complimented his cooking.

"You said you met Henry," Fowler said. "How? What did you think of him?"

"I was covering a booksellers' convention in San Francisco," Prohaska said after swallowing a piece of steak. "We were talking about how the conglomerate bookstores were edging out smaller operations. He was telling me about his problems in the area, with the big outfits in Ohio buying all the local chains and running them like rubber stamps. I said I'd like to do a story on it, so he bought me a drink and we talked for several hours. Got quite a story out of it. Ran two three-minute segments in Sacramento. I like books and bookstores, so we met about a month later in San Francisco and visited all the old bookstores around Union Square. He seemed a very intelligent, friendly guy. I invited him and his family to visit mine in Sacramento if they ever came up. But he said he wasn't married. Something of a swinging bachelor, I gathered."

"He did okay with women."

"Then, when they died, I covered the basics of the story for my station. But I couldn't believe it had happened the way the police said. Now, you tell me all this about Jordan Taggart looking out for haunts and I'm not so sure he wasn't crazy."

"Stick around."

"I intend to. One way or another, it's a story."

"But it isn't news any more. How do you justify following up old news?"

"Not all modern journalism is flash-and-go."

"Sounds like a rare bit of wisdom," Fowler said. He stood and began to clear the table.

"We're both breaking the law, you know," Prohaska said as he stacked the plates in the sink. He lifted his can of beer. "Breaking, entering, stealing."

"Yes, and I wonder why we haven't been approached yet."

"Nobody knows you're here. Bishop's pretty far away and things are kind of slow up here." He walked into the living room and looked through the front window. "It's going to get slower, too. It's starting to snow." He turned back to the kitchen. "You're nuts, you know. Believing ghosts could have killed them."

"Not directly killed them," Fowler reiterated. "Besides, it was Jordan's idea, not mine. I was brought up here to check it out. And there's evidence—of a sort."

"But do microwave emissions—and I'm no physicist, so you can fool me—always indicate spooks?"

"No. I don't know what they indicate. They're just part of the environment surrounding the event, which was in itself like nothing I've ever experienced. Until something else happens—"

"You sound positive it will."

Fowler smiled. "Until something else happens, you'll

have to take my word for it. There *is* something peculiar going on here."

"Think its connected with Lorobu?"

Fowler shook his head. "I doubt it. Lorobu's a long way from here. I haven't been keeping track of it much. I thought it would end up nerve gas or something, and we'd never really know what happened."

"Whatever it was, it's sealed tight as a drum. Nothing leaks out of that town now."

"Sounds like the defense department to me."

"Yes," Prohaska said, "but our station got a few stories from eyewitnesses. A highway patrol officer, before he shut up, and a state trooper. Sounds very much like what happened here. Which reminds me—shall we tie bells around each other's neck? Might be safer that way."

"I think staying awake will be enough."

"Your advantage," Prohaska said. "I had a long drive today. I'm sleepy already."

"Then how about a walk after cleanup?"

When the dishes were rinsed and dried, they put on parkas and stood in the doorway, looking across the gravel drive, the two cars already sprinkled with snow, and the quiet, cold night. "Is this Taggart's jacket?" Prohaska asked, holding up one arm.

"Jordan's, I think," Fowler said. The reporter nodded.

"Weather forecast was for about a foot of snow tonight. The roads won't be clear until late morning tomorrow."

"I don't intend to go anyplace," Fowler said. "Not outside of walking distance, anyway. I found a trail that's clearly marked, but we'd better stick to the drive tonight. Perhaps follow the road."

"Real exciting stuff," Prohaska said. "I'm missing the camera team already."

"I want to keep my head clear. The cabin is comfortable, but I feel vulnerable inside."

"How much more vulnerable outside, then?"

"We can see what's coming."

Prohaska laughed. "Jesus, I feel like I'm in an old Ghost Busters movie. Lon Chaney and Bob Hope. I can't write anything useful about this kind of crap."

They walked along the side of the road for several dozen yards, saying little, keeping their shoulders hunched against the cold air and drifting flakes. Through the quick-flying snow clouds Fowler could see a few bright stars. Then something crashed in the woods to their left and Prohaska jumped. "What was that?"

"An animal," Fowler said softly, standing his ground, looking sideways through the black trees. "A deer perhaps."

"Or a bear," Prohaska said.

"Want to turn back?"

"No," the reporter said, reaching into his coat pocket for a cigarette. "Does smoking bug animals, you think?"

"I don't know. I'm not much of a woodsman."

"Funny, I thought you'd be the Sierra Club type."

"Nope, just a well-to-do young executive."

"What in hell are we doing out here, then?"

Another crash, farther away, decided the question for them. "That was back by the cabin," Prohaska said. Fowler nodded. *It can move things,* he thought.

"Let's go back and check it out," he said. "I feel pretty refreshed already."

"That's the word, is it? I'll remember. Refreshed."

The gravel drive was covered by a thin blanket of snow. Everything was still around the cabin and its clearing, as though the snowflakes were absorbing all sound. Fowler walked past the Z, idly brushing snow off its roof. Prohaska was behind him, his cigarette a red star in the dark. The porch light cast a yellow glow across the snow-patched front yard. "Hold it," Prohaska said behind him. "There's something in front of my car." Fowler turned and saw the reporter take two steps to the station wagon. "Somebody's moved a bag under the wheels."

Then the reporter stopped. Something in the line of his back made Fowler stiffen. "Come look," the reporter murmured. Fowler walked up behind him and bent down by the car's bumper. Three great swaths had been cut out of the gravel in front of the station wagon. The dirt, gravel and snow had been piled up under the front wheels, then tamped down smooth to form a slushy mound.

"It'll freeze around the tires and you won't be able to get out," Fowler said. "Let's dig it out."

"No, look on this side. Just beyond the tire." Prohaska pulled out his lighter and flicked it on. The flame was steady in the still air. Fowler looked at an extension of the mound. "It's like a head," Prohaska said, bending lower with the lighter.

The shadows fell at the right angle and they stared at a crude sculpture of a face. There was a long, flat-ended nose and two deep depressions for eyes. "Like a pig," Prohaska said.

It looked like the boar that had tried to pull Fowler under the gravel. But as they watched, the features seemed to blur and subside, until only shadows remained.

They dug out the mound and spread it back across the drive.

CHAPTER TWENTY-THREE

THE TEMPERATURE WAS DROPPING RAPIDLY.

"I think it's starting again," Fowler said.

"What, just like that? Like clockwork, this thing, huh?" Prohaska paced back and forth across the cabin, clapping his arms against his sides and breathing into clasped fingers. "How cold is it?"

"Fifty in here. Dropped eighteen degrees Fahrenheit."

"Oh, and how much centigrade?" Prohaska asked sardonically.

"Celsius nowadays," Fowler said. "I don't know. I'd have to compute it . . . about ten degrees."

"Fine. Now I know. What in hell is it doing?"

"I think it's gathering energy for something."

"What?"

Fowler shrugged and smiled wanly. "You tell me. Last time, nothing happened. Nothing that I saw."

"Good, good. They should have you on Fright Theater. Real low-key horrors. Pardon me if I'm glib when I'm worried."

"That's okay. My girl friend's the same way."

"Have to be properly introduced some time. Could this be due to catastrophic failure of insulation?"

Fowler shook his head, still smiling. This was a little better—introducing another human being to the unknown was much more agreeable than facing it alone. It was almost fun, in the same way scaring the shit out of each other had been fun as kids.

"Down to forty-five, inside and out," Fowler said, looking at the graph as it crept through the chart recorder. "Microwave emissions up and at a plateau."

"Mind if I smoke?"

"If you can get your match lit, go ahead."

Prohaska struck a match and watched it flicker in his hands and go out. "Something wrong with the oxygen around here?"

"No. I don't know what causes it. Look at the fireplace." The flames were darkening, just as they had the night before. "It's sucking all heat out, radiant heat, heat in the air, in the ground, the wood. Everything."

"How the hell could it do that?"

Fowler shrugged. "Okay—now look at this. I want you to see everything I'm doing." He set up the camera in the window and recorded the shutter speed and film type— infrared. "I'm going to make a scan of the front yard around our cars."

He snapped the pictures and turned the camera between each shot. Then he brought out another camera and shot pictures inside the cabin with regular Tri-X film. "I've also got pieces of black-and-white negatives in my camera bag." He removed several small sheets pre-wrapped in black plastic. He proceeded to pin them to the walls around the cabin. "Radiation streaks will show up on them, if there are any."

"And on your film in the camera, too."

"Maybe."

Prohaska bent over the chart recorder and looked at the digital display on the thermometers. "Down to thirty. It's below freezing."

"Yeah. The air's very moist, too. Pretty soon you'll have frost all over you. Careful you don't get chilled." Fowler handed him another coat and suggested he put on ear muffs.

"This is incredible," Prohaska said, huddled on the couch, trembling uncontrollably. "H-how much longer?"

"I don't know. Maybe it's hungry."

Prohaska shook his head. "Stop being funny," he said.

"Funny, hell. What other kinds of m-motivation could it have?"

"Maybe it's after our souls. Out to scare us to death. Maybe it j-just hates human beings, can't stand being around them."

The chart record levelled off at twenty-nine degrees Fahrenheit, about two degrees below zero Celsius. "Okay," Fowler said. "It has enough now."

"Enough for what?"

"Patience."

Something slammed against the door. They both jumped. "There are two of us," Prohaska said. "If it doesn't like people, now it's twice as mad as when just you were here."

"Might have been a bird. An owl."

"Flying into the door in the dark. Jesus, there's frost on the logs in the fireplace!"

"I told you about that," Fowler said.

"Now I believe you."

The thump on the door came again. Fowler brought up the camera loaded with infrared and snapped two pictures of the door.

"Maybe we should answer," Prohaska suggested.

"You answer."

"I'm not insured for that sort of thing."

This time, the thump became regular, insistent.

"It's the old problem," Fowler said. "Do you keep the door closed and stay afraid, wondering what it is, or do you open it and know for sure?"

"Neither."

Fowler laughed grimly. "A man after my own heart. But that isn't a very scientific attitude. Maybe someone wants in." In a louder voice, he called out, "Who is it?"

Prohaska yelped. "In the window," he said. "There's something in the window!"

Behind the curtains, Fowler could see two points of light, like eyes, moving back and forth on the other side of the glass. He started to move closer, hesitated, then forced himself to look at the lights squarely. He was barely a yard from whatever was outside. Behind the curtains, he could see the two spots were moths, each burning with the red glow he had seen before.

"They're insects," he said.

"They're moving like eyes."

Something tinked against the glass, then again. It became a suggestive, metallic rain of tiny stones, and then it stopped. Prohaska's breath was ragged. The cabin was not getting any warmer.

"Build a fire," Fowler said. "Let's get some heat in here." He didn't bother checking the thermostat and the gas heater—the pilot light was probably out. They pulled logs out of the hopper and stacked them above crumpled newspapers, then lit a match and started the blaze. Fowler looked up and the moths were gone. For the moment, the noise had stopped. Prohaska held his hands out to the fire and sighed.

"How did this thing get the old man to kill his son?"

"How the hell should I know?" Fowler said, suddenly irritable. "Possession."

"You're suggesting it's a demon of some sort?"

"Jordan Taggart didn't think it was a ghost. It doesn't behave like a ghost—no human form, for one thing."

"How about a poltergeist?"

"I don't think so."

"But don't demons have to be conjured up or invited in or something?"

Fowler shook his head. "I'm no expert, Sam. I've only done scattered reading, and I'm sure none of the authors I've read knew what they were talking about. They express everything in religious terms, applying a ready-made metaphysic to it. Maybe this isn't connected with religion. Maybe it's a natural phenomenon."

"I find that hard to believe."

"It's happening, isn't it?"

Prohaska held up his hands helplessly. "Not at the moment. I don't believe a thing when it isn't happening at the moment."

Rocks began to fall against the roof. "Now there," Prohaska said. "As a reporter, I can handle rock falls on the roof. That's an old poltergeist trick."

Again the door was hit by pebbles. "Squirrels playing baseball," Fowler said. The muffled thumps resumed, and resolved into a steady knock. "It wants in."

"By God, I feel like an asshole," Prohaska said. "What if somebody is outside, hurt or sick?"

Fowler didn't answer. He stood by the couch, looking steadily at the window. Nothing was visible except a dim reflection of Prohaska and himself.

"If it can't get in, I don't see why we should let it in," he said steadily. His hands were shaking and he stuffed them into the jacket pockets. "If it's any consolation I feel pretty stupid, too."

"No consolation at all."

"Then open the door."

Prohaska screwed his face up like a kid faced with a particularly unpleasant dare. "If it wants in, it can break a window. It hasn't tried yet. It's only seen people go in and out the door. So it isn't very smart, is it?"

"I don't think so."

"Good, good. We begin to establish parameters. If it isn't an injured hunter dying while we futz around in here, it's some sort of immaterial force that gets energy by freezing things, and it isn't very intelligent. But it doesn't like people."

"I have to go to the john," Fowler said.

"And leave me alone out here?"

Fowler chuckled. "You'll survive until I return." He walked down the hall and left the door open as he urinated. A thin layer of ice melted under his warm discharge. He flushed the toilet and turned to look in the tub.

The growth was back, worse if anything. The crayonlike marks had started to make a pattern. It resembled a body curled up in the tub, drawn with a thousand frenetic lines. The smell was awful. "Sam, bring some disinfectant and come in here. Bring the cleanser, too."

Prohaska rattled under the kitchen sink, then came to the bathroom and stood by the tub with Fowler. "You sound like this has happened before," he said softly.

"It goes away with cleanser." Fowler picked up the scrub brush and poured disinfectant into the tub. "I don't know what will happen if it keeps growing," he said. The amber fluid poured toward the drain. Where it touched, the mould began to dissolve. He sprinkled green powder into the tub. The disinfectant crossed a few puffs of green and met the head of the figure.

It flinched.

Fowler backed up against the wall. Prohaska stood transfixed. "Did you see that?" he asked.

"Let's clear it out." Fowler returned to the tub and took the bathroom scrub brush from its holder near the toilet. Bending over, holding his head as high above the tub as possible, he began to erase the lines with the brush. He ran water and repeated the procedure. A dull stain remained this time, but the buildup vanished, and with it the suggestion of a curled-up body.

"They found Taggart—Jordan Taggart—in the bathtub," Prohaska said. He licked his lips. "I need something to drink."

"I didn't know they found him here," Fowler said. He stood, holding his dripping hands away from his pants. "What about Henry?"

"Outside, on the porch."

The door rattled.

"Don't say it," Prohaska warned.

"Say what?"

"That it's Taggart outside."

"Hell no, he was much too polite."

They looked at each other for a moment, and tears welled up in Fowler's eyes. A cloud of sadness and loss seemed to rise around them. "Why couldn't it be friendly?" Fowler said.

"What?" Prohaska voiced the word cautiously, as though he knew what Fowler meant, but the question was still necessary.

"It killed my best friend and his father. We haven't done anything to it, but it wants to kill us, now. Why?"

"Maybe we're thorns in its side." Prohaska seemed to struggle for the proper phrasing, his lips working. "Have you ever been in a room with a very dull person, and watched the hate grow when he met a smart person? The resentment, the hackles rising, all covered by society?" He leaned against the bathroom door, head lowered as if he was going to be sick. "The stupid person knows that the smart person can destroy him if he wants."

"I don't understand—not completely," Fowler said.

"If that thing outside is not intelligent, if it's dull and slow like a porcupine, it thinks we're dangerous. At the very least, irritating. If it's stuck here, stuck in the ground, in this valley maybe, we're not. We can go where we please. It hates us because we're freer than it is."

The door was hit by something infinitely heavy and slow. The air in the cabin seemed to thicken, growing more and more pungent. Fowler looked at Prohaska and suddenly loathed him.

"Your ideas don't make any sense," he said thickly. His tongue was like glue. He could hardly talk. "I have to get out of here, I'm going to be sick."

"Me, too," Prohaska said. They lurched against each other in the hall and Fowler felt like striking the reporter. They went to the kitchen tap and immediately began to slurp handfuls of water, butting against each other in their haste. Prohaska raised his hand, his eyes heavy-lidded.

"I feel dull too, now," Fowler said, jerking his eyes back and forth between the raised hand and Prohaska's face. "It's making me stupid. Dense. Can hardly move."

"A weapon," Prohaska said. Fowler could hardly hear him. "It gets rid of us by making us like it . . . is . . ." He lowered his hand and looked at it sheepishly. "Don't you feel it? Plodding, slow, but clever somehow . . . able to get into our minds and pick out the loathsome things, the things rotten with age. The fear. The bigotry. The greed. It knows these things, it knows how to use them."

"Stop talking," Fowler commanded. "Your voice hurts my ears." Every word seemed to pierce and irritate. He wanted to listen to something else but Prohaska was preventing him by chattering. That something else was the fall of gravel on the roof, soothing like rain. Perhaps it was rain. Rain had always lulled him, made him grow dull and sleepy. Now he wanted to sleep. He walked one step to the couch, to lie down, but stopped himself. "If we go to sleep, we've had it," he told Prohaska. The reporter raised his head and looked at Fowler listlessly. There were tears in his eyes now, too. "It's so sad," Fowler said, nodding.

"It's lonely," Prohaska said. "It needs company." He turned slowly and faced the living room. "If we're so fucking pure at heart and capable, surely we can teach it, make it more like us!" He walked toward the door. Fowler reached out to stop him, but his hand missed and dropped to his side. Prohaska stumbled on the throw rug and fell against the door. The infinite, single pound, in the lower registers of hearing, continued to roll against the outside, demanding, insisting, and now—Prohaska was weeping with it—pleading to be let in.

"Don't," Fowler whispered. He was crying for the Taggarts, not for what was outside. His mouth was thick despite the water. He turned back to drink some more. His fingers twisted the faucet handle and he held his hand out.

Brown water poured from the tap across his fingers and palm. The odor was sharp and poisonous, like smelling salts and sewage. He backed away, holding out his hand. Then he saw it was clean, just wet, and the water was clear. It was a distraction. He heard Prohaska unlatch and unlock the door.

"No!"

The door swung open and the reporter backed away. At first, there was nothing outside but darkness. Then, in the light through the door, Fowler saw a dark, hulking shape, oddly textured. He tried to place the texturing in his memory—where had he seen it before? He stood in the corner of the hallway, just beyond the kitchen, leaning against the wall. Prohaska was placing his hands over his eyes, unwilling to see what was outside. A stream of glowing things poured through the door in a rectangle, like an extrusion of gelatin filled with burning flecks, pushing against Prohaska. Mosquitoes and flies clung to his coat and pants and nestled in his hair. Fowler watched and gasped. The shape outside the door moaned and moved. It had tusks, ill-defined because of what it was made out of—tusks, a flat nose and huge, powerful shoulders. It stood on four thin legs, stomach low to the ground, and two red eyes peered into the cabin, searching, flashing like coals in the wind. They fastened on Prohaska.

Fowler remembered where he had seen the texture before—in the drive. The thing was made of gravel. He shouted to warn Prohaska and ran to close the door. The burning insects struck him like a shower of sparks, stinging his skin. With eyes closed, he braced his shoulder against the door, pushing with all his strength while Prohaska stood dumbly behind. It was a losing battle.

Fowler was flung aside like a toy. The door slammed against the wall. Lying against the couch arm, he saw the boar coil itself to leap. He made a weak gesture to kick Prohaska back, but he was too late. The boar poured through the opening, striking the reporter in the head and chest, knocking him to the opposite wall, muffling his screams as gravel filled his mouth. The pig collapsed into a mound of rock and covered Prohaska as he slid to the floor.

Fowler stood, swayed in shock, then lurched forward. Everything was still. With one hand he shut the door, latched it and locked it. Then he turned to look at the reporter.

He lay on the floor, at least a foot deep in gravel, his face bleeding. Fowler knelt down by him and gently touched his forehead. ''My God,'' he said. Prohaska's arm moved, dislodging a few pebbles and sending them skittering across the floor.

Fowler rolled the man's head to one side and tried to pick pebbles out of his mouth.

Outside, in the drive, it sounded like a giant foot was stomping their cars into the ground.

CHAPTER TWENTY-FOUR

APPROACHING LOROBU ON HIGHWAY 54, TRUMBAUER LOOKED at his watch and announced, "Four-ten. Should be there in a few minutes." Jacobs was sitting across the back seat, holding his leg so it wouldn't knock irritably against a water tin.

"How do you feel, Miss Unamuno?" he asked. She was in the front seat and turned to look back at him.

"I don't feel anything," she said, puzzled. "It's not at all like it was. I mean, it could just be a normal day and nothing changed. Except—there are a lot of worried people ahead."

"Intuition or psychic or both?" Trumbauer asked.

"Just a lot of worried signals."

"I'm feeling them, too," Trumbauer said. "Franklin, could you get me a glass of tea from the thermos?"

Jacobs poured the cup and handed it across the seat. "FBI people, I suppose," he said. "What do we do if it's sealed off?"

"Turn around and go home, I suppose. Maybe the hotel will take a message from that clerk in Washington."

Jacobs frowned skeptically. "I wonder what they've found."

"Road block ahead. Detour," Trumbauer said.

A soldier dressed in kelly green, wearing dark glasses and a baseball-type cap, waved them over as they approached a wood and sand-bag barricade.

"What's your purpose, please?" he asked, bending down to Trumbauer's level.

"We've come to do research," Trumbauer said. Jacobs lifted his eyes at the tactless response.

"We've already told you people, flying saucers had nothing to do with this."

"Not about the town directly," Jacobs said, leaning forward in his seat. The dark glasses stared at him implacably. "We're here to inquire about several people—"

"Inhabitants?"

"We don't know. We have a list of names."

"Can I see identification?"

They took out their driver's licenses and handed them to the soldier, who had called for several others to join him. Three men and a woman, all in the same uniform, surrounded the station wagon.

"Mr. Jacobs, what's your interest in this?" the soldier asked.

"Mr. Trumbauer requested my services."

"Why do you need him, Mr. Trumbauer?"

"I—I—"

"Tell him, Arnold. He already thinks we're crazy."

"I represent a group of people with unusual abilities," Trumbauer said. "Psychics, actually. Miss Unamuno here has the . . . uh . . . ability. And we—that is, the people I represent—were all brought down ill at the same time. . . ." He stopped and swallowed. The dark glasses registered no change in expression, but seemed to convey disdain.

"Go on," the soldier said.

"They were all made sick by what happened in Lorobu," Trumbauer finished.

The soldier nodded and walked around the car to talk to his companions. Trumbauer glanced back at Jacobs and shook his head. "We're in too deep," he said. "They won't have anything to do with us."

"Too deep?" Jacobs asked. "We're concerned citizens. There was a time when that meant something."

The soldier returned and took off his dark glasses. His eyes were blue and he was really quite young, Jacobs saw—no more than twenty-three. "Were you planning on driving around the town? There's a detour."

"I don't believe so," Trumbauer said. "Our business is in Lorobu."

"Lorobu is closed off for now. No admittance. I'm sorry you had to come all this way. If you'll give me your list of names, I'll let you——"

"Sorry," Jacobs said, waving his hand. "If anything turns up, we'll get in touch." The soldier shrugged and backed away as Trumbauer turned the station wagon around.

Janet Unamuno sat silent as they drove away. "They don't even know what's happened," she said a few minutes later. "They think it's an act of terrorism. That somebody gassed the whole town."

"He was thinking that?" Trumbauer asked. She nodded. "Maybe he wasn't in on it."

"I'm treating for dinner," Jacobs said. "You've all been very good sports."

"We'll stop over in Santa Rosa," Trumbauer said. He glanced up in his mirror and frowned. "Or maybe we won't." Jacobs turned and saw a Jeep pursuing them about a mile behind, lights flashing.

"Slow down," he said. Trumbauer slowed the station wagon and pulled over to the side of the highway. The Jeep parked in front of them and a man and a woman in kelly green got out. The woman took a position by Unamuno's side as the man stood near the driver's door.

"Mr. Franklin Jacobs, please," the soldier said.

"I'm him," Jacobs said, getting out. The soldier backed away nervously.

"Are you the Jacobs—the Mr. Jacobs who inquired about a list of names, specifically—" And he read off the first three names of Unamuno's roster.

"I am."

"Could you please come with us? Just turn around and head back for Lorobu. We'll follow."

"My call to Washington must have aroused some attention," Jacobs said as Trumbauer brought the car around.

"Then maybe they do know more," Trumbauer said.

"Or maybe they suspect us."

"No," Janet said. "They're scared, but not of us."

They were flagged through the barricade and escorted down the main street.

CHAPTER TWENTY-FIVE

EXCEPT FOR THE MEN IN WHITE BODY SUITS AND SCATTERED soldiers in kelly green, Lorobu was deserted. Barbed wire had been placed around the town, even around the outlying shacks common near desert communities. Portable generators had been set up near mobile command trailers, and their noise provided an aural backdrop to the emptiness.

The Jeep pulled alongside and the woman told Trumbauer to park his car in front of the Lorobu Inn.

"How are you feeling?" Jacobs asked Miss Unamuno.

"A little frightened, but not sick."

"Then it's gone," Trumbauer said. "I don't feel anything unusual, except the emptiness and the nervousness."

The young soldier opened the car doors for them and asked them to come into the inn. They walked by the restaurant entrance, which was sealed with an official notice of quarantine, into the hotel lobby. A staff sergeant was stationed behind the front desk. He snapped to attention as a Colonel came down the stairs and approached the group of three.

"Hello," the man said cordially, offering his hand to Trumbauer, then to Jacobs, and finally to Miss Unamuno.

"I'm Colonel James David Silvera, in charge of research here in Lorobu. I understand you're interested in recent events here." He was in his forties, with wiry gray hair and a weathered olive complexion. His nose was a match for Jacobs'.

Trumbauer introduced himself and the others. Jacobs examined the lobby casually, noting the line of portable bulletin boards, new television monitors, and a pile of electronic gear neatly stacked by the old elevator. "Sir," he said, "is this all top secret?"

"Yes, Mr. Jacobs, it is."

"Then you can't tell us anything."

"I wouldn't say that. We feel very obligated when citizens express an interest in our work." He brought a folded piece of paper out of his jacket pocket and opened it. "You requested information on a list of names, most of them military personnel at one time or another."

"All of them," Miss Unamuno said.

"Where did you get the list?"

Jacobs looked at Miss Unamuno.

"I gave it to them," she told the Colonel.

"Were you acquainted with any of these men?"

"Of course not," she said. "I believe they're all dead."

Silvera nodded. "Who gave the list to you?"

"The names were conveyed to me by—" She hesitated. Silvera waited, then smiled and said, "Don't worry, Miss Unamuno. Nothing will seem very strange after a few hours in Lorobu."

"By the spirits of the men themselves. I think. I'm not positive. I was very ill."

"What made you ill?"

Trumbauer broke in. "Lorobu made many psychics in New Mexico ill, Colonel."

"Yes. I can see that. Over eight hundred people dying in one day. Very traumatic."

"That wasn't what made them ill," Jacobs said wryly.

"Colonel, we're being frank with you. In exchange, I hope you can confirm or deny some of our suspicions."

"As much as I'm able. My office is upstairs." He turned to the staff sergeant and requested that the mess truck provide them with sandwiches, coffee and milk. "That's all we have for now, I'm afraid. The restaurant is closed down." They followed him up the stairs.

Silvera's office was a converted guest room. Some of the rooms were sealed off, others were being used as offices and storage areas. Silvera explained that all the soldiers were billeted in tents on the other side of town, or in the Holiday Inn farther down the road. "It was almost empty when this happened," he said. "Frankly, I think the rooms here have more charm."

The room was in western style, with furniture made of tamarisk and decorations consisting of a weatherbeaten oxen yoke, some unidentifiable piece of flattened mining machinery, and an old saddle standing near the door on a converted parking-meter pipe. Silvera's office equipment barely intruded—a portable steel desk, a file cabinet, and several new telephones, only two of which were connected. The wires ran out the window, presumably to a field-communications trailer nearby. A portable typewriter squatted lightly on the desk. He sat down on one of the twin beds and offered a chair to Miss Unamuno.

"Perhaps you should begin first," he suggested.

"First, a question," Jacobs said. Silvera nodded. "The list that we gave you—are those names by chance classified?"

Silvera nodded again.

"Is Lorobu connected with secret government tests?"

The Colonel shook his head. "No. Lorobu was not wiped out by nerve gas, secret Army plagues, or anything of the kind."

"Fine," Jacobs said. "Arnold, I think we should tell the Colonel all we know."

When Trumbauer finished the story, the sandwiches and

drinks arrived and they ate quietly. Silvera made notes on file cards and stacked them neatly on the bedstand. It was dark outside. A big truck pulled in behind the inn, its lights briefly illuminating a wall beyond the window.

"We know very little, ourselves," Silvera said after wiping his lips with a paper napkin. "We're in the position of police investigators who have no clues and no hope of solving the case. They've been known to call in psychics, so why can't we? Well, in this case we're concerned with more than a single murder, or maintaining press security to prevent copycat crimes. Since you've come up with something that matches what little evidence we have—"

Jacobs raised his eyebrows.

"—I think you're fairly legitimate. I'm going to make a request that security checks be run on you, and that you be given clearance to help us here."

"I already have a security clearance," Jacobs said. "I was in the Navy."

"Good. That'll expedite things. For the moment, since you probably already suspect something, I'll give you this much information. Some of the names on your list we've already investigated. Several were recorded around the town by former citizens."

"Recorded how?" Trumbauer asked.

"I thought you might have read it—it was reported in a newspaper back East. One name was written all over the inside of a shack where a wino lived. Others were scrawled in phone booths, doors, desks, chairs, all sorts of places. Apparently the people in Lorobu were receiving something similar to what you picked up." He looked at them quizzically. "Is that what you think?"

"Did the people on the list live in Lorobu at one time?" Miss Unamuno asked.

"Only one," Silvera said. "The first name—Lieutenant William Skorvin. He lived here in the thirties. Went into the Navy in 1941, became a pilot, and was killed in World War Two.''

''How was he killed?'' Jacobs asked.

''My orders are to prime the pump a little—to see if you have anything more of interest to offer. But let's wait and see if you're cleared.''

''He was killed—'' Miss Unamuno began. She paled and put her hand to her mouth. ''No, he was shot down and taken prisoner.''

Silvera looked at her steadily, then turned and picked up his file cards. ''You people are as spooky as this town. If you're cleared, will you be willing to work as civilian contractors?''

Jacobs hesitated, then nodded.

CHAPTER TWENTY-SIX

TIM SAT QUIETLY IN THE PRINCIPAL'S OUTER OFFICE WHILE HIS brother talked inside. He could guess what they were saying: Tim is sensitive, Tim may have nightmares, this is a new experience for him. He felt very helpless. He was homesick, but of course there was no home to go back to.

Except with us, Tim

And he knew that was no good, because all those voices were dead. Somehow they had established an outpost in his head where they could talk to him, pester him, but they were not anyplace he could go while he was still alive.

"I want to be alive," he said softly to himself, biting his lower lip and looking around. The secretary hadn't heard; she smiled at him. She was pretty. He didn't want anything to happen to people like her. Something had to be done, but he didn't know what just yet. He had to talk to important people, people who would believe him. If he said anything more to doctors or to Rick he would simply be put in a hospital for good. He couldn't do anything in a hospital. He had seen shows on TV about such hospitals. Even if you said you were sane they laughed at you and beat you up. The doctors in Albuquerque had been a little

bit like that. Everything you said was suspect to them,
even if you only wanted to go to the bathroom in the
middle of talking. "Are you trying to avoid something,
Tim?" they had asked.

I'm trying to avoid *you*. And *them*.

Rick came out of the inner office and the principal
followed him. The principal was a tall, big-boned man
with a dry, light hand grip. His hair was feathery and there
wasn't much of it, so he oiled it carefully and made each
strand count. His eyes were friendly and he probably knew
everything there was to know about kids.

"Tim, I think you're going to have a good time here,"
he said. Tim nodded.

"I've taken Tim around the school, so he knows the
classes and everything," Rick said.

"Just in case, let's give him a map and introduce him to
the first class," the principal said.

It was just after lunch. His first class after lunch was
Utah history, he discovered. The teacher was a young
woman with a hairstyle remarkably like Suzanne's. They
went through the uncomfortable ritual of introducing Tim
and all the kids looked at him blankly, trying to decide
where he would fit. Most didn't care much one way or the
other. That was okay. He preferred to be ignored. Rick
left.

The teacher assigned Tim a seat, promised to give him a
textbook as soon as they could bring one up from the
repository, and spent an awkward five minutes trying to
fill him in on Utah history up to the point they'd reached,
about 1890.

What would Brigham Young have done about Lorobu?
Tim had seen a movie about Brigham Young and what had
happened to the Mormons, being driven from state to
state. He was sorry he'd missed the best part of the class.
He had liked history as Mr. Parker had taught it in Lorobu.

Mr. Parker is still with us, Tim

The next class was arithmetic and he talked to a boy with glasses who told him what the teacher was like (the kids stayed in the room but the history teacher went away and the arithmetic teacher came in; he would also stay for civics, the boy said). The boy's name was Archie Gerald. Tim thought that was a funny name but didn't say anything. They both liked to build models.

"I got to stop that kind of kid's stuff soon," Tim said.

"Why?" Archie asked.

"Time to grow up."

"That's a funny thing. Why would anyone want to be a grownup?"

"Reasons," Tim said. Archie didn't have time to press him. The new teacher arrived and the kids became quiet. The teacher noticed Tim and said hello to him, then marked his position in the class. Tim was a little ahead of the school in arithmetic for his grade. He settled back to cover old territory, feeling better now that he had met Archie.

After civics, Archie walked with him to the front of the school, where the buses and parents in cars picked up all the kids. They talked about football for a little bit, but neither of them cared very much, so then they talked about television, which was a better subject. Tim noticed that Archie had a limp and Archie explained he'd had an accident as a little boy. "I lost my foot under a train," he said.

"Geez!" For a moment, Tim couldn't think of anything to say. "That must have hurt."

"Hurt like hell," Archie said. "But I was only four and I don't remember too much. So now I got a fake foot. I do pretty well on it. You'll even see me at recess. I play mean tether ball. Want to play tomorrow?"

"Yeah, sure."

"Where do you live?"

"I'm not sure how far it is from here. It's on a street called Marchand."

"Sure—I know where that is. I live about three miles away. Maybe we could get together on the weekends."

"That'd be great," Tim said. He saw Rick's car. "Gotta go."

"Sure. See you."

Tim started to walk to the curb, then stopped and turned. "Hey," he said.

"Yeah?"

"Everything's pretty normal around here, isn't it?"

"What do you mean?"

"Like, everybody's nice, and all that sort of stuff, aren't they?"

"Sure," Archie said. "See you."

Tim got into the car and Rick asked him how everything went. "Fine," Tim said. "I met somebody named Archie. He's a nice guy."

"Good," Rick said. "You'll like it here."

That was the problem, Tim thought. If anything happened to these people, it would be awful.

CHAPTER TWENTY-SEVEN

PROHASKA GROANED AND SAT UP IN THE BED, THEN FELL BACK. His face was badly swollen and the cuts and scratches radiated around his nose like a starburst. He had two deep gouges in his chest—from the boar's fangs, apparently— and he was now shirtless and bandaged. "What happened?" the reporter asked, his voice muffled by puffy lips.

"You opened the door," Fowler said.

"An animal jumped on me. How did you get it out?"

Fowler held up a small plastic bag filled with gravel. "With a shovel, mostly," he said. Prohaska tried to focus on Fowler sitting in a chair next to the bed, then gave it up as a bad job. "You're lucky," Fowler said. "Your eyes aren't hurt bad—just scratches on the lids. Most of it is bruises and shallow cuts. You'll be sore for a week or two."

"What was it?" Prohaska asked.

"A pig. A large boar—very large. Four or five feet at the shoulders, built like a nightmare. Built out of a nightmare, too, I'd say."

"Is it gone?"

"I don't know. There's enough gravel in the driveway to build one or two dozen of them. If it runs out of that, then it might go to dirt and sticks. Either way, I'm not going outside until daylight."

The reporter felt his face tenderly and groaned again. "All this for a curiosity story," he said.

"Go back to sleep if you can."

"Brave guy. Stay in the house alone with an injured man. Why don't we try to leave?"

"Because the cars are wrecked," Fowler said. "Windows smashed, hoods caved in. I haven't gone out to see if they're drivable, but I doubt it."

"Calling out?"

Fowler took the bedroom phone extension off its receiver and held it to Prohaska's ear. A sound like the rush of wind hissed out of the earpiece.

"What is it?" Prohaska asked.

"I don't know. I found it when I tried to put through a call to Dot—Dorothy, my friend in Los Angeles. No luck. We're stuck until someone comes to get us. Or we can hike out in the morning, if this thing isn't still busy."

"Is it snowing?"

"No. Clear as a bell and fairly warm for this time of year. Snow is out for the next few days, and that may be in our favor. We can walk out of here and hitch a ride on the upper highway. Not many cars pass through the valley."

Prohaska closed his eyes and folded his hands on his chest, then winced.

"You've been gouged in two places around the sternum, but they're clean now."

"I should get a tetanus shot."

"Maybe. We'll see when we get into town. For now, sleep."

"Sleep, and dream," Prohaska said, his voice fading. Fowler tucked the blankets in around the reporter's shoulders and stood back. His face was lined with worry and fatigue. It was almost midnight. The microwave level had dropped from its earlier plateau, and the climate of the valley appeared to be back to normal, but that was no guarantee the night was going to be quiet. He needed to sleep, but didn't dare.

In the living room, his equipment waited faithfully, the chart recorder humming slightly. It would be time to put in a new roll of paper soon—perhaps an hour or so. He wondered what good the records were going to do. If something showed up on the photographs, how would they interpret it? What would all of the information mean when it was assembled? He sat down in the lazy boy and pulled the recliner back, then picked up one of Jordan Taggart's books.

Tomorrow, if the schedule was being followed, the new dam would release overflow water into the valley. The lower driveway, just before the highway, would be flooded to the depth of a foot or so.

Jordan Taggart's cabin would sit on an island of two acres, surrounded by a slow, shallow river. The stream boundaries had been marked by stakes and flags. His eyes closed and the book started to slip from his hands. Then he sat up abruptly, grabbed the book, and cursed in surprise.

Somewhere in Taggart's library, he had read that vampires couldn't cross running water. He searched the shelf for the particular book and located it—*The Vampire in Europe*, by Montague Summers. It quoted an extensive passage from Apuleius' *Golden Ass* about an early vampire. Fowler began to search through the other books for more documentation.

And then he found it, in an old, crumbling paperback on

witchcraft and black magic. Spirits and the undead could not cross running water.

"It's a conductor," he mused, putting a piece of paper into the book as a placemark. "It shorts them out. They can't cross over it if they're bound to the Earth." He was beginning to feel excited, but the tiredness was overcoming the new energy and he lay back, eyes blinking. If the thing returned, it would announce itself. Sleep was very important to health. At three in the morning, Fowler slept and the chart recorder ran out of paper.

Old.

Living with magnetic flux, born in other spaces, not a part of the human progress. A separate, predatory thing, always angry, cunning but not bright . . . as creative as the moulds in the forest floor. Master of the germ, the weak, delighter in decay. A thing halfway, yet on neither side. Primal hater. Antithesis. Opponent. Plague.

Something roared and he awoke. Outside, it was bright. Fowler looked at his watch and groaned. Eleven-thirty in the morning. There was a car in the drive.

He got off the couch and peered outside. A sheriff's car, two people inside. Shaking his head, resigned, he walked to the back bedroom and looked in on Prohaska. The reporter was tangled in his sheets and blankets. Like Fowler, he must have had unpleasant dreams. Fowler gently shook him awake. The swelling had gone down. Prohaska looked at him through gluey eyes and managed a weak smile.

"They're on to us," Fowler said.

"What?"

"The sheriff is here."

"Christ."

"Are you strong enough to get up?"

"I think so. Ouch—these bandages are tight."

"Just as well that they're here. We'll get you to a hospital and let professionals look you over."

The knock on the front door was familiar and even welcome this time. He straightened his clothes and looked at his hair briefly in the bathroom mirror—noticing the tub was clean today—then went to answer.

He swung the door open. "Yes?" The sheriff looked at him, frowning indecisively. Dorothy left the car and walked to the cabin.

"You're Lawrence Fowler?"

"Yes, sir."

The sheriff was about thirty, husky and not to be fooled with. Dorothy stood in the middle of the drive, among the potholes and bare spots, looking around, frightened.

"My name is Parkins, Howard Parkins. What the hell are you doing here, Mr. Fowler?"

"I'm playing amateur investigator," Fowler said, smiling weakly.

"No . . . I mean, what happened around the cabin?"

Fowler stepped out of the door and looked at the clearing and woods. Besides the wreckage of the cars, the underbrush and trees around the cabin looked like a thousand bears had been set loose on them. The bark was stripped from the trunks, the branches broken and bent and bare, and the turf lay scattered in yard-wide divots.

"I'm not sure," Fowler said. "I was asleep."

The sheriff shook his head and walked back to the car. "I'm going to call in, say you're all right. Is there a reporter here with you?"

"Sam Prohaska, yes. He was injured last night—not serious, I think."

Dorothy approached him, hands clasped in front of her. "There was no call," she said, her lips tight. "I was very worried. I flew up here and chartered a flight to Lone Pine . . . Larry, there's water over the road now."

"I know. A dam overflow."

"What happened to the trees?"

"Same thing, I think, that happened to the cars. I don't know whether it happened last night or this morning. I must have been zonked. Prohaska was attacked last night."

"By what?"

"A giant boar." He couldn't prevent himself from laughing. He leaned against the doorjamb, feeling relief and anxiety and a bubbleheaded lightness he couldn't explain.

"Oh, Larry," Dorothy said, touching his face with one cool hand. She was wearing a safari suit tailored to fit, with high-fashion leather hiking boots that came to her calves. Her hair was dishevelled. He took her in his arms but she didn't come easily, seeming to resist, then give in complacently. He caught the signals right away. She was furious with him but didn't want to show it.

The sheriff returned and Dorothy broke from his embrace.

"Mr. Fowler, you're occupying these premises illegally. You've broken a seal and I don't know what else, and it looks like you had a drunken ball around here. I don't know whether to arrest you or just kick you the hell out. Any damage in the cabin?"

"No, sir. I've been keeping it clean. Cleaning the bathroom regularly." He managed to hold back his smile this time, but just barely. The sheriff pierced him with a glance.

"You still stoned?"

"I have not been stoned, and what you see now is relief. You've just saved me from a task bigger than I could handle."

"What would that be?"

Fowler pointed to the cars and the trees. "I didn't do any of this. How could I? Take a look at the cars." His eye fell on the dirt where the gravel had been removed. He walked over to the bare spot and pointed at a hoofprint in the dirt.

"Do you have pigs this large around here?"

"No pigs at all."

Prohaska came to the cabin door, dressed in his fawn-colored suit, walking awkwardly. "Hello, Howard," he greeted the sheriff.

"Sam, are you all crazy here? This woman tells me her boyfriend is camping out in a secured cabin, fighting off ghosts—what in *hell* happened to you?"

Prohaska shook his head. "I wasn't drunk, and I was here for the same reasons as Mr. Fowler. But I don't know how to tell about it. You're a pretty level-headed fellow."

The sheriff nodded.

"All the worse," Prohaska concluded. "Come in, have some coffee—for my sake, please—and I'll try to tell you. Mr. Fowler isn't crazy, and he has all kinds of evidence to prove it."

Fowler took Dorothy's hand and led her into the cabin. In the kitchen, she helped him prepare the coffee and warmed up a few frozen breakfast rolls. The sheriff ate hesitantly, uncertain about the legalities, as Prohaska related what had happened.

Fowler drained his cup and swore softly.

"What's the matter?" Dorothy asked.

"The chart paper has to be replaced. I let it go last night—broke the record." While he worked over the recorder, he talked about the equipment and mentioned he had first come to the cabin at Henry Taggart's request.

Parkins sipped his coffee slowly, not reacting to anything yet, his eyes going back and forth between Fowler and Prohaska.

"You knew Henry Taggart well?" he asked.

"Went to high school together. Kept in touch after I came back from Vietnam."

"You dabble in this occult stuff?"

"Never have before. And I hope never to again."

"Mr. Fowler, Sam, I don't know *what* to do with you. Sam here has done five or six stories on this area, he's a smart fellow, and fair, too. I don't know about you, Mr. Fowler. I'd trust almost anything Sam says. But Jesus, you're telling me a pig made out of rocks did all this damage, wrecked two cars and ripped up a forest?"

Fowler nodded. "And worked over Sam."

"You need a doctor, Sam?" Parkins asked.

"Not immediately. I can wait for a couple of hours. But I'm sore as hell."

"There aren't any birds outside," Dorothy said. "I couldn't hear anything singing or moving. It was so quiet."

"Water's all around the place now," Fowler said. "I don't know how it will react."

CHAPTER TWENTY-EIGHT

FOWLER MADE A LAST CHECK OF THE CABIN, TO BE SURE EVERY-thing was as it had been, then took Henry's key from his pocket and locked the front door. The emotions he was feeling were too mixed to sort out and identify, but he knew he had failed.

What evidence he had was ridiculous, useless to convince a world even more incredulous than he was—had been. No, he was incredulous still—despite what had happened, he hardly believed the past few days himself.

He took Dorothy by the arm and walked with her to the police car.

"I'll have a tow truck out here by tomorrow morning," Parkins said. He opened the rear door of his car for them. Fowler started to get into the back seat, then hesitated and snapped his fingers. "I left the bag of gravel in the kitchen," he said. Prohaska looked at him from the front seat and nodded.

"It'll wait. We'll get it to you by mail, if it's so important," Parkins said.

Fowler agreed meekly and stepped in. Dorothy sat beside him, hands folded in her lap, silent. Her face was rigid. He glanced at her, then turned away to look at the cabin. As if nothing had happened, it was unmarred—but for a few scratches on the front door—and serene.

The sheriff backed the car out, turned it around, and drove down the gravel drive.

"It'll be glad to see us go, I think," Fowler said. Dorothy flinched.

They were almost to the new stream when a loud bang and the car's sudden wobble made the sheriff brake to a stop. They all sat mute for a second. Prohaska looked out the window. "Blew a tire," he said.

"I don't believe it," Parkins said. He opened his door and walked around the car to examine the damage. "Mr. Fowler, you'll have to help me move your equipment to get at the spare."

Fowler waited for him to open the door on his side—there was no interior handle—and pulled his cases out of the trunk, laying them carefully on the gravel. Together they hoisted the tire and jack out and carried them to the front right fender. "You know how to set this kind of jack up?" the sheriff asked. Fowler nodded.

"Can I help?" Prohaska asked.

"Just get out of the car, both of you. Mr. Fowler and I will handle it."

"I'm not helpless, you know." Then, under his breath, "It wants us to stay for lunch."

"*Stop it*," Dorothy said firmly. "I don't want to hear any more about it."

Fowler placed the jack under the car frame and began to pump the handle. Slowly the car lifted from the deflated tire. "Okay, that's enough," the sheriff said. "Here, there's a safety on the jack." He pointed and Fowler flipped the little clip. Using the pry-bar, the sheriff removed the hub cap and began to strain at the nuts. "Goddamn electric wrenches put these things on too tight," he said.

Fowler grinned sympathetically and helped apply pressure on the other nuts. They slipped the tire off and replaced it with the spare.

Fowler slapped at a mosquito, then looked at his palm. He had hit it. There was the evidence—a smear of blood, fragments of insect. The blood smear turned black. The fragments powdered and fell away. He put his hand down slowly and looked around. "Better hurry," he told the sheriff.

"Why?"

"Just hurry."

There was a crashing in the woods behind them. Prohaska jerked and moaned as his bruised hand hit the open car door. Fowler held the nuts out to Parkins one by one.

"What will it do when it finds out it's trapped?" Prohaska asked. Fowler glanced at Dorothy, whose face was stony, and shook his head.

The tire was on and the nuts were tight. He put the hubcap in place and the sheriff slapped it with his palm. It refused to clamp in easily. Each time he hit one side, the other flopped out. They hit it together, tangling their arms, and it clanged into place.

Parkins stood and brushed off his knees. Fowler approached the open door as the sheriff let the car down and pulled the jack away. He was lugging it to the trunk when more snapping and crashing noises came from the woods. Fowler looked up the gentle slope toward the cabin. At the crest of the rise, a two-legged figure was standing, arms raised.

"Hold it," Parkins said. "There's someone up there."

"Get in the car," Fowler said. *"Please!"*

"It's gray," Prohaska said, gripping the car door. "Sheriff, get us out of here."

Parkins packed the jack away and sighed raggedly. "You lift your equipment in, I'm going up to see what he's doing here."

"Sheriff—"

"Mr. Fowler, don't tempt me to change my mind about you! Nobody is going to wander around this area, is that understood?"

"It's not some*one*, look at it!"

The road was covered by tree shadows and the figure was indistinct across the thirty yards. Parkins squinted, then held his hand over his eyes to cut the sun glaring in his face from the West. "Stay here," he said. Fowler quickly loaded his cases while Parkins hiked up the incline. Dorothy and Prohaska got into the car.

"Whoever you are, you're not supposed to be here," the sheriff said loudly. The figure didn't move. Parkins swatted at flies buzzing around his head and repeated what he'd said.

"What's happening, Larry?" Dorothy asked.

"I don't know."

Prohaska leaned out the car window. "Howard, stay away from it!"

Parkins stopped and put his hands on his hips. "You! You heard anything I've said? Come down from there."

The figure lowered its arms and appeared to hunch its shoulders. A low hum rose from the woods. Parkins backed away a step and put his hand on his pistol. "Down from there right now," he growled, unstrapping the holster flap. A cloud rose around the figure's feet, as if a dust devil was swirling. The sheriff started to walk backward.

Fowler ran toward him and grabbed his left arm, leaving his gun hand free. He tugged and Parkins stumbled after him, still trying to face the crest of the rise.

Fowler aimed him for the driver's seat. "Get in, get us out of here or you'll need a tow truck for this car, too." Parkins started the engine and Fowler climbed into the back seat, grabbing the window edge to pull the door shut.

The dust around the figure cleared and Dorothy sucked in her breath.

"The pig," Prohaska said, looking back.

It was at least as large as it had been the night before. Bits of gravel rose from the road bed and collected on its surface, adding to its bulk as Fowler watched. It advanced one foreleg, then the other, awkward, as if remembering how to move. The car lurched forward.

The boar leaped and scrambled. The entire forest shrieked.

It knew. Fowler pushed Dorothy into a crouch and covered the back of his neck. The gravel beast bounded into the air as the car skidded toward the new creek. Its forelegs crazed the rear window and punched a hole through, sending a shower of pebbles onto their necks. It bellowed with a nauseating, slate-squeaky edge and kicked at the rear of the car. The front tires hit the water and the car slewed on fresh mud and silt until it lay half in the creek. Parkins put it into reverse and backed up, ramming something heavy and unyielding, like a post.

Fowler didn't dare look back. Dorothy was hyperventilating and trying to scream, unable to make any effective noise.

"Fucking hell!" the sheriff bellowed.

The engine died. At the same moment, the boar's attack stopped. Parkins turned the key and the wet engine sputtered. The longer they stayed in the water, the less chance there was that the engine would start.

Dorothy began to pray in sobbing half-audible syllables. Fowler wondered if a cross would help. Somehow, he didn't think the creature was religiously observant. It was too primal.

He raised his head and looked back through the cracked rear window. He could see a dark shape lumbering behind them, and through a hole in the glass he discerned the pebbled skin.

All around the car, the trees were shivering.

The shape vanished for a moment. The car bounced as the thing landed on the roof. A stony hoof crashed through the rear window and stopped against the back of the seat, flexing this way and that.

He pushed Dorothy against the door and backed himself up to the rear seat. The hoof withdrew. A dancing series of beats on the roof followed Parkins' attempt to start the engine again.

The engine caught, coughed, then held. The sheriff gunned it and put it into drive. The car leaped forward and the boar fell off the roof, lancing another hole through the window, catching one leg and being dragged, wailing, across the creek. The car raced up the last portion of the drive and skidded onto the road, almost across it into the field beyond. Parkins straightened it out and floored the accelerator. Tires smoking, they bounced and wobbled across the asphalt until the tread grabbed and they were off.

Fowler shook his head and began to laugh helplessly. He could think of no more appropriate reaction. The boar— what he could see of it—had broken up as soon as they crossed the creek.

They were home free.

It was trapped.

CHAPTER TWENTY-NINE

HAVERSTOCK, ILLINOIS, WAS A BEDROOM COMMUNITY FOR CHIcago. Each day, twenty thousand commuters took trains and cars into the city, and each night they returned. The town itself was old and honorable, with new housing tracts surrounding a central downtown district. The sprawl had been fast and unorganized in the forties, and now there were only a few open areas, broad fields and empty hillsides, between the developments.

In three acres of such open space, Charles Q. Taylor had built a geodesic cabin and set up a business which was riding the wave of current fads. His front and back garages and toolsheds were filled with stacked lengths of rod and piping. As a showplace and training area for salesmen, the acre in front of the round house was littered with samples of his stock-in-trade: pyramids.

The hollow frameworks, some covered with plastic sheeting and some open to the winds, gave a playgroundlike air to the yard. The pipes and rods were painted in rainbow colors. Accessories were placed in a neat single-wide mobilehome parked twenty yards from the house. The whole area was enclosed by chain-link fencing.

Taylor was a bachelor and alone for the first time in a week. The night was cold and still, clear enough to almost reach up and touch the stars and moon. He finished his dinner at seven-thirty and stood on the back porch, smoking a pipe and casually looking for constellations. There was a kind of turbulence or cloud cover to the west, a rippling effect not unlike the northern lights, which he had seen once from the general vicinity of Haverstock, but of course not in the west. He wondered if he had missed the sunset results of a rocket misfire.

Taylor, unlike many people in his business, genuinely believed in his merchandise. He had put tiny pyramids in his bathroom and bedroom, and in them he kept his razor blades, bars of soap, even bottles of vitamin C, to preserve them. When he swore an oath about his merchandise's efficacy in concentrating the pyramidic energy of the cosmos, he was honest and devoted.

Despite the clarity of the air, this night he had a headache. He wasn't prone to headaches, not as bad as this at least, but a combination of meditation and sitting under the main pyramid in the front yard usually did the trick. He picked up his tobacco pouch, put on a sweater and walked out the front door.

When names flashed in and out of his head, he wasn't alarmed. He'd gone through Dianetics and est and knew the sources of many irrational things. No doubt the name that kept occurring to him had been heard by his mother many years ago, when he'd been an impressionable fetus. That name stuck with him now, called back by the energizing of some buried engram.

What had Corporal S.K. Percher to do with his mother? He shook his head and grinned. Best not to inquire, sometimes. That was the good part about being cleared of the hangups of the past—past lives, parental lives, and the past of the current life. He hadn't gone far enough in any discipline to achieve that state. He admired those who had—but for him, there hadn't been enough financial incentive. He hadn't found the right wave to ride. No central figure controlled the sale of pyramids or pyramid literature— no franchise interrupted the flow of profits. Pyramids were something he could dedicate himself to completely.

He pulled out a plastic cushion and placed it on the cold concrete base of the open pyramid. He took out a key, unlocked the light switch and flicked it. Neon tubes on the metal piping flickered, then steadied into a bright blue glow. That was better. He squatted on the pad, pulled his feet and knees into a lotus position and tamped his pipe onto the cement.

He sucked in a breath and released it with a resonant, loud, "Au*ooooooommmmm* . . ."

A dark room, tiny windows

"What?" His concentration was broken. He frowned and took up the mantra again.

Exercise detail. In the yard of a concrete building

"Au*ooo* . . . darn!" He stopped and rearranged himself to face north. The sweater was usually enough under the big pyramid, but now he was shivering. Best to raise the heat from the center of his energy-being. Best to concentrate and—

Tiny drone, high above

"God damn!" He stood up and grasped the poles of the pyramid, almost ready to shake it down. He'd never had this much trouble before. The headache was worse. He was feeling very depressed now, worse than he'd felt in a long while. "Bad vibes tonight, very bad vibes." He looked to the west and saw that the ripply patch was gone. Then he felt his shoulders tingle, as though someone were watching him. Not someone—a crowd.

Incineration

He just had time to see the stars above waver as if distorted by rising heat. Then his hands were glued to the bars of the pyramid. To his horror he saw it was because the skin was charred and the joints were cooked solid. The neon lights shattered and sprayed powdered glass across the lawn. All the other pyramids were glowing with something like St. Elmo's fire, but it was red, and it was melting them as he watched. They crumpled into slag, more like wax than iron or aluminum.

His shoulders began to smoke.

Before he could scream, he was done clear through.

The trees in the yard began to squirm, then to blacken, like burning hands grabbing for the sky. In the house, potted plants wilted and fell away in brown shards.

Quietly, mildew began to grow along the inner walls, on the bedclothes in the upstairs room, and up and down the curtains across the plate-glass windows.

The the sky stopped shimmering, and the blight moved on.

In downtown Haverstock, Mrs. Lenora McCarthy, a widow, sat in her modest apartment, reading a new *Ladies' Home Journal* and waiting for a quiche to cook in the small, chipped oven. She heard a scream downstairs and did nothing—there were always noises in the old building, and unless they kept up for minutes at a stretch, it was best to ignore them. She had lived in the apartment for five years, and had adapted. Her husband had left her enough money to get along, and in another year she would be eligible for social security.

She looked up from her reading and scratched her shoulder absently. An old memory was returning, not an unpleasant one now, but she hadn't thought about the war years for a long time. Why the memories should press on her at this moment was unaccountable.

"Stanley," she murmured. Then she saw him, far off in the living-room mirror. He looked worried.

She stood up and let the magazine drop to the floor. The

figure in the mirror was trying to say something to her: Go away, leave.

She became frightened. Stanley was dead, had died—the memory of the government telegram came to her, *Missing in action, presumed dead*—thirty-three years before, destroying their dream, ending that stage of her life. She had subdued all these pains. Now they came back to her. If those disastrous days had never been, she would now be Mrs. Percher.

Go away, leave

She heard a sound like airplanes, high above—no, a single airplane, faint as a mosquito. Then she saw that Stanley was no longer alone in the mirror.

This confirmed the dream she had had, thirty-five years ago—a dream of Stanley in a gray little room, with a tiny window, leaving to exercise in a gray-concrete yard, and flowers blooming along the top of the wall, beginning to burn, becoming bright and painful. He had not died when his plane went down.

"What happened to them, Stan?" she asked. The screams were louder and more insistent. Stanley was crying. She looked down at her arms and hands. She could see the bones in them. The glare was intolerable for a moment. Then she saw the skin was burned and scarred, but it didn't hurt. Her hands began to glow, lighting up the little room. She couldn't leave now. It was too late.

They—and their pain, their hell—were in the room with her, and would not let her go.

An hour later, the police sirens began to wail.

CHAPTER THIRTY

Trumbauer leafed through the paper, concentrating on each story, trying to calm his nerves. Jacobs looked out the window, which opened on a fair view of the north side of Lorobu.

"You notice something?" Jacobs asked.

"Notice what?" Trumbauer murmured.

"All the trees are dead. All the plants and bushes. This morning, when we went for a walk with that soldier, all the bushes in front of the inn were brown."

"And?"

"Just musing out loud," Jacobs said. "Maybe they haven't been watered—but there's a cactus garden around the side, by the pool and patio, and it's all brown and gray, too." He looked at his watch. "Two days we've been here. This is an important project. You'd think they could cut through the red tape and decide whether we're spies or not."

"Sure," Trumbauer said. "It's important, but it's not getting anywhere. The Army and the FBI and everybody else can't begin to accept what's happened here. They're blind, as it were, and can't see the elephant that just stomped on them.''

"Colorful turn of phrase, there. You're a poet, Arnold.''

"No need for sarcasm, Franklin.'' Trumbauer dropped the top of his paper and peered over it at Jacobs.

"My patience is wearing thin and I get irritable. So you should put up with me. I put up with your poetry, you put up with my criticism. Edmund Wilson I'm not.''

"Yeats *I'm* not," Trumbauer said, grinning.

"You're so agreeable I may not be able to stand you. What do you think is holding them up?''

Trumbauer's grin vanished and he turned back to the paper. "How should I know? You're the one who's had military experience.''

A light rap on the door made him sit up and fold his paper. "Mr. Trumbauer, Mr. Jacobs?'' It was the staff sergeant who manned the desk in the lobby.

"Yes?'' Jacobs said.

The sergeant opened the door and stepped in. "Colonel Silvera would like to see you and Miss Unamuno.''

"Then let's go,'' Jacobs said, standing slowly. "We don't want to keep the Colonel waiting.''

Miss Unamuno was already in the Colonel's office, sitting stiffly in the room's desk chair. Silvera greeted the men without a smile and motioned them to sit on a couch, newly imported from the lobby.

"We've had some difficulty,'' he began, riffling file folders on his desk.

"And?'' Jacobs prompted.

"You've been cleared, Mr. Jacobs. You've done nothing to nullify your security rating. But Mr. Trumbauer . . .''

Trumbauer dropped his gaze, then raised it almost defiantly.

"What about Arnold?'' Jacobs asked.

"Mr. Trumbauer participated in potentially subversive activities in 1959.''

"I was a member of the Communist Party for two years," he said.

"You didn't mention it in your affidavit," Silvera said.

"I'm a private citizen. I offered to help you in your investigation, not to reveal my whole life."

"And you've had a record of . . . unusual sexual preference."

"I have been celibate for fifteen years."

"But weren't you active in recent homosexual political groups?"

"Not in any immoral capacity, Colonel Silvera. I am a good citizen and there is no reason you should doubt my good faith."

Jacobs looked back and forth between Silvera and Trumbauer. Suddenly he slammed his open palm on the couch arm and leaned forward. "In the name of God, Colonel, are you telling me that Arnold's political or sexual inclinations have anything to do with what's happened in Lorobu?"

"No," Silvera said. "But our investigation is being conducted under tight security. We haven't eliminated the possibility of enemy action—"

Janet Unamuno stood up. "Colonel, you and your Army and your investigation can go straight to hell. We already know more about Lorobu than you do."

"That is not strictly true," Silvera said defensively.

"Arnold Trumbauer is one of the most decent human beings on God's earth," Miss Unamuno said. "And if he is to be excluded for such ridiculous reasons—Colonel, he is no longer a Communist, and his sexual affiliations are not important as far as Lorobu is concerned."

"Exactly," Jacobs said.

"I said there were difficulties—"

"Do you need our help, or are we to be treated as interfering lackeys?" Jacobs said.

"I have never been accused of treason or lack of faith in

this country," Trumbauer said. "I became a Communist out of sympathy for friends who were being repressed by the government in the fifties. My attitudes changed during the Cuban missile crisis. My leaning is still toward the left, but in my dotage I've become very conservative. I am interested in human beings, not nations."

"All right, all right," Silvera said. "I understand your point of view, Mr. Trumbauer, and I sympathize. I have no doubt you approached us in good faith. But my superiors are more hard-line than I am, personally. And there is precedent for their convictions."

Jacobs shook his head. "Colonel, politics has nothing to do with what happened in Lorobu. Something terrible is loose—"

The door to Silvera's office opened and a black woman in the standard green uniform entered carrying a newspaper. "Sir, I'm sorry to interrupt. It's on the networks, radio and TV, sir, too. General Machen has been trying to get through to Washington."

She dropped the newspaper on his desk and stepped back stiffly. Silvera unfolded it and looked at the headlines. Jacobs craned his neck to read them.

"It's in Chicago now," Miss Unamuno said without looking at the paper.

"Have Mr. Rittenhouse and Colonel Harrison meet me in the lobby as soon as possible," Silvera said. The soldier saluted and left. Silvera looked up at them. "Could you have predicted this?" he asked.

"If I had known where the people on that list lived, yes," Miss Unamuno said. "The third name—where did he live?"

"He was a Colonel," Jacobs said.

"I know," Silvera said. He picked up a piece of paper. "He lived in Waukegan . . . no, he was born in Dayton, Ohio. His wife lived in Waukegan until she died in 1956."

"They all died in World War Two, didn't they?" Miss Unamuno asked.

The Colonel nodded.

"They were all prisoners of war, weren't they?" Trumbauer asked. He looked at Jacobs. "I was trying to put it all together. They died all at once. My guide protected me, but some of it came through and I've been sorting it ever since."

"Do you know where they died?" Silvera asked.

"Is Mr. Trumbauer cleared to work with all of us?" Jacobs asked.

"We don't bargain—but—" He raised one hand to fend off Jacobs' birthing protest. "I don't think we'll have to worry about Mr. Trumbauer. I'll give him my personal support and that should be enough—unless and until I'm replaced, which could be any time now. Do you know where they died?"

"In a prison," Miss Unamuno said, closing her eyes. "Flowers bloomed on the walls of a compound, bloomed and burned."

Silvera shook his head. "Please be patient with me. We think you're right—but we don't want to give out information that may prejudice your . . . uh . . . sensitivity."

"What information?" Jacobs prodded. "Janet, do you know what happened to those men?"

She shook her head. "I don't think they know what happened to themselves, not really."

"Why are they still here?" Trumbauer asked quietly. He had slumped in his chair and looked older, more frail. He refused to meet Jacobs' direct gaze.

"What do you mean?" the colonel asked.

"If they're dead, they should have passed on," Jacobs explained. "But I think we're all avoiding the major question. These little things are just the prelude to a real biggie— \why in hell are they killing people?"

\ilvera reached into a desk drawer and brought out a

thick folder. "This is our dossier on the men whose names you've brought to us. We can tell you, without any worry of prejudice—since it's all a *fait accompli*, and Miss Unamuno seems to be guessing anyway—that Lieutenant William Skorvin lived in Lorobu—"

"You've mentioned that," Jacobs said.

"And," Silvera continued, pointing to the paper, "Haverstock, Illinois, just outside of Chicago—Corporal S.K. Percher lived *there*." He held the paper out to Trumbauer, who took it reluctantly.

Jacobs looked over Trumbauer's arm. "Sixteen hundred people dead and wounded," he read. "But not the whole town. Why not all of Haverstock?"

"Maybe because it's limited," Silvera said, "whatever *it* is. And we're by no means sure you people are right in assuming it's supernatural. General Machen's staff has a long list of possibilities, among them biological warfare—"

Jacobs snorted.

"—which isn't farfetched, considering the increased growth of bacteria in the area."

"Or the death of plants?" Jacobs asked.

"That, too."

"Who would be responsible for that, the Russians?" Jacobs asked facetiously.

"Not necessarily."

"Oh, the Chinese, then. The Russians are the ones responsible for crazy-rays from space. Or a satellite came down in Lorobu filled with deadly space-dust."

"I saw that in a movie once," Miss Unamuno said.

Silvera stood and gathered the papers on his desk into a manila folder. "I don't think any of those ideas are more farfetched than the possession of a whole town by ghosts. Mr. Jacobs, I'd like you to come with me. Mr. Trumbauer, Miss Unamuno, we'd like for you to return to Albuquque and resume your normal lives—with the additi few security men. We'll need you in a few

Lorobu is not a pleasant place to stay. We'll call you back when—'' He stopped and tapped the folder on his desk. ''I've said too much already. I'll have your car waiting outside. I apologize for any personal distress. This isn't an easy time.''

''I didn't know you were a Commie,'' Jacobs whispered to Trumbauer as they walked out of the office in front of Silvera.

''Oh,'' Trumbauer said, ''I suppose that means it's obvious I'm a fag?''

Jacobs gave him a glance of mock shock and patted him on the shoulder. ''Someday I'll let you know what I am.''

''I know already,'' Silvera said behind them. ''You're a gardener.''

Miss Unamuno smiled briefly.

CHAPTER THIRTY-ONE

SATURDAY MORNING WAS BRIGHT AND WARM ENOUGH TO RE-
quire only a sweater. Suzanne put one on Tim as Rick
looked on, munching a donut.

"You're feeling okay now, you're sure?"

Tim made a face. "I'm sure," he said.

"This boy, Archie, he's a nice kid, isn't he?" Suzanne
asked, fussing around his buttons. "Is he a Mormon?"

"Oh, for rice cakes, Suzie," Rick said. "Let the boy
play and have fun. We can convert him later."

"I'll sing in the choir," Tim said, grinning.

"Right," Rick said, pushing him gently to the door.
"Just be back by lunch."

"I will." He stood on the doorstep and saw Archie
walking down the street. "There he is now. 'Bye!" He ran
across the yard, calling for his friend, one hand digging
into his pants pockets.

The forty-two dollars were there, all wadded up and
covered with a gum wrapper and a rubber band. He didn't
know how long it would take Rick and Suzanne to notice
the money was gone. He had to act fast.

He wanted to tell Archie first, though. He had to tell

someone. Of course, they'd probably go to Archie when he was gone, and Archie would have to tell them. But they might guess anyway.

"Hi," Archie said. "All ready?"

"Sure. Where?"

"There's a nice park near here. I thought we'd go over there. I know a guy works in the hot dog stand. Maybe he'll shave a couple of dimes off some drinks for us."

"Great." They walked along the sidewalk, Tim making sure not to step on any cracks. Archie noticed—he was sharp that way, Tim decided—and laughed. "Not going to break your Mom's back, huh?"

The little ugly bastard

"My Mom's dead," Tim said. It seemed so far away, so long gone, and it hadn't been three weeks yet. The two weeks in the hospital had taken forever. (I like him, be quiet. Not now.)

"I thought that was your Mom in the door."

"That's my Aunt . . . no, I mean my sister-in-law. Archie, are you a Mormon?"

"I don't know. Dad's a Catholic, Mom's a Mormon. Every week I go to a different place. They're pretty loose about it. I guess all the Mormons think Mom is a fruitcake, and all the Catholics think Dad is. Pretty good arrangement, nobody bothers us." Then Archie thought a moment and saw Tim's pensive look. "Gee, I'm sorry. I guess it must be pretty rough."

"Let's not talk about it, huh? I've got a secret I want to tell you. Later."

The park was busy with children and picnickers. T boys took horseshoes from a stand and played in a nea sandpit, but neither was very good. Tim felt vaguely en barrassed. Then they climbed a tree and sat on the lower branches, flicking ants off the bark and not saying much.

"You like car models?" Archie asked.

"Sure," Tim said. "But I like airplanes better."

"I put together customized jobs. You know, the ones that take putty and sanding and stuff."

"I tried that once, but I could never get the pits out. And besides, I'm not very good at deciding what extra piece looks good on the front, or anything."

"I suppose it takes a knack," Archie said. "I'm still learning. I want to work in a garage when I grow up, for a little while anyway."

Jim Townsend swam briefly before Tim's eyes. The voices came up again.

Don't let him talk to you that way

What way?

"I've been thinking a lot about what I'll do when I grow up," Tim said. "My Dad worked in a garage."

"Where did you live before you came here?"

Tim didn't answer for a moment. "A town in New Mexico," he said finally. "But I don't really want to talk about it."

"Where will you work when you grow up?"

"I might be a policeman. They help people. They get things done."

"Naw, policemen have all sorts of trouble. My uncle is a policeman. He says they can't arrest anybody because they might get in trouble if they look at the crooks cross-eyed."

"He was probably exaggerating."

"Maybe, but I went with him once in a patrol car. He had to pick up a drunk. Geez, the guy was all scuzzy, with stuff leaking out his mouth . . . yechh."

Carrying the fire

Tim remembered Kevin Land and frowned. "I knew a drunk once," he said, trying to appease the voices. "He was just sick, that's all. He was in bad shape. My Dad rented some land to him cheap so he could live away from the streets."

"Yeah, but I wouldn't want to go around handling them

all the time, anyway. So cops have to do lots of dirty things, arrest pushers and whores—''

''Whores?''

''Sure. My uncle used to work on vice.''

''What was that?''

''Boy,'' Archie said, sighing, ''you did live in a small town, didn't you?''

''Pretty small,'' Tim said softly, looking down at the ground.

''Vice is where they arrest whores and pimps and raid porno joints. They used to be able to bust porno joints all the time, but now they have their hands tied. Both Mom and Dad say it's because Satan has control of the government.''

''You ever seen a whore?'' Tim asked curiously.

''Naw. My uncle still gets to bust them pretty often, though.''

''What do whores do?''

''Geez, you don't know? Ever watch *Police Woman* on TV? She gets to play whores—hookers—all the time. My Dad watches that show. Mom likes *Kojak* better.''

''Yeah, but what do they do?''

''They let you stick it in them for money.''

''Stick what?''

Archie blushed and muttered something about not asking too many questions. ''Ain't you been through sex ed yet?''

''Oh,'' Tim said. ''That.''

''Yeah, that.''

''I might have known a hooker once. At least, there was talk she went out with guys for money.''

''I guess every town has them.'' Archie adjusted his fake foot and swung down lightly from the tree limb, dropping to the ground. Tim noticed he let his good foot take the shock.

''You're pretty handy with that thing,'' Tim said, landing beside him.

"Yeah. Lots of practice. I don't want to be gimpy."
Archie walked away. Tim bent down to tie the laces on his
tennis shoe.

Put him out of his misery

Then he stood up and ran after the boy. "Anybody ever
razz you about being . . . you know?"

"Sometimes. I just punch their lights out. You know, I
can kick pretty hard with this thing, like a horse hoof.
Doesn't hurt me, unless I twist the leg wrong, but it sure
kicks the hell out of anyone who bugs me. Like the Bionic
Man, you know?"

"Yeah." Tim laughed.

"You like comic books?"

"Some."

"Which ones?"

"Oh, I like Superman and Batman."

"Geez, those are *old*!" Archie said, snickering. "You
should look at the Marvel stuff."

"They're dumb," Tim said. "Everybody talking all the
time, and that idiot Spiderman."

"Some of them are pretty good, though. I read a lot of
DC stuff. Ever look at *Howard the Duck*?"

"What?"

"It's about a talking duck, wisecracks and all sorts of
stuff. Pretty good. But if my Mom knew what the duck
talked about, she wouldn't let me read them. He has this
girlfriend, a woman, not a duck, and he sleeps with her
and everything."

"A duck, with a woman?"

"Sure."

"That's *really* dumb."

"Yeah, but it's funny, too."

They came to the bushy edge of the park and simultaneously ran for the playground equipment. On the swings,
they tried to outdo each other. They came out even. "Ever
go around all the way?" Archie asked, yelling from the
peak of his swing.

"No!"

"I did, once." Swing. "Boy, was it great!" Swing. "I almost wet my pants."

"Hey, Archie." Swing.

"Yeah?"

"I got to—" swing—"tell you something."

"Your secret?" Swing.

"Yeah."

"When?" Swing.

"Now." They skidded to a stop.

"Okay. What is it?"

"I'm going to run away."

Archie looked at him as if he was crazy. "Why would you want to do that?"

"I have to. I've got some money and I'm going to the bus station. I have the schedules and everything. I can pick up a bus near the park and it'll take me to the Trailways terminal. I'm going to buy a ticket and go back to my home town."

"Geez." Archie looked abashed. "You don't like it around here?"

"No, that isn't it. I *have* to."

"Why?"

"I can't tell you that."

"You know what my uncle told me about runaways? He said that they get picked up by weird guys who take them out and bugger them. Or they get hopped up on dope by some pusher and he makes them go out and steal TV sets, or do the murders for gangs because they won't get the firing squad if they're caught."

"I have to do it. It's very important. I have to talk to people."

"You going to leave today?"

Tim nodded.

"Where'd you get the money?"

"I . . . you won't tell anybody?"

Archie shook his head slowly.

"I stole it. Borrowed it, really, because I'll pay it back. But I have to find out something, tell people about things. People who'll believe me."

"I don't know," Archie said. "Maybe you shouldn't have told me."

"Why?"

"I don't want anything to happen to you. Couldn't you just stay around here and play with me? I don't have all that many friends. I can't afford for them to run away."

"I don't have any choice."

"Tim, if I let you run away, I might have to be all kinds of guilty if you get caught, or . . . you know . . . if somebody buggers you and strangles you. You don't know what kind of monsters are out there. My uncle warned me about some of them, but sometimes my Mom makes him shut up."

"Nothing will happen to me."

"You don't know that! Tim, I'd be awful scared for you."

"You wouldn't tell, would you?"

Awful slimy crippled bastard coward

"Geez, I don't know. I don't think it would be right to let you do something stupid like that."

"You mean you'd tell?"

"You stole the money and everything."

Tim got off the swing, fists clenched. "You'd tell?"

The eyes

Archie climbed out of the swing backward. "Tim—"

"Goddamn you to hell, you fucking little snot!"

"Hey, enough of that! Nobody talks to me that way."

"I should kick your balls in, you wretch!"

"You try and I'll put you down for the count." Archie looked at him levelly, arms raised in defense. "What's the matter with you?"

"I have to go," Tim said calmly.

"Okay, but you touch me with one little finger and I'll—" He hefted his fake foot and made a jabbing motion with it. "Right in the crotch. I've had to fight before."

Tim laughed. Part of it sounded like a boy, but another part was cold and distant and full of hate. "You won't tell anybody. You know where I come from?"

"I don't know, I don't care."

"Lorobu, you fucker. I survived Lorobu."

Archie's eyes widened. "I don't believe you."

"I'm the little kid left alive. I'm the one left to carry the fire for the town."

"What are you talking about?"

"I can call things down on your head you wouldn't believe." Is that true? he asked the voices, very frightened by the words coming out of his mouth. They didn't answer.

"Yeah? Try it. I dare you." Archie backed away. "You're crazy. Go head and run away, get buggered. See if I care."

"On your head!" Tim said coldly.

"Up yours!"

Faster than Tim could believe, he ran forward, reached out and grabbed Archie's shoulder. The blood was on his hands clear as could be. Archie's fake foot lashed out automatically and caught him in the shin. His leg exploded in pain. He raised his fist, fingernails extended.

The eyes

"You squealing asshole."

A large, gnarled hand grabbed his arm, nearly lifting him off his feet. It was a tall, stocky old man in gray overalls. "What's the matter with you, kid?"

"Let me go," Tim said slowly, looking directly into the man's tired green eyes. He tried to kick him but the old man hefted him away just in time to leave his foot flailing.

"He's crazy!" Archie said. "He just went nuts!"

"Where do you live?"

"I know where he lives," Archie said.

"I'm going to call the cops and have them take you home right now."

"I'll kill you," Tim said. "I'll make your skin fall off and your guts hang out. *They'll* get even for what you did. What all of you did."

"Who's that, kid?" The old man's nostrils were flaring. "You," he said to Archie, "go over to the superintendent's booth—the equipment place—and have him call the cops. Tell him where this boy lives, too."

"Sure." Archie ran off.

"If you were a grownup, I'd beat the shit out of you for what you just said to me," the old man told Tim. "If I were your dad, I'd take a cane to you and raise welts all over."

Tim, deep inside, thought, *This man is as nuts as the rest of them. Make them angry and they turn into animals.*

The old man shook him by the arm until his joints popped. Tim screamed and the man let him down. Then his foot had opportunity to connect. The old man clutched his knee and groaned, going over backward. Tim picked himself off the ground, where he had fallen from the force of his kick, and ran.

He would find the bus, he would go to the bus station. He had to get to Lorobu. He was sick. He'd hurt somebody if he didn't.

CHAPTER THIRTY-TWO

PROHASKA AND FOWLER TOASTED EACH OTHER WITH CUPS OF coffee in the restaurant booth. Fowler took a napkin from the dispenser and a felt pen from his pocket and began a list of priorities.

One, he wrote. *Dorothy's bugged. Mollify her.*

"We survived, at least," Prohaska said.

"I'm not so sure I did," Fowler said. "I left quite a few shattered personas in that cabin. How can I go back to designing and marketing computers after that? It would be anticlimactic."

"There's a story in it somewhere, but I'm damned if I can find the angle."

"You mean, who's going to believe us."

"Exactly. My station doesn't go for this sort of thing at all. I could sell a half dozen stories to the grocery store tabloids, but what good would it do? That kind of exposure only makes acceptance more difficult."

"So?"

Prohaska shrugged. "I still can't back away from it. There's something here that cries out to be investigated. You have a scientific bent—doesn't it interest you?"

"Yes, but I've fulfilled my obligation. I've shown that Jordan didn't kill Henry—that he was forced."

"And who will believe that? Just you? Were you out to vindicate their memory just to yourself?"

Fowler looked down at the table. "I don't know."

"Seems to me your job won't be complete until you convince the public at large there's something in the valley."

"How do I do that?"

"Not alone, that's for sure. Together, we might be able to make a dent."

"And what's your stake?"

Prohaska pointed to his bruised face. "Two stakes. One, well—let me ask you a question first. What's the prime requirement in a scientific experiment?"

"How do you mean?"

"Repeatability. Someone else has to be able to replicate the lab results, or witness the phenomenon. I'm almost certain the thing in the valley is willing to repeat its act over and over again. Like clockwork. Just add people. So I'm sitting on the biggest story of our time. First affirmed, studied demon. My second stake is revenge."

"Very well, then, how do *we* go about it?"

"First, we stay here in Bishop."

"Forfeit our jobs?"

"It comes down to that, doesn't it?"

"To follow up some. . . ." Fowler stopped, disgusted, and x'd out the list he had made on the napkin. He turned the paper over to start again. "Dorothy'll hate me. If we can bring the scientists and our beasts together on common ground, *then* we have something."

"Then we can sacrifice our private lives for a good cause." Prohaska rubbed his eyes gingerly. "How much are you willing to sacrifice?"

"Willing isn't the word. You've brought up that old devil Duty again."

"So to speak." The reporter grinned.

"Dorothy was pretty shook by what happened. I'm not sure she'll take to the idea of staying—especially if I forfeit my job."

"Where is she now?"

"Napping in the room. She doesn't talk about it."

"I don't blame her. How is Howard going to explain a beat-up car to his superiors? He's probably already making up a story."

"Demons don't pass in this society," Fowler said.

"So we should abandon it, let that thing run amok after the creek freezes over, maybe kill more people? That's another reason we can't let it lie. We can call up Duke University."

"The hell with that. They're interested in ESP, not demons. And they don't know much more about it than anybody else. But . . ." He tapped his fingers on the formica. "I have a friend at UCLA, a physicist. Maybe we could show it to him, and he could bring another friend and show it to *him*, and we'd be on our way."

"What about the military?"

"What about them?" Fowler asked, frowning.

"They might be interested."

"How?"

"When I called my station, I talked to a friend, a broadcaster, and he said the nix is out on stories about Lorobu. The government has wrapped tape around anything having to do with the town. No one can get near it. We can report all we want, but we don't write stories unless we have information."

"So how does this connect with Lorobu?"

"Maybe your monster moonlights."

"Hell," Fowler said, "it's purely a local phenomenon. It's trapped now, and besides, it never left the valley."

"Positive?"

Fowler held up his hands. "No, but I'd stake a few bucks that this thing and Lorobu have no connection."

"Maybe not directly. But you know the story about Lorobu, don't you? Everybody went berserk, started killing each other. Three people survived. In a hospital several days later, one of the survivors killed another and committed suicide by jumping out a third-floor window. Now doesn't that sound similar to what happened with the Taggarts?"

"Yes, but Sam, eight hundred people died in Lorobu."

"All the more frightening, isn't it? If there's no direct connection, maybe there's a generic relationship. Maybe they come from the same family. Big brother, little brother."

"That's crazy."

Prohaska laughed. "Then it has a ring of familiarity, doesn't it?"

"I think the thing in the valley is a natural phenomenon. What happened in Lorobu—" He stopped, frowning. "You know, Jordan Taggart said something to me . . . about ants and sticks and things. He said something was going on, that he could almost feel it, and that we were ants being stirred up. And that this thing in the valley was another kind of bug, also being stirred up. Like a common stimulus—a giant, invisible stick." He shook his head slowly. "I'm not sure that makes any sense, though."

"But shouldn't we tell the authorities anyway, have them check it out?"

"If we do that, we lose all claim to it," Fowler said. "They'll slap a security rating on it just for the sake of practice. We'll lose everything."

"Even movie rights? Larry, we're not talking about a story *property*, we're talking about news and how to spread it around. That's a duty, not a privilege."

Fowler finished his cup and let the waitress pour him another. "I've got six thousand dollars in savings, enough to keep my life-style going for about three months, five if I let my beach apartment in Malibu go, and sell my Z for payments. Sell, hell, what Z? Well, if I turn in the insurance claim and get it passed, I can keep the money—if any—left over after completing payments. So five months tops. Then I'm broke, out of a job."

"So go back to LA and keep your job. Come up here on weekends and help me."

"And what about you?"

"I've got a novel payment coming in by the middle of February. I can muddle through until then. Larry, I think we're both honorable men. We can't let this pass."

"This is a theoretical question, but—why not?"

"Because it could blow the lid off our entire century. Consider—a living thing without a material form. This could provide a basis for ghosts, demons, even UFOs . . . maybe even life after death."

Fowler looked out the window, squinting in the bright late-morning sunlight. "I have never thought of myself as a noble, sacrificing man. You know what this world of ours does to crackpots?"

"I have a fair idea."

Fowler nodded. "Okay, then, who do we show it to first? My friend at UCLA, or some military type?"

"Let's go the civilian route first."

CHAPTER THIRTY-THREE

JACOBS SAID HIS FAREWELLS TO TRUMBAUER AND MISS UNA-
muno, then followed Silvera across Main Street to an
olive-green trailer parked on a dirt lot. A woman in a
laboratory smock was standing near metal steps under a
closed steel door, smoking a cigarette.

"Good morning, Colonel," she said.

"Mrs. Beckett. This is Franklin Jacobs, a writer—"

"Yes, I've read one or two of your books, Mr. Jacobs.
Pleased to meet you."

She was about thirty-five, with close-cropped red hair
and a utilitarian appearance which almost belied a striking
facial structure. Jacobs smiled his most charming smile
and bowed slightly. "I enjoy meeting my readers."

"Until a few weeks ago, I thought you were full of the
most intriguing garbage," Beckett said, dropping her cigarette into the dirt. "Now I'm keeping an open mind. What
does the Colonel have planned for you?"

"Mr. Jacobs is going to be an advisor," Silvera said.
"I'd like to show him the trailer."

"Certainly. Have you brought a specimen of ectoplasm
with you?" Her smile reduced the sarcasm somewhat.

Jacobs took a liking to her instantly. She had energy and conviction—if she were to oppose him, the fight would be an entertaining one.

"You'd be disappointed by genuine ectoplasm," Jacobs said as she reached up to open the door. A red light came on above the entrance. "It's mostly water and dead skin."

She cocked her eyebrows. "This way, Franklin. My first name, by the way, is Judith. Not Judy."

"Of course." The trailer was filled with electronic equipment, all of it used-looking, all carrying that overpainted, spotlessly clean stamp of military hardware. At the rear, through a door just light enough to escape armored status, were banks of quiet computers and memory consoles. These were less identifiably Army and looked like fresh installations.

"Mr. Jacobs has a B clearance for this project, Mrs. Beckett."

"That means I can tell you most of what I know," the woman said, pulling a computer terminal out of concealment. "Do you know anything about computers, Franklin?"

"Next to nothing."

"This trailer is the coordinator and memory for all the research teams around Lorobu. We have microprocessors and small computers elsewhere, but by the end of the day everything has to be put through the unit in the back. On this side of the door is communications equipment, auxiliary terminals, and a hotplate for coffee. None brewing at the moment."

"Has any of it helped you discover what happened in Lorobu?" Jacobs asked.

"No. But we have all kinds of information. Would you like to see some of it?"

"Yes."

"What in particular?"

"What do you have on bacterial growth rates?"

She led him to a CRT and typed instructions into the

keyboard. As he watched, growth curves and comparable norms of several major bacteria were quickly sketched. She punched a continuation button and three more appeared, and then again.

"We have a biology lab analyzing samples from around the town. This one here is particularly virulent—ever heard of post-mortem sepsis?"

"Yes," Jacobs said.

"I'm surprised. It's not common any more. But if anyone conducting autopsies on the dead citizens of Lorobu pricked his finger on a piece of bone or a scalpel, and couldn't get antibiotics treatment, he'd probably die in great pain. They were all filled with streptococcal bacteria. Much more than would be expected, in fact. Their bodies decayed very rapidly—within twenty-four hours, before adequate morgue facilities could be set up by the police and National Guard. That morgue has been burned to the ground. We now conduct our biologicals in a special trailer parked near the elementary school."

"What about plant diseases?"

Silvera interrupted and said he had to attend to work in his office. "Mrs. Beckett, if you can spare the time, could you finish Mr. Jacobs' tour?"

She frowned, then nodded. Silvera smiled and shut the door behind him.

"I'm not even a civil servant," Beckett said. "The government called me away from a conference on genetic engineering."

"But the disaster wasn't caused by bacteria," Jacobs said.

"No, that's already been eliminated. The increased growth rate happened after they died. Now the plants—you asked about them." She requested more graphs and figures. "All the diseases are endemic to Lorobu, but their populations are greatly exaggerated. The plants died partly because of that—and partly for unknown reasons. Except for algae in the sumps and some hardy varieties of cactus and wild grass, all plant life is dead here.''

''I think I know why there are so many little live things now,'' Jacobs said. ''Though of course my idea is from an unpopular viewpoint.''

''Why, then?''

''For thousands of years, spirits have been blamed for plagues. Vampires were supposed to bring plague in Medieval times. Fairies could make people fall sick. Gods have been known to bring pestilence down on the unfaithful.''

''And?''

''Whatever killed the plants and made the bacteria prosper, whether on purpose or inadvertently—the latter, I'd say, considering the undirected nature of the growth—was of a spiritual nature.'' He paused and took a deep breath. ''If a scientist will excuse the sacrilege.''

''Not at all,'' Beckett said, looking at him quizzically. ''Silvera is putting you on as an advisor? They're getting . . . desperate, pardon the expression.''

''You haven't found anything you can blame on the Russians,'' he said by way of defense.

''Not a damned thing. Shall we take a look at the other labs?''

Walking around the trailer and across the lot to a cluster of modular buildings, Beckett offered Jacobs a cigarette and smiled when he refused. ''Are you into health foods and stuff like that?''

''No. I grow many of my vegetables, but I'm not averse to modern conveniences.''

''I think your books were more upsetting to me than the Bermuda-triangle garbage. Probably because you tickled my metaphysical bone, and it hadn't been touched for years. All scientists have one, you know, except maybe B.F. Skinner. Even him; I'd be interested to be around when he's on his deathbed.''

Jacobs chuckled. ''What was so provocative about my books?''

"The one about spiritual hierarchies—I forget its name—"

"The Realm of Light and Death."

"It was so logical, compelling. It infuriated me. All this absolutely ridiculous stuff about . . . well, I don't have to repeat it to you. But now I'm not so sure."

"There are no atheists in foxholes . . . or Lorobu?"

"We've had lots of psychological problems among the soldiers and staff here. Even the FBI people have felt it. Such a sense of depression and foreboding. Something really awful passed through, whatever it was."

"I know."

"You know what it was?"

"Not exactly."

"Is it unprecedented? You're an expert on folklore. Has anything like this ever happened before?"

"We say *this* and *it* so often—haven't we any names? Of course—but they are swear words to the scientists and the liberals, as much as sexual language is to the conservatives. We are talking about a possession of some sort, but no, I know of nothing like it—except perhaps the invasions of nunneries and monasteries, or incidents of mass hysteria."

"Like *The Devils of Loudun.*"

"Yes. But they were not chiefly violent episodes—not so violent as Lorobu. I tell you what—I've coined a word, a rather clever word, for the thing that came here, and probably to Haverstock, also. I don't think it'll be of much value to scientists . . . but I call it a psychlone." He spelled it out carefully.

"Franklin, you're nuts. You may be just what we need to break the ice."

"I don't appreciate being called 'nuts.' I'm a crackpot, perhaps—I wear that epithet with honor in some company—but—"

"I mean, we've run out of sane theories. Your ideas have been restated by a surprising number of staff people

here. Lorobu has us all spinning inside. Do you understand
how horrible it was?''

Jacobs shook his head. "I can't say that I do."

"I was brought here while they were identifying and
trying to preserve the bodies. Men, women and children,
hacked to death or strangled, sometimes by their own
hands. Animals pounded to flat smears. Rooms covered
with blood. Some of them drew on the walls before they
killed themselves, or were killed by somebody else—the
most vile, incredible things. I'll never forget them. What
happened here was patently evil. But I still don't believe in
the devil, Franklin. You know, I—"

"I don't believe in the devil either. Not in the Catholic
concept."

"Yes, I remember. Anyway, I was saying, rather than
take you through the trailers first, would you like to see
the remnants of what happened? Most of the town has
been investigated and the buildings are open to project
members. None have been completely cleaned up."

Jacobs put his hands in his pockets and scowled. "I'm
not much for gore," he said, staring intensely at Beckett.

"Then you don't belong on this project, do you?"

"Lead on," Jacobs said. "May I take notes?"

"By all means." She pulled a steno pad from one of her
smock pockets. "These are all numbered and registered.
After you're done with it, return it to me or Silvera. Don't
make notes on anything else, or write about the project in
any way that's liable to reach the outside world."

"They must learn about it sometime."

"The working philosophy around here is that they
shouldn't know what's going on until we do. For the
moment, I agree."

Six electric carts were parked near a long trailer marked
MDP 4. She commandeered one and they drove across a
fresh dirt path to Main Street.

"First we'll go to a respectable family dwelling. It be-

longed to the Townsends. Have you heard about them
yet?''

Jacobs shook his head.

"Their youngest child, a boy, is the only survivor. I
suspect the project leaders are going to pick up Tim soon—
that's his name, Timothy—and put him through some
rigorous testing. Nothing inhumane, but he was under the
jurisdiction of the FBI and civilian hospitals until a few
days ago. Now he's in Salt Lake City. He may be able to
tell us an awful lot, whether he says anything or not.''

"I don't like the sound of that," Jacobs grumbled.

"This is a plague situation, Franklin.''

"I'm not used to being ruthless.''

"Nor am I. We won't be ruthless, if I have any say, but
we may have to be stern. Uncompromising.''

"The distinction can be hard to make.''

Beckett nodded and turned the cart in to a residential
section—a single street lined on each side with five tract
homes. The yards consisted of cactus gardens or bare
gravel. She stopped the vehicle in front of a pleasant-
looking building with a flagpole in the yard and a basket-
ball hoop mounted near the peak of the garage.

The interior of the house was deceptively well-ordered.
Beckett showed him the living room with its tile floor
covered by a large throw rug, and the kitchen, where
plates from the last meal were still on the table and sink.
"Everything was peaceful in here," she said. Then she
showed him the family room and bedrooms.

The smell still lingered—an indefinable mix of blood
and fear, like an abattoir. Dark stains arced across the
walls and ceilings like splatters on a Pollock canvas. Jacobs had seen the dead and dying before, and thought
himself inured to the idea—but this evidence of slaughter
made him feel faint.

"The little boy saw all this?''

"He must have. He was found with blood all over his
hands.''

"What was the sequence of events?"

"As close as we can tell, the first one to be killed was James Townsend, the father. Georgette Townsend then committed suicide, but not before she tried to kill Timothy."

"How did the boy face it and stay sane?"

"We can't be sure he is sane. He acted normal afterwards—with the usual signs of buried memories and trauma—but—"

"Did he participate?"

"We don't know. He doesn't either—not that we could tell. Hell, I'm saying 'we'—the FBI and state police did most of the investigating then. We were brought in a few days after. Timothy was in the control of a state hospital before we could ask him questions."

"Horrible," Jacobs said. Horrible and fascinating—death, destruction, the hidden interiors of the human mind, the human body. The incredible fragility of life, the vulnerability of man's sack of fluids and bones. . . .

"Enough of this," Beckett said, taking him by the arm. "Mrs. Townsend blew her head off with a shotgun in the bathroom. Timothy escaped about the same time, probably before, and was found wandering down Main Street by a highway patrol officer."

Jacobs wished either Trumbauer or Miss Unamuno could be with him, to see if the house carried any residue of the events. A capable seer could differentiate between the slowly fading imprint of violence and evil left by such an act, and the true presence of the souls of those involved. Such violence, imposed from the outside, could be disastrous to a confused personality.

Beckett watched him from the front door. "What are you thinking about?" she asked, breaking his reverie.

"I was . . ." He hesitated. "I'm not sure you'd appreciate my ramblings yet."

" 'Yet' . . . I like that. You think our metaphysics will get quite a scrambling, don't you?"

"I'm more worried that mine will. I've been writing about parapsychological phenomena for so long, but I've never had to put my ideas to a crucial test."

"You may be one step ahead of us. At least you recognize the possibility. We're still kicking in the dark. Come on. More houses, more grue."

The next house up the street was worse. Obscene drawings covered the walls of the rooms. Jacobs stared at the chalked outlines of five bodies, three obviously of children. White dust spotted conspicuous tabletops, sliding glass door surfaces, doorknobs and the few drinking glasses left whole on the counter. "Family of five, the Frenches," Beckett said. "The FBI dusted for prints before concluding the family killed each other." Cheap chrome chairs with patent-leather cushions were scattered across the kitchen. The odor was stronger here, a smell of burnt metal and rotten oranges. With a start, Jacobs realized he knew the smell—not from experience but from descriptions.

"The hell with being circumspect," he said sharply. Beckett turned to face him, looking expectant. "If we're going to work together, we can't be afraid of each other's opinions. Do you smell something strange here? Not blood—not death?"

"Yes," Beckett said. "Like smelling salts, only different."

"That is the smell of evil. Don't laugh—not until I can find a less melodramatic choice of words." He looked around the kitchen and dining room, wide eyes absorbing the mayhem. He was trying to reconstruct what it must have felt like. "I need Trumbauer here," he said. "He could tell us a great deal. When something drastic happens to a human being, he leaves a residue almost anyone can sense—a residue of disgust, despair. Hatred. Whatever. It's interpreted by the lowest levels of our minds, those connected with the olfactory sense. Whether we actually smell the residue or pick it up some other way I don't know—but it's here. The smell of evil, fear, the urge to destruction."

Beckett nodded. "I can't deny what I smell. So what did happen here, Franklin?"

"Passover," Jacobs said. "Something horrible flew over, much worse than any angel of death. Look at this symbol here." He stood by the wall between the kitchen and the garage. A few holes had been kicked into the plasterboard above the floor and the dark of the garage was visible. Above the holes was a large, wide eye, drawn in what appeared to be feces. Under the eye were obvious dancing flames.

"Yes?" Beckett asked.

"The spirit in hell," Jacobs said, his index finger following the outlines a few inches above the surface. "The eye that sees, the soul, in eternal agony."

"Something out of hell, then."

Jacobs whirled and stared at her, his face reddening. "No! This is no silly, simple possession by devils. A child drew these, and may also have kicked the holes. Why? Trying to escape—and giving up. But a child would know nothing of these symbols. They are sophisticated, enormously old cultural symbols—but they are not the ones a child would use."

"Would a simple child use shit to draw with?"

"Yes—if there was nothing else, and he—"

"She. Two daughters."

"If the child had to express what she felt, or undergo something even worse than death."

"You're not very clear, Franklin."

"Perhaps because I'm very unsure of myself. Look at the other drawings—foul, adult stuff, scrawled at an adult level. But down here, within the children's reach, more elemental drawings." He walked into the living room and pointed to a series of pictures on the brick fireplace. "At five or six feet, this. . . . " A hideous fanged mouth was ready to swallow a smear just barely identifiable as a vagina with a baby's head poking out. "And below, along the floor, these." Stick-figures with limbs falling off, eyes menaced by fire, a crude head splitting down the middle, the edges of the cut jagged liked torn paper.

"They must have drawn these before they killed each other," Beckett said, staring at the walls and fireplace, face pale.

"They must have cut themselves beforehand to do it," Jacobs said. "They used blood, urine—if this is urine—and feces."

"We also found chocolate syrup. They used everything they could find."

"Why? Perhaps they were trying to communicate what they saw and felt, knowing they were doomed."

"Very melodramatic."

"Mrs. Beckett, I appreciate healthy cynicism in its place. But you must take me seriously, listen to my experience, or none of this will be passed on—and they meant it to be. In their insanity, they knew something bad was happening to them, and they were trying to convey what it felt like."

"But not what it was."

"They didn't know any more than we do."

"Did Silvera tell you about the names found in other houses?"

"Yes."

"Did he tell you where those names came from?"

"No."

"What reason did he give?"

"He didn't want to prejudice our observations," Jacobs spat. "I think perhaps the Army doesn't want to know what happened here."

"Well, I know where they came from. I'm not supposed to know—I'm only a civilian contractor—but considering all this, the source may be important."

"Yes?"

"Let's go outside first." In the gravel yard, with a cold desert wind blowing down the empty street, Beckett stood looking at the ground, hands clenched tight in her pockets. "I thought I was used to it," she said. "I'm not. It's horrible, what happened in there. . . . ."

"Who were they?"

"They were bomber pilots . . . some were, anyway. They were all prisoners of war taken to Japan for internment. They were held in Japanese cities."

"Which cities?" Jacobs said. A spark seemed to leap in his mind, vaguely lighting a huge mass of unconnected ideas.

"Hiroshima and Nagasaki," Beckett said.

Jacobs' mouth dropped and his eyes became round.

"I found out because there was a clipping in an old paper in a junk store in Albuquerque. The names were released last year, but nobody seems to have made the connection except myself—and the Army, of course. They've known all along. I have a habit of wandering through junk stores. I find it soothing. My husband thinks I'm just acquisitive."

"How did they die?"

"When the bombs were dropped, they were about a quarter-mile from ground zero. In Hiroshima, that is. I'm not sure where they were in Nagasaki. There was a fairly large prisoner-of-war camp there."

"Then they were Americans, killed by atomic bombs."

"As far as I can check, yes."

"And now they are coming home."

CHAPTER THIRTY-FOUR

Tim stood in the bus terminal, trying to decide how to buy his ticket. It was possible the man behind the grimy brass bars wouldn't ask him any questions and he wouldn't have to lie. But if questions were asked—how would he answer?

Then he knew. He stood in line, fingering the wad of bills in his pocket, trying to look inconspicuous. Soon the police would be looking for him. Perhaps they already were. If they stopped the buses to look for him, or alerted bus stations in Provo, Gallup or Albuquerque, that was the end of it. But he hoped he had an hour or so head start before the police became too active. He watched the clock and examined the televised bus schedules, snapping his fingernails nervously in his sweater pockets. He hoped the buses were warm. It was dumb not to have taken a good coat. It only proved he wasn't grown up yet.

"I'd like a ticket for Albuquerque, please," he told the man behind the bars. He unwrapped his money and presented the bills.

"Sure, sonny," the man said. "Where are your folks?"

"They're off looking at magazines and getting a lunch

183

for me to eat on board," he said. "They have my suitcase, but they told me to get in line before it got too long."

"Okay," the man said. "But all big luggage has to be checked in at baggage before you get on the bus."

"I only have an overnight case," Tim said. The man handed him his ticket and change. There was enough to buy a lunch someplace.

"Bundle up," the man said. "It's cold along the way."

"I will."

The bus was scheduled to leave in fifteen minutes. He stood in the next line, fingering his ticket, waiting for someone to see him and call out his name. It was awful. He *had* to go home. He hoped he wouldn't hurt anybody if they did catch him. The old man he had kicked—that was bad enough.

The driver opened the door leading outside and took their tickets as they passed through, giving them stubs and a brochure on the trip. Tim clambered up the steep steps and found an inconspicuous seat in the middle, next to a window. An elderly woman with a purple fuzzy coat and a green handbag which almost dragged on the ground sat next to him, smiling with even ivory-colored teeth. She smelled of perfume. Tim didn't mind that—it blocked out the funny bitterness in his nose.

In ten minutes, the bus driver got in, made a check the length of the bus, and sat in the driver's seat. "Next stop, Provo," he said over the loudspeaker.

Tim settled into the seat and looked out the window as the bus backed away from the terminal. He was tired—running, walking, fighting, and nervousness had taken his energy away. He didn't want to sleep, but it looked like the only thing to do.

He didn't know how he'd get from Albuquerque to Lorobu. Hitchhiking was dangerous. That was what his folks had always said. Now he was on his own, however. The voices that came were muddled, impersonal; he couldn't make out anyone he knew. Besides, he wouldn't listen to them if he could.

An oriental man and his wife lurched from the front to the back, heading for the restrooms. The man said something and the woman responded. Tim guessed they were speaking Japanese.

He frowned. It sounded familiar. It was hard placing sounds and words he didn't understand in the first place. Perhaps he had heard Japanese being spoken in old war movies on TV. Then he knew. The screaming and humming behind the images of the people from Lorobu, behind the images of S.K. Percher and the others—they were using the same language. But it wasn't speaking. It was a screaming in the head, like stepping on the tail of some awful cat, or listening to a desert wind blasting through the boards of an old shack.

CHAPTER THIRTY-FIVE

FOWLER PULLED CHANGE OUT OF HIS POCKET AND COUNTED the quarters to see if he had enough to complete the call. He fit the stack of coins into the telephone slot and waited for the switching-equipment sounds to give way to strong ringing. It was seven o'clock; he was trying Burnford's home phone.

George Burnford had been a party-going acquaintance in the early days of Fowler's marriage. Since then they'd talked over the phone off and on. It wasn't the sort of friendship that allowed the kind of request he was about to make, but Burnford was the best choice—the only choice— for what he had in mind.

"Hello." It was Burnford's wife, Sheila. Fowler remembered her clearly—tall, classically proportioned, with a hard-edged beauty that was almost masculine, and a warmth that was entirely feminine. Fowler had often daydreamed about her, but he was an honorable man. He had never actively moved in on married women. Not even his wife—but he cleared the accusation away quickly.

"Sheila, this is Larry Fowler."

"Larry . . . good to hear from you. It's been kalpas."

"Uh . . . yes, yes. Long time." He had always felt a bit inferior to George and Sheila. Their minds seemed to absorb knowledge on a plane quite different from his own. "Something important has come up and I have to speak with George."

"Sure. He's in the garage—just a moment and I'll bring him to the phone."

Fowler waited in the booth, looking across the restaurant at Prohaska's back. They'd just finished dinner and the reporter was having a last cup of coffee. There wasn't much else to do in Bishop, not when they couldn't keep their minds off the cabin. Dorothy had eaten with them and was now back in the hotel room.

She and Fowler had made love the night before. It hadn't been very good for either of them. She wouldn't talk about it, but Fowler thought he knew what was going on. She was even more of a "realist" than he was, a confirmed agnostic with a distaste for anything religious. She had been brought up in Catholic schools and had been, in her own words, "inoculated against religion, and now the antibodies are very, very strong."

Burnford approached the phone, shouting something to one of their children. "Larry! I thought you had a big sale going in Antarctica. Haven't heard from you in—"

"George, I'm about to impose on you."

Burnford paused, wary. "Oh? What is it, you need advice on semiconductors for your fifth-generation computers?"

"Nothing so easy. Before I ask, do I sound crazy to you?"

"No more than usual. You still going with the woman in that Greene and Greene house?"

"Still going."

"Good. I like her."

'She's here with me now—in Bishop. I'd like you to come up here, too."

"Something happen, Larry?"

"No accidents, nothing like that. But we need your experience and advice. Hell, I'll be truthful—we need your prestige."

"What's going on? Where the hell is Bishop—no, wait, is that up past Lone Pine, out in the boonies?"

"Sort of. I've found something very interesting up here and I need you to confirm my ideas on it."

"Don't tell me. You've found a meteorite and you don't want to let anybody know until you've had it assayed and sold."

"No. Good guess. Something maybe much older than a meteorite, not nearly so solid."

Burnford paused again. "You willing to spring for plane fare?"

"Absolutely."

"Put me up for a couple of nights in a ritzy hotel?"

"You've got it."

"Hell, this is beginning to sound like a free vacation. I have a seminar to finish up, then I have about a week free before . . . wait a sec, let me look at the calendar here. No, Jesus, Christmas break is coming up. All the time in the world. My seminar is over tomorrow. Is this as important as you make it sound?"

"It is indeed. I couldn't hope for anything more important. I think you'll be impressed. So far, it's been very reliable."

"Larry, are you drunk?"

"Sober as a judge. Too much coffee, in fact."

"I'll ask Sheila—"

"George, wait. I don't think you should bring Sheila. This is business."

"Sheila knows my business and enjoys it."

"I'm having trouble with Dot. She saw what I'm talking about. It's upset her quite a bit—I don't want to get anybody else involved if I can avoid it."

"You're sounding ominous now. What in hell do you have up there?"

"I don't know. But if you can figure out what it is, you'll probably get a Nobel. Either that, or you'll be banned from every university in the country."

There was silence on the other end of several seconds. "Larry, tell me truly now—are you imposing on me, or is this really important?"

"It couldn't be more important." He decided to use his trump card. "It may help us understand what happened in Lorobu." Having said it, he almost regretted it. "And Haverstock." Prohaska had read stories about the closing off of several square miles in the Illinois suburb; they had put two and two together.

"Nobody's supposed to know about the connection with Haverstock," Burnford said.

"Then how do you know?" Fowler asked, suddenly catching the physicist's change in tone.

"Larry, we could all get in a lot of trouble if this is a hoax. Can you tell me any more about it?"

"Not a thing. You'd stay away from here like it was the plague if I came out and told you."

"Shit." The expletive was quiet and deliberate. "Never mind paying for expenses. I'll take care of it. I'll leave Sheila here, and I'll give you three days to show it to me—whatever it is. Fair enough?"

"Perfect."

"I'll call you when I get plane reservations. No, wait, I can give them to you now. I'll be there at three o'clock tomorrow afternoon, a private flight. We'll talk then." He hung up without saying good-bye. Fowler put the receiver on its hook and stared at the black phone book for a moment. Something funny was going on. There was no way Burnford could afford to privately charter a plane. And Burnford was apparently not used to the idea yet, either.

Fowler walked back to the counter and sat on the seat beside Prohaska. "Well?" the reporter asked.

"He's coming tomorrow. It sounds like he's canceling an important seminar to be here. And he's coming in a privately chartered plane."

"You didn't say he was rich."

"He isn't."

"So?"

"I think we're getting in deeper than we thought."

"That's pretty deep," Prohaska said, lifting his cup to drain it.

CHAPTER THIRTY-SIX

THE BIOLOGICAL LABORATORY WAS HOUSED IN LOROBU'S CLINIC. Special modular units had been brought in to supplement the clinic's meager facilities, and trailers filled the parking area and a dirt lot behind the building. Generators hummed monotonously in the still afternoon air.

Jacobs was very tired. Since breaking for lunch, the apparently tireless Beckett had taken him through ten or twelve buildings, and now was prepared to show him the heart of the project. He held up a hand in protest, took a deep breath, and sat in one of the chairs in the clinic lobby. "This is too much, all at once," he said. "Give an old man a chance to rest."

Beckett sat beside him and apologized. "We just don't have much time."

"The third name on our list—after Percher in Haverstock—that man lived in Dayton, Ohio. There was a gap of three weeks between Lorobu and Haverstock. How long before something happens to Dayton?"

"You think the connection is that clear-cut? Whatever it is is going to follow Miss Unamuno's list?"

"I would hate to gamble that it won't."

"Why would it follow any list?"

"I don't know," Jacobs said. "Do those coffee machines work?" He pointed across the lobby to a bank of vendors along one wall.

"No, they're off-limits. Silly that they should be, but they are. I'm sure the staff has some coffee brewing. I'll get you a cup."

"Make it strong," Jacobs said. "I'll wait here." He leaned his head back against the wall and closed his eyes. Facts and figures whirled inside. All the men died at Hiroshima or Nagasaki or both. Where did they die in the cities? Were they executed before or after the bombings, or were they killed by the bombs themselves? Beckett wasn't sure—she wasn't privy to such important data—and he couldn't make any worthwhile guesses until he knew.

Still, a theory was already forming, one so incredible he was unwilling to voice it.

The spirits of the dead did not behave in such a fashion. Unless . . .

He sat up straight and rubbed his eyes. That way led to madness. All his life he had believed that there was life after death, and his experience with mediums and psychics had reinforced that belief. At the same time, the world had become increasingly more materialistic, less willing to make a commitment regarding things beyond matter and simple energy. The usual flurries of "spiritual reawakening" had swept the country, but they had been weak outbursts, hardly affecting the practical side of the nation's life. His career had been looked upon by friends and critics with a kind of impatient, liberal tolerance, much as Jacobs looked upon any homosexual dalliance Trumbauer may have engaged in in the past. Each to his own . . .

And he himself had often looked upon his work with the same amused indecision. Even regarding his own death, he had never felt impelled to fear the possibility of total extinction. Any existence afterward was icing on the cake.

Now he felt more than half a fool. The world was so full of disasters, fears, hatreds—to actively suggest that ghosts of dead servicemen were responsible for the deaths of several thousand people was more than he could do. But he couldn't do otherwise. He believed in Miss Unamuno and Trumbauer and what they had found, along with their reluctant comrades. He couldn't help but believe in the correlation between Miss Unamuno's list and the names scrawled in many of the houses.

Most vivid in his mind was the shack of Kevin Land, an alcoholic. "Lieutenant William Skorvin, USN" had been written all over the ragged walls, along with rough pictures. The instrument had been a marking pen. Before it had run out of ink, to be discarded under the metal frame bed—where it still lay, secured with a piece of masking tape—Land had recorded an astonishing history of boyhood in Lorobu. Since Skorvin had lived in Lorobu, Beckett guessed they had been boyhood friends. In the hours before his death, before mortally wounding the sheriff, Land had relived those years. The record was heartbreaking. Schoolrooms, constructing a clubhouse, double-dating, repairing old cars . . . and then Skorvin getting married, going off to war, his wife dying in an automobile accident in 1944 (the year came from old town records). Land, after the war, realizing the world would never be the same, guessing that Skorvin's body lay rotting in some jungle in a tangle of rusted metal (that drawing was particularly clear), had become disgusted with the world. Drink and delusion followed. For twenty-five years, Land had worked at odd jobs, with long periods of abstinence alternating with equally long periods of binge.

Now they were gone, leaving only the pictures. And not even in death could they rest, if Trumbauer's early guess was accurate. The psychlone had snatched them up, forced them along. But how could the souls of a few dozen, even a few hundred, men do such a thing? In all the history of psychic phenomenon, there was no parallel. Lorobu and Haverstock were completely new. Why?

Beckett brought the cup of coffee and sat beside him again. "Maybe we should call it a day, go have some supper and turn in."

"No. There's too little time, as you said. Give me a few minutes to call my wife. I have to tell her to do some things in the greenhouse. I forgot to do them myself before I left. Then you can take me through the labs. I'm very interested."

His conversation with Millicent over an Army phone in the clinic office was attended by a security officer and lasted five minutes. He was careful to say nothing and answer all her questions obliquely. He was allowed to tell her he couldn't say much for the moment, and she didn't press him. The garden was doing well, she said, despite the cold weather. It had rained a little, not enough to matter. His publisher had called. Was the second third of his new book ready for final typing, and could it be sent off to satisfy the editors? He supposed it was, and told her to carefully correct his spelling and grammar. She always did that. She was the only person he trusted to clean up his often sloppy prose. She had once said, "Franklin is the strength, I am the finesse," and that was true.

"You sound tired," she said toward the end of the call. "Are they treating you all right?"

"Sure. By the way, Arnold and . . . Arnold is going to be in Albuquerque, in fact, he's probably there already. He can't tell you any more than I, but call him and remind him we're thinking of him."

He self-consciously hid his mouth and whispered a few obligatory sweet nothings, then hung up. "It's not enough to talk with loved ones over the phone," he told Beckett as they walked down the main corridor of the clinic. "Where is your husband, by the way?"

"In Alaska, on a little island called Afognak, just off Kodiak."

"It must be very secluded."

"It is. We haven't talked in two weeks. He's a zoologist, studying elk herds in isolated areas. We went to school together at Stanford."

"Sounds like an interesting relationship."

Beckett brightened and took him by the arm. "I think Dan would like to meet you. He'd tear you apart in a debate, or try to, though. He's even more of a realist than I am. But he was the one who brought your books home. He scoffed and snorted, but he read them."

"Many of my readers are like that. It's fashionable to scoff and snort, but curiosity is primal, above all fashion."

She showed him a lab module—a balloon, actually, fitted with remote-control manipulating arms, encased in a box of transparent lucite. It was eight feet on a side, and within were several dozen boxes filled with a variety of laboratory animals. The module wasn't in use at the moment. "We were hoping what happened would happen again. If it affected the animals—like it did the first time—we might determine the cause. The plastic cube is filled with sterilizing gas at a lower pressure than the outside air. The balloon's pressure is slightly higher, but still below the outside. Two lines of defense."

Other modules contained gardens and vats of various algae. Still smaller units carried complete culture equipment for microorganisms.

One cubicle, larger than the others, was filled with a foggy gas. Dimly visible in its interior was a human cadaver. Beckett didn't elaborate.

"Whether time is short or not, I think that's enough for today. You're walking like a zombie. Why not have dinner with me, then I'll escort you to your room. Silvera will probably want you up early tomorrow."

Jacobs agreed and followed her to the cafeteria, several olive-drab mobile homes parked and connected lengthwise. The food was plain but acceptable, nothing like what Millicent would have fixed at home.

"My wife always does the sauces and plans the menu, and I do the mechanics of cooking," he explained as they walked back to the inn. "That's the secret of success in marriage—both partners must be master chefs."

Beckett laughed.

Silvera was standing in the lobby. He greeted them and Beckett left for the communications trailer.

"I'm waiting for a special phone call," Silvera said. "Did you find the tour educational?"

"That's not the word, exactly," Jacobs said.

"No, I suppose not. This call may interest you."

"If it concerns Trumbauer and Miss Unamuno, yes."

"It does. I'm sure we can use you on the project, if only as a backup man in case science doesn't save the day. The Army likes to cover its tracks."

"But you aren't so sure about Arnold and Miss Unamuno."

"Why do you always call her 'Miss'?"

"I don't know. It's the name she prefers, and Arnold senses that, and I follow Arnold's lead. Am I right about them?"

"Yes."

"That's why you sent them to Albuquerque."

"Partly," Silvera said. "But there was another reason. If we can use them, we'll want to send them someplace, and we can move them faster from there than from here."

"Where would they go?"

"I'm not free to say. Not right now. Just be sure you understand my position."

"I'll try. In the meantime, I'll rest for tomorrow. Mrs. Beckett—Judith—tells me there's a long day ahead."

He walked up the stairs with a heavy tread. He doubted he would sleep very well. His mind was engaged, running full speed, even though he was exhausted. The facts weren't connecting properly. He didn't have the expertise. But then, who in the world did?

CHAPTER THIRTY-SEVEN

TIM STOOD IN THE ALBUQUERQUE BUS TERMINAL, SHIVERING, staring at the rack of magazines. Faces of pretty women stared back, smiling happily. He wiped a tear off his cheek and swore under his breath.

This was it. This was the end of the trip. It was too cold outside to go anywhere with the clothes he was wearing. He was already sniffling. Off and on, he wished he had stayed in Salt Lake City, but that was purely selfish and he knew it. He would have killed somebody if he had stayed there much longer. He had to face the fact that he was not equipped to get very far in the world. Nor could he solve the problems that had ruined his family, his life. They were beyond him.

It was hard to take. Being twelve years old and powerless was something Tim had never thought about before, and he resented the force of the realization. Kids were put upon, but more than that, they were sequestered, controlled, looked after, given the secrets about survival piece by piece instead of in one grand, practical course. And kids were small, weak, born victims.

It would be years before he was grown up.

It won't be that way with us

It wasn't that he was afraid of dying—though he didn't like the idea of being where his parents were now—but giving up when he had come this far made him furious. The tears started to flow freely. He tried to stop them, to be a man, to be tough like his father had been (except when Grandmother had died) but it didn't work. Until now, he hadn't cried at all. It was all bottled up.

He kicked the magazine stand and hurt his foot. He bent down and ripped at the faces of the pretty women, scattering bits of them across the dirty tile floor. A clerk tried to grab him, but he kicked and clawed and broke away, screaming with rage and grief, then ran through the swinging doors into the cold.

It was dark and the stars were out. Wind blasted around the corners of the buildings, luffing his sweater as he ran. His face stung. A group of Mexican boys in ragged coats and parkas turned in unison to watch him. He stopped. Something warm to wear.

You can get it

He didn't want to, but he was cold.

A hand touched his shoulder. He turned and saw a heavy-set man in a long tan coat. "Tim Townsend?" the man asked. Tim ran and collided with a tall black man in a dark suit. He pinned Tim's arms effectively. Tim glared. The tears came again and he opened his mouth in a silent wail.

"Here, boy," the black man said, taking off his suit coat and wrapping it around Tim. "Come with us. We have warm food and hot cocoa for you."

CHAPTER THIRTY-EIGHT

"WHAT WILL IT DO IF THE RIVERS FREEZE?" PROHASKA ASKED.

"I don't know. The water runs pretty fast, and it isn't that cold at night yet. We should have a few more days." The wind whipping across the small airport runway was sharp. Fowler could feel the winter getting deeper; when the ice was frozen, he knew the thing would be free again. He didn't want to think about it. Dorothy watched them from the windows of the small airport restaurant, bundled up in a coat with a fur collar. Prohaska lit a cigarette and puffed on it quickly, leaning his head back. "At any rate," he said, "with the whole valley to run around in, it'll come after us if we go back to the cabin. It hasn't failed us yet."

"Maybe it's been frightened by the trap. Maybe it won't come near the place again, just hide in the woods."

"Be optimistic. Either way, we win. If it doesn't show, we don't have to face it again. If it does, we'll be vindicated and Burnford will get his Nobel."

"If it doesn't show," Prohaska said, "I won't have any story to write and my station will fire me. You'll look like a fool. Hell, the sheriff is already denying he saw anything."

"When did you hear that?"

"Stories have leaked out. Parkins is doing his civic best to keep the town from storming the valley, or panicking, or whatever he thinks they'll do. But I know him better than that. He's sure there's something up there. I doubt he'll go back with us."

A speck broke through the scudding clouds. Fowler pointed at it. "There he is, I think." It was a twin-engine Cessna, banking to make the turn to the runway. The wind knocked Prohaska's cigarette ash away.

The plane wobbled on its approach, then swerved, but made a good touchdown and taxied to the apron. Fowler walked over and stood nervously by the wing until the props were still. He waved at Burnford. The doors opened and the physicist and his pilot stepped onto the wing, then down to the cement.

"That's a government plane," Prohaska said, walking up behind Fowler. He pointed to the letters on the door and the side.

"Larry, good to see you," Burnford said, shaking hands. Fowler introduced him to the reporter. The pilot walked around the plane and joined them. "Larry, Sam, this is Fritz Williams. He's my sidekick for this trip."

"George, are you working with the government on something?" Fowler asked, squinting at him suspiciously.

"You better believe it," Burnford said. "Let's go inside where it's warm."

"This way," Fowler said, pointing to the restaurant. Inside, Dorothy was gone. As the others seated themselves at a table, Fowler asked the waitress about her. She had called a cab and left a few minutes before. "Did she say where she was going?" The woman shrugged. He rubbed his neck and returned to the table. Prohaska raised his eyebrows but Fowler shook his head.

"What are you involved with?" he asked Burnford.

"I'm not at liberty to discuss that, as the screenwriters

put it,'' Burnford said, looking through the menu. He hadn't changed in ten years. He was still youthful-looking, with tanned, smooth skin and a meticulously neat, short haircut. His moustache was full and added weight to a stubby nose and heavy eyebrows. "Iced tea," he told the waitress, "and a tuna sandwich."

The pilot shook his head. "Nothing so chilly for me. Hot coffee, a bowl of soup—if it's bean soup like the menu says—and a cheese sandwich."

"We've already eaten," Fowler said.

Williams stacked the menus and handed them to the woman, then waited until she was gone. "Gentlemen, Mr. Burnford is in my care, and I take my duties seriously. He's less used to government red tape than I am, so I may interrupt him or tell him to shut up occasionally. Please don't take offense. I'm just doing my job."

"Now you understand why I said you'd better be serious, Larry," Burnford said. "These people mean business. What do you have for us?"

Fowler looked warily between them. "I don't know if it has anything to do with Lorobu," he began. "But the *modus operandi* is the same. A friend of mine and his father were driven to murder-suicide in a cabin not far from here. We stayed in that cabin for several days."

"And?"

"We know they weren't responsible for what they did. Something got into their minds, drove them mad. I think we've captured it now."

"Captured what, and how?" Williams asked.

"It's natural, it's not anything mystical or from a horror movie—"

"Bullshit, pardon the expression," Prohaska said. "You scientists will spend all day trying to tell us what it isn't." He looked at Williams. "It's a demon. Maybe not in the modern conception, but in the Greek conception. A demon. An immaterial being."

Burnford took his iced tea from the waitress and drank a sip, waiting for her to leave. "Okay," he said, putting down the glass. "Do you have any hard evidence?"

"Several days of chart record from thermometers and a microwave detector, plus some film we haven't developed yet. We saw it; it beat up Sam pretty badly."

"I was wondering about those bruises," Williams said. "What did it look like?"

"At first, nothing. Then, a giant pig, a boar with tusks. I think it took the image from our minds, or perhaps from the Taggarts' minds—the people who were killed. Jordan and Henry, father and son. I went to school with Henry and he asked me up here to investigate odd things around the cabin. This was before Lorobu—or maybe about the same time, I'm not sure."

"You think they're directly connected?" Williams asked.

"No, I don't," Fowler said. "But I won't rule out an indirect connection. I believe it stays in the valley. But now it has an even smaller range. A few days ago, a new dam started trickling water through the valley as part of a planned runoff. The water forms two creeks around the cabin, which is on a rise. The thing doesn't seem to be able to cross running water."

"The water will freeze soon," Prohaska said, glancing at Fowler. "We don't know if it can get across frozen water. We'd like you to see the place as soon as possible."

"What kind of a demon is it?" Burnford asked.

"You ask that so calmly," Fowler said, smiling. "You aren't just humoring us?"

"We're dead serious, Mr. Fowler," Williams said.

"It behaves partly like a poltergeist, throwing rocks and stuff, making noises, causing hallucinations. I don't know if poltergeists can cause hallucinations, but this thing can. Delusions. It can move objects and shape them. The cabin has a gravel road. It manifests itself as a boar made out of gravel. The gravel fell on Sam and that's what bruised him."

"Damned thing threw a few hundred pounds of it right at me. My ribs are bandaged, but nothing serious. All the same, I'd like to get revenge."

"Why does it do these things?" Burnford asked.

"Because it hates people, or wants to be alone," Fowler said. "How can we be sure of its motives?"

"I mean, is it evil, or just like a wild animal?"

"More like a wild animal," Fowler said.

"I feel differently," Prohaska said. "But Larry's right, we can't be sure."

"What do you think?" Burnford asked.

"When that load of rocks landed on me, I could feel it controlling me, gloating. It hated my guts and it had fun hating me. It may be natural, but as far as I'm concerned, it's evil as hell."

"From hell, you think?" Williams asked.

"No, Larry's right there. It seems to just stay in the valley, like a moose in its territory."

Williams nodded slowly, then picked up his leather folio and brought out triplicate affidavits. "Gentlemen, if you'll sign these, we'll get on with the investigation."

Fowler looked at Burnford. The physicist shrugged. "It's the in thing to do," he said. Prohaska read the paper and pushed it away.

"No," he said. "I'd be compromising my duty."

"Mister Prohaska, whether you sign the affidavit or not, any of the information you've given us is secret. For the moment, you have no story. But if you wait a while, you may be the first to write about it. We've gathered a lot of strange people into the project, but no reporters."

Burnford leaned forward and crossed his hands. "I know what you're objecting to. The government has no right to cover up matters of obvious importance to the general public. I had my doubts, too, when they first approached me. But one thing is clear—if what happened in Lorobu and Haverstock is going to happen elsewhere, and if we can learn to predict it, we'll have to evacuate entire cities. Any slipshod handling of information could kill thousands of people."

"I'm not used to this sort of thing," Fowler said, but he signed his paper with Williams' ballpoint pen.

"No stories for the duration, from anyone?" Prohaska asked. Williams nodded. "Then I'll sign, too."

"Excellent," Williams said, putting the affidavits away and clicking the pen. "Do you have a car?"

"A rental. Our cars were destroyed," Fowler said.

"Then let's go."

The restaurant phone rang and the waitress answered just before accepting their money for the food. She muffled the mouthpiece with one hand and asked, "Anyone named Prohaska here, or Fowler?"

"I'm Prohaska." He took the phone and listened for a moment. "Howard," he said, "that was a stupid thing to do. Yeah. We're on our way now." He hung up and motioned for them to leave. Williams flopped down a ten-dollar bill. Outside, Prohaska swore and stamped his foot on the asphalt. "Goddamn Parkins, he's a Catholic. He went to confession and told his priest. Now he says the priest has gone to the valley. He just learned about it a few minutes ago. Dorothy told him we were at the airport."

They climbed into the car and backed out of the stall, tires squealing as Prohaska twisted the wheel and accelerated for the highway. "Dorothy must be at the hotel, then," Fowler said. Nobody paid any attention. Williams was busy making notes, compensating expertly for the jolting of the car.

CHAPTER THIRTY-NINE

THEY STOPPED AT THE HOTEL BRIEFLY. FOWLER RETRIEVED HIS synopsis of the chart record from the room. Dorothy wasn't there and her luggage was gone. There wasn't time to worry about it. On the way to the valley, he explained the instruments and results to Burnford.

"Microwave increase during all periods of peak activity," Burnford said. "Absorption of heat from most available sources. Apparently the heat is absorbed across a volume and not a surface. That would make it a four-dimensional absorbing hyper-volume."

"Extra-dimensional?" Fowler asked.

Burnford shook his head. "I'm only guessing."

It was dusk by the time they reached the lookout point. They descended into the valley. The trees darkened the road enough to require headlights. "Who is this Parkins?" Burnford asked.

"A sheriff," Prohaska said. "Not a very bright one, apparently."

"Religious crisis of some sort, eh?" Williams prodded.

"How the hell should I know? He didn't say much. I didn't even know he was a Catholic."

"Did he say what the priest was up to?"

"An exorcism, he thought."

"I don't believe it," Burnford said. "Ordinary priests don't do that sort of thing."

The car's lights reflected off tail-lights ahead. Prohaska slowed.

"How far from here?" Williams asked.

"A hundred yards."

"Park behind him and let's go." The car stopped behind the sheriff's car and they got out. "Which way?" Fowler pointed to the gravel road leading to the right.

"Apparently Howard didn't want his car banged up again," Prohaska said. They walked the first dozen yards quickly until they reached the stream. It was flowing freely, though there was evidence of ice. Fowler and Prohaska hesitated.

"Where's Parkins?" the reporter asked.

"He must be in there."

"And the priest?"

Williams pointed to fresh tire tracks leading up to the creek. "Looks like he drove right in."

"Howard!" Prohaska called. "Do you hear anything?"

"Nothing," Burnford said, shaking his head. "Well?"

"This is its boundary," Fowler said.

"Do we cross or not?"

Williams stepped back and jumped across the eight-foot stream lightly. "Come on, gentlemen," he said. "We won't learn anything by being cowards."

They followed suit, Prohaska landing with one ankle in the water. He shook it and stared angrily at Williams' back as the man walked ahead. "He doesn't believe there's anything dangerous here, does he?" Burnford turned and smiled.

"He knows his duty. That's to protect me, under all circumstances. So he goes first."

"Damned stupid for us to even be here," Prohaska said.

His foot squelched as they followed. "Howard!" he called again.

"Is it an air demon, or a ground demon?" Burnford asked. "I know it's a funny question, but—"

"Ground demon," Fowler said. "Caliban without Prospero."

"No relation to Ariel then, hm?"

Fowler shook his head.

" 'Graced not with human form,' as the bard said," Burnford tried to quote.

"I didn't know you were into Shakespeare," Fowler said.

"I'm not."

"And he misquoted," Williams said. "It's 'honor'd not with a human shape.' "

"Quiet," Prohaska said, getting down on one knee at the top of the rise. He motioned for them to do likewise. Faint moans came from the vicinity of the cabin. They advanced slowly, crouching, feeling a peculiar pressure all around them. With the last tree trunk out of the way, they saw the cabin and a small green Volkswagen, the priest's car.

One man, dressed in black with arms stretched out, stood just in front of the porch. He was oddly still. Straightening reluctantly, they approached the Volkswagen. Williams looked without evident concern at the two smashed cars parked nearby.

The sheriff was kneeling on the gravel beside the Volkswagen, hands clenched. He was crying and praying. "What's with the priest?" Burnford asked.

Williams approached the still man and Parkins got to his feet quickly, screaming, "Don't touch him!" Fowler grabbed Williams' shoulder and jerked him back. Frost covered the priest's hands and the back of his neck. Fowler circled and saw the man's face was caught in a grimace of fear, his eyes white with rime.

"What's the matter with him?" Burnford asked.

"He's frozen," Prohaska said, taking hold of Parkins' arm. "Let's get out of here."

"No, wait," Fowler said. "This happened to an animal the first morning I was here. It thawed and was okay."

"That's ridiculous," Burnford muttered.

"Prohaska, see if the sheriff still has that tarp in his car," Fowler ordered crisply. He repeated his warning to Williams. "Leave him be. Don't touch him."

"Come on," the reporter urged Parkins, pushing him down the road. Williams walked to the front porch and pointed at a wooden crucifix lying on the steps. "There's gravel all over here. And he must have thrown this. I wonder if it did him any good." He bent to pick up the cross.

The forest reverberated with a deep, bass roar. Fowler's body hair and scalp prickled. Burnford flinched and backed away. "Jesus Christ!"

"Didn't help, I guess," Williams commented dryly. "You think the boar was here, and he threw the cross at it?"

"I don't know," Fowler said. He bent down to look at the priest's legs. The priest wasn't as stable as the lynx, standing on two legs instead of four. The toes would be under great strain. Anything—

The trees shivered and twisted with the next roar. This time the sound ended in a high-pitched, animal scream of pain and rage. Burnford walked backward, away from the cabin. He spun quickly and looked at the forest, eyes wide.

The priest began to wobble. Fowler instinctively reached out to grab him. His hands connected with the man's suit and burned with cold. The arm cracked and came away in its sleeve. Fowler let go in horror and turned away as the body hit the gravel. The head snapped and rolled.

Burnford retched. "Let's get the hell out of here,"

Fowler said, choking. They stumbled and ran down the road. Behind them, a cloud of darkness rose above the cabin, grasping at the last of the daylight. Oily rainbows swirled. Like Lot's wife, Fowler had to look back. He almost fell head-long on the shadowy road.

Over the trees, surrounded by sparkles of deeper black, was a massive crow's head with a red eye like a dying sun. The beak pointed straight up, half-open, and a green glow rose out of it.

They jumped into the creek up to their knees and splashed to the opposite side. Fowler dragged Burnford from the water and they crawled across the road, their breath coming in harsh whistles. Behind them, the bellowing grew louder.

"Now we've done it," Williams said, standing over them.

CHAPTER FORTY

WHEN JACOBS ANSWERED THE DOOR, RUBBING HIS EYES, A stiff young man in khakis handed him an envelope.

"You're to be dressed in five minutes, sir. We have a car waiting to take you to the helicopter pad. We're getting you to the airport as soon as possible."

"What's this all about?"

"Colonel Silvera's orders, sir."

"What time is it?"

"Five a.m." The man backed away, turned sharply, and walked down the hall.

"Where will I meet you?" Jacobs called after him.

"Oh, yes, sir," the man said sheepishly. "In front of the inn. With your luggage."

Jacobs shut the door heavily and went into the bathroom to bring himself fully awake. Ten minutes later, he lugged his suitcase down the corridor and the stairs and across the lobby. Silvera stood by the Army staff car. "We have something right up your alley, Mr. Jacobs," he said. "You're going to Albuquerque, where you'll join Mr.

Trumbauer and Miss Unamuno on a charter flight for
California.''

   "I expected to be going to Haverstock.''

   "Not yet, perhaps not at all. We need you elsewhere.''
The car's driver helped him load his bag.

   "Good luck,'' Silvera said as he shut the door.

CHAPTER FORTY-ONE

TRUMBAUER WAS TREMBLING WITH EXCITEMENT. THEY WALKED across the concrete to their small passenger jet, escorted by four soldiers. "Are they going to use us, or just drop the whole thing?" he asked Jacobs.

"Haven't they told you anything?"

"Nothing," Miss Unamuno said tightly. "We've been kept in a hotel room under close guard. I've lost my job by now, I'm sure."

"We're going to California. I think, for the moment, they plan to use all of us. I don't know why."

"We're experts," Trumbauer said, triumphantly. "We're the only experts they have."

"I don't know," Jacobs said. "I have the feeling we've just touched the tip of the iceberg."

"Do they accept our ideas?" Trumbauer asked.

"I don't know." He shook his head—no further questions. They climbed the ramp and were seated in first class. The rest of the plane was empty. As the door was sealed, the guards talked quickly and formally to two stewardesses. They nodded, pale-faced, obviously upset at the hurry and secrecy.

The engine noise increased and the plane began to roll.

CHAPTER FORTY-TWO

TIM ATE HIS DINNER SLOWLY, MEASURING EACH BITE. THE TALL black man read a newspaper on the other side of the table, but Tim knew he was being watched closely. The old stucco house was cool, but not cold. The furniture was spare but pleasant. Judging from his father's experience with property, Tim decided the house was rented, and recently, too. It was too clean and uncluttered to have been lived in long, too bare to have assumed the personality of an owner.

"Good stuff?" the black asked, nodding at Tim's plate. Tim said yes quietly and scraped the final few bites onto his spoon.

"Enjoy yourself and don't be nervous, son," the man said. "Everything's going to be fine."

"I'm not nervous," Tim said.

"We've brought someone to help you."

"I want to go home."

"I know. We'll talk about that later."

Tim heard a car drive up and park in front. The curtains on the windows were drawn. He couldn't see the people getting out, but he heard three doors slam. He should have made his move earlier, if he wanted to make it at all. Against one man he might have a chance. Against four—nothing.

The black stood to answer the knock on the door. He walked out of sight, into the hall, and Tim tensed. Then he relaxed. It was no use. They'd have him before he could climb the fence in the backyard. His eye surveyed the entire house. There was nothing he could use as a weapon—no heavy bookends, no knives and only the plastic fork he had been given to eat with. The plate was Melmac—almost impossible to break. He could shatter a window and get some glass, but he'd cut his hand doing that. The voices insisted he do something, but there was nothing to do. A dull throb made him shut his eyes and squint.

Shit-eating nigger kill

He opened his eyes and edged back in his chair. In the kitchen entrance stood a tall, thin man, very old—looking older than anyone Tim could remember. His hair was white and long, reaching almost to his collar. He wasn't smiling, but his face seemed to embody humor.

"Timothy Townsend?" the man asked. His voice was resonant, full. Tim thought his accent might be English. "My name is Edward. I've heard a lot about you, and I've decided you need a friend now."

The old man's body seemed so insubstantial that for a moment Tim thought he might be a ghost, like his parents and the fellow named Percher. But he reached out his hand to take Tim's and the grip was warm, strong and dry. When they touched, Tim's headache vanished. Their hands still clasped, the old man spoke again. More than one voice seemed to come from his mouth.

"You have no need of the dead now, Timothy. They are past. Relax and let the hatred flow from you, into my arm. I have ways of disposing of it. Someday you can learn these ways and feel much, much better than you do now. May I have the hatred?"

Almost against his will, Tim shut his eyes again and felt his body tingle. For a second he wanted to cry, and then that was gone, too. The man let go of his hand.

"Who are you?" Tim asked.

"I'm a vagabond, in a way. A hobo, Timothy. I spend my life going from place to place, trying to learn about people and the things inside—and outside—of them. How old do you think I am?" Tim shook his head and the man laughed. "I'm quite old, by your standards. But my teacher lived to be a hundred and twenty years old. I'm short of that by forty years."

"Where did the others go?"

"Excuse me for a moment. I haven't unloaded my arm yet—full of all that stuff you gave me." He made a face and pulled up his coat sleeve, then unbuttoned his cuff. With three curving motions, he swung his hand. Something snapped like static electricity. "There. Down to the center of the earth, where it won't last long."

"What are they going to do with me?"

"I imagine they want to talk, Timothy. Myself, I want to listen. You've come to tell us what happened in your town, and I'm here to be told. You aren't afraid, are you?"

"No," Tim said. "What are you?"

"I'm not sure even yet. Let me tell you a story, though. Once, when I was not much older than you—and this was back in the days before there were many cars, and horses drew buggies through the streets, and before the World Wars—I visited my grandmother. She was dying. Her skin was yellow because her liver was failing. She had been a very proper Victorian woman, serious and concerned, but now she was quiet. She was ill and too weak to do much besides lie in her bed and look at the people who came to visit her. My mother said I should say good-bye to her, for she was going to die soon. That scared me. No one in my family or among my friends had died, except a little sister I hardly remembered. When I came to her bed, my grandmother took my left hand. Actually, she just opened one of her hands on the counterpane—where the covers are folded back—and I put my hand into hers. Her fingers were cold, but her palm was almost hot. 'Edward,' she said, 'there are many, many people in this room, and I tell no lies.' But I could only see my mother and father and a nurse. 'Listen to their voices,' she said, and she opened her mouth. What came out of her mouth only I heard, apparently—many, many people laughing and singing. There was also a sound like wind through the trees, and something I didn't recognize until perhaps ten years later—like the noise a radio makes between stations, when the airways are quiet. My mother came forward to make sure Grandmother wasn't frightening me. It was obvious she neither heard nor understood. 'I've been privy to these sounds ever since I was a little girl,' Grandmother went on, 'but I never told anyone, for it wasn't the right time. Now I see you have the same gift, but it hasn't opened the doors to you yet. I can see it all around you. We are privileged persons, Edward. When I die, I won't come back to see you. There's too much to do. But I will expect you to carry on.' She opened her mouth wider again and the music was very plain, light and dancing as if it came from an orchestra made of crystal. And then she shut her eyes and her mouth and she was dead.'' The old man sighed and pulled a chair close to Tim's seat. ''Now you hear voices, too, but you don't have the power. Something is forcing itself upon you that has no business in a boy. Am I right?''

Tim nodded.

''I have friends, allies actually—you can't see them, and I rarely do. But they are very strong in me now, because you need their help. Will you accept them, Timothy?''

Tim felt his heart in his throat. He swallowed and blinked back more tears. ''But they're my parents,'' he whispered. ''My friends.''

''You know they're not in control,'' Edward said. ''They need help as much as you do.''

''How can you help?''

''These people are from the government. You know that. You're a smart lad. All together, we are going to free your parents and friends, and free you. I'm not sure just how yet, but we're certainly going to try. Do you hear the voices now?''

''No,'' Tim said.

''Good. Some of it is already happening. Do you believe I'm your friend?''

''Yes.''

''Then let's go into the living room and have a long talk. This time, I'll listen.''

BOOK THREE

CHAPTER FORTY-THREE

THE LOOKOUT HAD BEEN CONVERTED TO A LANDING PAD FOR helicopters. The highway had been blocked off for a five-mile stretch, where it meandered around the valley, and Jeeps patrolled regularly. The road into the valley was empty. Except for a special truck, which had been allowed in three hours before, no vehicles or humans were in the valley.

It was four o'clock in the afternoon. Fowler nervously checked his watch, sitting in the back of an Air Force personnel van. He was going to be allowed to use the phone in about fifteen minutes. He was miserable.

Dorothy had apparently returned to Los Angeles. He could guess at some of her reasons, but why she was running away from him, and not just the valley, he didn't know. When the possibility of losing her became clear, he realized how much he needed her. Not someone like her—but Dorothy herself. His misery came because he couldn't remember ever telling her that, and now it might be too late. For the first time, he actively hated the thing in the valley. This was the second relationship it had snatched—was snatching—away from him. When he thought of Henry

Taggart his eyes grew moist and he wanted to curse. But he kept silent.

Across from him, Prohaska sat reading a newspaper, a cigarette dangling from his lips. Burnford and Williams were playing chess in the next seat forward. He leaned over the seat and watched them.

Snow was predicted for the evening. It had been clear enough the night before, when five officials in plain civilian suits had watched the beast present its display. Tonight, the rumor was that real experts would be called in. To Fowler and Burnford, that meant more civilian contractors. Both doubted the military or government kept active experts on demons and psychic phenomena on the payrolls. The persistent rumor that the President would also be present had been quashed by the presiding General Machen late in the morning. The President didn't dare risk exposing himself to a potential farce.

A major tapped on the outside of his window and Fowler looked around. The man indicated his phone was ready. Burnford glanced up at him as he walked down the aisle. "Don't be long," Williams said. "We're going into the valley in an hour."

Fowler walked to a small communications truck with his escort. The back doors opened a crack and a hand passed out a small headset and mike. The major took it and asked Fowler what the phone number was. "The guy inside will get it for you," he explained. Fowler told them and waited while hums and buzzes crossed the line. "You know the routine by now, don't you?" the major asked. Fowler nodded.

"I'm not to say anything meaningful. No clues or hints. All is calm, all is quiet."

"That's why we're calling this operation Silent Night," the major said, grinning. "Don't mind me. I'm a pro at this sort of thing, like a doctor."

"Sure," Fowler said. The phone at the other end started

ringing. After four rings, Fowler began to lose hope. But
the receiver was picked up and Dorothy answered.

"Dot," Fowler said, "hello from where I sit."

"Hello, Larry," she said, sounding tired. "I had to
leave."

"Listen, everything's in control up here. I'm fine, we're
in good hands—"

The major nodded approvingly.

"—and everything's going to be fine. Why did you run
away, honey?"

"You can't guess, not after all the things I said? I'm
sorry, Larry—"

"What things? Dot, you just left."

"About being upset. I couldn't take it. I've never been
through anything like that."

"Neither have I."

"And I don't intend to ever put up with such delusions
again. It was unreal. I can't take that. Maybe you can, but
I just can't."

"But you left *me* up here, not just—not just the cabin."

"I have to think things over." Her voice was unsteady.
He put his mouth closer to the mike, trying to find some
semblance of privacy. The major casually looked the other
way.

"Honey, why did you leave without talking to me?"

"You're all wrapped up in it. You wouldn't listen. You
would have done the same thing you're doing now, try to
get me to stay—come back—and I can't."

"I don't want you to come back—not for this, I mean.
For me, yes. I would have told you to go."

"Sure." Her voice was flat, almost nasal.

"Honey, you're not being rational."

"Rational? *I'm* not being rational? Larry, you *laughed*
about it. I saw you and I couldn't believe—you laughed at
it! Jesus, if that's rational. Here we all were going crazy,
seeing things, and you were the worst of all. What can I
tell you, Larry? I never saw you like that before."

"Maybe it was guts, some kind of crazy bravery. Did you think of that? I was coping. If I hadn't laughed, I would have gone mad, had a heart attack or something. We weren't seeing things, Dot, not the way you mean." The major looked at him sharply. Fowler ignored him.

"I just couldn't take it. You laughing. I was scared shitless."

"You think I wasn't?"

"But you believe it was there! I *saw you believing,*" she said, her voice reaching a high peak.

"Dorothy, a lot of important people are waiting to make sure. Some have already seen."

The major raised his arm and made a cutting motion. Fowler nodded and held up his hand. "I can't talk about it now. I want to. I want to show you you're not taking this right, that being scared is fine, but ignoring it is foolish. I can't ignore it."

"You know I'm into firm things," Dorothy said. "I want solid realities. I couldn't put up with parochial schools. They always wanted to show us what Hell was like and I couldn't take it. So I left. All those people suffering, just so I could have a pretty, fatherly God. That was too much. And for the same reason I can't handle this. I'm sorry. I have to go now."

"Wait, Dot. Think about it. Remember that I love you. Remember! *I love you.*"

"I'm thinking, but . . . oh, shit, Larry. Leave me alone. Let me get this all straightened out and don't try to mess me over."

"I'm not trying—"

"I have to go now." There was a pause and Fowler expected a click. Instead, she said, "Larry, come back, soon."

"I'll try." Then she hung up. He handed the set back to the major. "You aren't going to put a guard around her, or anything silly, are you?" he asked.

"No plans, as far as I know," the major said. "We checked her out. She's safe."

"Yeah," Fowler said. He thanked the man and walked back to the bus. A gray-and-white helicopter was landing on the lookout, raising dust. He shielded his eyes and climbed into the bus.

"Any luck?" Prohaska asked, folding the paper.

Fowler shook his head. "I don't know."

"Keep at her," Burnford said. "I like that girl."

Fowler returned to his seat and watched the passengers disembark from the helicopter.

Jacobs and Trumbauer ducked to avoid the last turns of the blades. Miss Unamuno, dressed in a wool skirt and plain black blouse, stepped down gingerly and followed them away from the craft. A marine in kelly green conferred with the pilot, who started the motors again. The marine backed off and the helicopter lifted into the air.

Jacobs and Trumbauer walked to the edge of the lookout and peered into the valley. The marine escorted Miss Unamuno to the edge.

"Is that where the cabin is?" Jacobs asked.

"Yessir," the marine said.

"When are we going down?"

"In forty-five minutes, sir."

"What's down there, son?" Jacobs asked.

"I don't know, sir. Follow me, please." He took them to the bus.

Burnford and Williams stood up as the new group entered. Fowler watched sullenly, slouched in his seat. The marine made introductions and then left. Jacobs approached Fowler, bushy eyebrows knitted together.

"Mr. Fowler, you're the man who found it first, aren't you?"

"No," Fowler said. "The first two are dead."

"I see. Can you tell us what it was like?"

"Be patient, Mr. Jacobs," Williams said, pushing a pawn. "We'll get there soon enough."

Burnford pounced on a bishop left unguarded and Williams groaned. "Never play chess with a physicist," Burnford warned. "We're skilled at getting grants and staying on faculties and research groups. Chess is very similar."

"We were supposed to go to Haverstock," Trumbauer said to no one in particular. Williams looked up, annoyed at him now. Trumbauer was puzzled. "Gentlemen, I've been—we've been subjected to secrecy ever since we got involved in this mess. When are we going to stop behaving like children playing spy games and start figuring out what happened?"

"My sentiments exactly," Jacobs said. "You—Mr. Williams—how do you government people expect us to help when we're ignorant?"

"I don't expect anything until the rest arrive," Williams said. "I've already warned a few of you—I'm a red-taper from start to finish. Everything is protocol and planning. After tonight, we'll put you all in a room and see what comes out. Until then, please sit down and be bored and restless. Mr. Burnford is undoubtedly going to win this game, and one of you can play him after."

"May I?" Miss Unamuno asked.

"Ho ho!" Burnford grimaced. "Playing with a mind-reader. By all means." He made a move. "Checkmate."

Prohaska turned in his seat as Jacobs sat behind him. "You're an author, aren't you?"

Jacobs nodded. "And you're a reporter."

"I'd like to have an interview with you when this is over. An exclusive."

Jacobs shrugged. "Put your name in with my appointments secretaries," he said. "Either General Machen or Colonel Silvera."

CHAPTER FORTY-FOUR

THE BLACK MAN'S NAME WAS VOLTAIRE SIMONS. AS HE FIXED lunch for Tim, he told the boy to call him Volt. "Other fellow, his name is Jack Davies. We'll be with you and Mr. Thesiger for a few more days."

Tim sat at the kitchen table and drank from his glass of milk. "I was going to Lorobu," he said.

"There ain't nothing for you there, son," Simons said. "Just a bunch of Army people and scientists. Most of them'll be pulling out soon."

Davies entered through the swinging door, holding a half-eaten sandwich in one hand. "Thesiger wants us to call Machen and get us a flight to Haverstock in two days."

"Will do," Simons said. "Tim, I hope you like corned-beef hash, 'cause we have a mess of it."

"I'll take a dollop," Davies said, sitting at the table.

"What about Thesiger?"

"He isn't eating much now. Says he works better on a fast. You like him, Tim?"

"He's okay," Tim said.

"Sure." Davies gave Simons a wink.

In the afternoon, Tim watched television with Simons and played Monopoly with Davies. He took a bath and ate dinner. Simons wrote in a small black book and Davies made numerous phone calls in another room.

"Who lives here?" Tim asked as he helped Simons with the dinner dishes.

"Nobody but us," Simons said. "Rented the place special."

"You trying to keep me away from people?"

"No—" Simons began, his tone betraying him.

"If you are, that's good," Tim went on. "I got to stay away from people until I'm grown up."

"Yeah," Simons said softly. "I know how that is. We're all here together, son. We ain't afraid of you, you shouldn't be afraid of us."

"I'm not afraid," Tim said. "Mr. Thesiger knows what's happening, I think."

Thesiger came out of his room in the back of the house at seven. He stood beside Tim's old overstuffed chair and smiled at the TV game show. "Gentlemen, do you mind if Timothy and I get back to work?"

"Not at all, sir," Davies said. "If you need anything, let us know."

"Ready, Timothy?"

Tim nodded.

"Then get your coat and come out in the backyard with me. There's a lot to do tonight. We're leaving here tomorrow, right, gentlemen?"

"Sure are," Simons said.

Tim slipped into his jacket and walked through the kitchen to the service porch. He zipped himself up, stuck his hands into the pockets—it was a new, bright blue, down-filled coat—and opened the back door.

Thesiger was standing in the middle of the small lawn. The fish pool and tool shed were clear in the moonlight.

"Have the voices been bothering you?" Thesiger asked, motioning for Tim to stand beside him.

"No, sir," Tim said.

"No headaches, anything like that?"

"Nothing."

"Good. Do you understand what was happening to you?"

"I think so. Everybody who died was trying to get me to come with them. I didn't want to go, so they made me want to hurt people."

"Why would they want to do that?"

"Whatever killed them was real mean."

"I see. Have you ever heard voices before, when you were younger, or seen anything unusual?"

"No. I had nightmares—still do, sometimes, but not like you mean. Not like I think you mean."

"You understand my meaning very clearly, Timothy. Would you like to see something marvelous tonight? Not see, exactly, but feel?"

Tim hesitated. "What kind of thing?"

"Nothing that will hurt. We're going to duck our heads into the water—below the water—and feel what lies far beneath. Not the fish pond, but all around us."

Tim dug his hands deeper into his pockets. "Why?" he asked.

Thesiger put both his thin, gnarled hands on Tim's shoulders and squatted down in front of him. The old man's eyes were as bright as a child's, without the bleariness or veining Tim had once seen in his grandfather's. "Because you're important to us now. We need you strong and capable. Grown up, even. To be sure you understand, I'm going to show you things related to what you've experienced. You're a lucky young man, actually. Very few people can be shown these things any more. They keep their feet on the ground so firmly they don't even know how to die. But you're young and flexible."

"How did you see when you were younger?"

"Remember the story about my grandmother? I knew I had the gift from that time on. So I travelled around the world, listening to people tell stories and camping in the countrysides, just *listening. Feeling.* I saw many of the things they talked about, and saw them clearer than most others had before me. My strength grew. And so must yours, but we don't have much time. I will give you advanced training now, because I believe you can stand it. You've already stood up to considerably more than most could."

Tim looked up. The sky was bright with stars and a close, observant moon. "Okay," he said. "If it will make me grown up."

"In a way, it will." Thesiger lay on the grass and stared up at the sky. "Lie on your back, feet pointing away from me, with your head against mine." Tim did as he was told and Thesiger adjusted himself until their scalps touched. "Good."

"Now, do you see the stars, Timothy?"

"Yes, sir."

"Between them and us, around them and us, there is a vast ocean which we seldom see. It isn't really our business to see it. Our business is to live in this world as well as we can, and to keep our kind alive. But some of us, now and then, have a glimpse of the ocean. We've interpreted it many ways. Some have been driven mad, others have become saints, others have lived their lives normally. But apparently something very bad has happened and this balance has been upset. Now we *must* look into the ocean, for there are sharks waiting. What kind of sharks, we don't know. The sharks got your town, Timothy. But sharks are very rare in this ocean. Look, feel. Listen."

"I don't see anything," Tim said, scrunching up his eyes. "Just stars and stuff."

"Listen."

After a few minutes, Tim's body began to tingle. The old man was very strong. Tim felt his eyes were sinking far back into his head. It didn't hurt, but it was peculiar. When he shut his eyelids, the illusion was complete and he swam in warm, empty darkness. Thesiger's voice was clear and distant. "Some of the ocean's inhabitants are huge. Feel them? They move between the stars, between and through us and our world, like leviathans—great whales, broad and slow, paying no more attention to us than we do to molecules of air. Feel."

A shudder passed through the boy. His eyes were locked and would not move. He was no longer seeing with them. His arms and legs were numb, yet he was moving. And from the darkness came a deep, shuddering mind-sound.

"There's one," Thesiger said without words.

"I feel it," Tim replied in kind.

The mind-sound passed back and forth across great distances, echoing yet not echoing, rising in pitch and falling, yet not. "It's singing," Tim said.

"Breathing," Thesiger corrected. "With every breath it swells past suns, and with every exhale it vanishes into a pinpoint. But it lives across a wider range than we do, so at no moment is it ever smaller in our universe than it is now. Or larger."

Tim didn't understand, but he didn't need to. The leviathan, whatever it was, had no care for them, no care for the world. It existed and travelled. Then it was gone and the ocean was empty again.

"The giants are very common," Thesiger said. "They aren't powerful, however. Smaller forms have a greater ability to influence our world. Listen for them—they chatter like birds."

Yet the chatter was a symphony compared to human speech.

"Are they God?" Tim asked.

"No more and no less than we are."

"I seem to know them."

"They play with our dreams sometimes like dolphins play with turtles. You know them, they know you."

"Are they angels?"

"Close, but no. The beings important to you and me are inaccessible without much deeper ability, or training. These things are harmless, trifling. Now listen again."

The next things Tim saw were shadows, small and shapeless. Tim could feel one realizing it was being observed. It suggested *horse* and Tim saw a long, dark horse swim through their sea.

"Occasionally, these creatures attach to a world and live there. It seems to be a stage in their lives. Once in a great while, something will go wrong—though I'm not sure that's the right phrase—and they will stay. The longer they stay, the more power they gain. Humans have seen them, used them, and been used by them."

"Ghosts and demons," Tim said.

"In a way."

"Can I see people who have died?"

"Not in this sea, Timothy. When we die, we go very much farther away. Sometimes it takes ages to get there, but time has little meaning. People must make their decisions, prepare themselves. Dying is very important, much too important to be left to amateurs."

Tim laughed and the laughter poured into his body. He seemed to be hollow, filled with a tide of humor. *This* was what it felt like to be grownup. If it was, he had never known anybody truly grownup. The sensation passed and he missed it terribly.

"Now, Icarus, listen to your guide carefully. We are going to fly much higher than we should, but only for a while, a very short while."

"I thought we were in a sea."

"And so we are, a sea of flying. Ready? Cling tight." It

was neither soaring nor sinking, but a dizzy expansion which Tim wasn't sure he enjoyed. "Open your eyes."

He opened.

"Close your eyes."

He closed.

And they were in the backyard again, lying head to head.

Tim wasn't sure what he had seen. A hundred billion earthworms crawling through a city made of flowers and wire and glass? Except they weren't earthworms, and there were no flowers, no wire, no glass. Or had it been a convention of holy men, their spirits like doves, walking through a maze of gardens and parks, singing, each song emerging like a golden cord from their mouths, and the cord forming a tapestry too bright to look at? He couldn't capture it, or remember it.

"What was that?"

"Don't ask," Thesiger said. "And don't try to remember. Just keep the feeling. Was it a happy feeling?"

"Yes," Tim said, feeling his chest fill. "Oh, *yes*."

"Good. That is our strength. Tomorrow we'll carry that strength into battle. Are you ready?"

Tim nodded, and their scalps rubbed together.

CHAPTER FORTY-FIVE

THE VAN DRIVER STARTED THE ENGINE. FLAKES OF SNOW WERE drifting across the closed highway in the pale-blue twilight. Fowler finished a game of chess against Burnford by conceding. Burnford packed away the pieces as the bus lurched onto the road through the valley. "Should have brought a magnetized set," he said, folding the board and sticking it into his valise.

Fowler looked at his watch. It was five-fifteen. Trucks big and small were following them. His stomach was upset. Williams offered him a thermos cup full of milk and he took it, sipping it slowly.

Burnford handed him a sketchpad filled with mathematical equations and a crude diagram spotted with Greek letters. "This is what it looks like, I think," he said. Fowler traced his finger along the diagram.

"Like a mushroom," he said.

"Sort of. The stem is its power link with the earth. Last night we were able to distinguish this rough shape, and a distribution of charged air masses. It can't cross the running water because that would interfere with its power supply." He grinned. "Actually, I don't have any idea what I'm talking about. How it converts energy, how it maintains a four-dimensional space surface, and what the hell it really is—none of us know. But we learned one thing. Microwaves bug the hell out of it. If it's sluggish tonight, we'll get it going with a few pulses. Or we'll lob another cross into the area.''

"Has anyone brought out the priest?" Prohaska asked.

"Not a chance," Williams said. "Nobody's going to interfere until we've studied the situation thoroughly."

"They're scared shitless," Burnford confided.

"And if the streams freeze?" Fowler asked.

"The first truck to go in today has a portable water heater. We'll tap into the water table to keep a flow." Williams put aside his much-handled newspaper and sat up in the seat.

Opposite the gravel road to the cabin, a meadow had been cleared and levelled. A bulldozer sat vacant in one corner of the lot. The van parked near the middle and the other trucks maneuvered around it. A staff car was the last to arrive. Silvera and Machen stepped out, escorted by soldiers armed with submachine guns. Fowler smiled and shook his head. "Are they expecting commando raids?"

"Even Chinese ghosts hate crosses," Jacobs said. He had been quiet throughout the trip, sitting in the front seat next to the driver. "Any explanation for that, Mr. Burnford?"

"None," Burnford said.

"Humans attach great significance to symbols," Trumbauer said. "They allow us to concentrate and gather our forces. I imagine if something hates us, it hates everything beneficial to us."

"You mean, the priest might have gotten out of there alive if he hadn't carried a crucifix?" Williams asked.

"By itself, the symbol is nothing," Miss Unamuno said. "One must have faith."

"You think a good exorcist could clear the whole area?"

Williams pursued, a small grin curling the edges of his lips.

"No," Jacobs said. "This is an elemental, not a fallen angel or a dead soul."

"Pray tell, do you believe in all those things?" Williams asked.

"That's enough," Fowler said sharply. He could feel the debate starting again—materialists against spiritualists—and he didn't want to hear it.

"Nervous, Fritz?" Burnford asked. The agent smirked and looked out the window.

"I saw it," Williams said. "I can't deny that. But attaching any religious significance to it grates on me."

"I agree," Jacobs said. "Mr. Burnford's attitude is best now. But Mr. Williams, we are here as experts, and if we don't offer our theories, what use are we?"

"I don't know," Williams said. "I wouldn't have called you in."

Trumbauer raised his hand like a conductor about to start his orchestra. The gesture was so patently dramatic that Fowler was about to laugh.

Then the ground trembled.

"Sunset," Jacobs said. The driver's face was pale.

"Feel it, Arnold?" Miss Unamuno asked. Trumbauer nodded. "So can I. It can't get across the river, but it can affect us out here, all the same."

"How much?" Burnford asked.

"Not strongly, I think," Trumbauer said. "It's very mild now. Just a hint. My . . . pardon the expression . . . my guide is very sensitive."

"Who is your guide, John Kennedy? Shakespeare?" Williams' voice was almost a snarl.

"Mr. Williams, that is enough!" Jacobs commanded. "Are you feeling all right?"

"This truck," Williams said. He was sweating. "It's so

damned small. You people are all senseless. Even you, Burnford. This is a crock of shit.''

"Settle down, Fritz," Burnford said. The agent was squirming on his seat.

"When is it going to start?" Williams asked.

Miss Unamuno reached across the aisle and took one of his hands, stroking it. "Be calm," she said. "It's trying to irritate us." He cursed under his breath.

Fowler's eyes met the driver's and they nodded simultaneously. The driver opened the cab door and stepped out. "Where's he going?" Williams asked.

Jacobs fixed his attention on the bulge in the agent's coat pocket. He tapped Burnford on the shoulder and walked down the narrow aisle to Williams' seat. Burnford saw what he was up to.

"Fritz, listen," he began. Williams looked at him wildly. Jacobs locked the agent's arm across the back of the seat and flapped the jacket open. Burnford grabbed the gun and quickly emptied the clip into his palm. Three soldiers approached the side door with Silvera following a few steps behind. The Colonel produced a key and swung the door open. Williams went limp and laughed as they pulled him out of the van.

"Jesus, what's going on here?" he asked, his voice high. "I was just talking. What in hell is all this?" The soldiers led him away. Silvera took his place and glanced at Jacobs, Burnford and Fowler, his expression demanding an explanation.

"Can it get us even across the river?" he asked.

"We can feel it," Trumbauer said. "It's weak. I don't think it could make us do anything drastic, but it's here, yes."

"Mr. Burnford, we're going to prompt the thing with a pulse and see how long it displays," Silvera said. He pulled six steno pads from a canvas bag and handed them around with pencils. "Record your impressions, please.

This van is wired for recording on tape, too. Your reactions are important. Don't hold them back.''

"Watch your soldiers carefully,'' Jacobs warned.

"We are. All weapons are being stored under lock. There was some irritation and nervousness last night. Nothing like Mr. Williams, though.''

"Everybody's so damned polite,'' Fowler said.

"You feeling irritable now, Mr. Fowler?'' Silvera asked, looking back at him. Fowler shook his head.

"I'm not feeling possessed. I know what that's like.''

"I hope you do. The driver will relay any messages to me. Please stay in the truck. A heater will be on to keep you warm. Here are penlights to write notes by.'' The small tubes were passed around. Jacobs stuck his in a pocket and put the notebook aside. Silvera shut the door.

Trumbauer raised his hand again.

Something darker than the night was coalescing above the cabin's small hill. Threads of pale-green luminosity shot through the mass.

"Recorder on,'' the driver said. Fowler trembled.

"My body's more scared than I am,'' Prohaska murmured.

The dark mass flickered with an oily sheen of rainbow colors. Burnford whistled appreciatively.

"I'm getting a headache,'' Jacobs said.

"It's in pain,'' Miss Unamuno said. "Whatever they're doing to it, it's in pain.''

"I can't feel too sorry for it,'' Prohaska said.

"Nor should you,'' Trumbauer said. "It feels no sorrow for us.''

The cloud began to writhe and take shape. A giant sparrow flashed in its depths, then wavered and vanished. Spots of fire flared up.

The van's occupants gasped in unison. A naked woman appeared in the cloud. She looked remarkably like Dorothy, Fowler thought. Jacobs saw a clear resemblance to Millicent. The form was split up the middle and disemboweled. The illusion began a ragged, bloody dance and then dissolved. A succession of animals were handled in a similar manner. The ground shook as if giant feet were stamping. Fowler wanted to vomit and was barely able to control himself. With each stomp, he could feel the horror he had known in the cabin returning with greater strength. The thing was mindlessly evoking terror, hatred. The smell of fear in the bus became acute. The parade of images was getting more and more obscene.

"It's drawing the images from us," Miss Unamuno said. "From the soldiers, the men around the streams. All the worst in our heads."

The mutations were horrible and fascinating. Fowler categorized them to subdue their physical impact on him. *Blood and genitalia,* he wrote. *Destruction of fetus-like forms. Combining insects with children, Things decaying. Monstrous animals. Crows with human eyes.* "Hatred," he said. "God, how it hates."

"We're less limited than it is," Jacobs said. "Something has gone wrong. It shouldn't be here. It knows that. It's been stunted in some way, while we are whole, complete. It's a natural force, but it doesn't belong here. It's trapped."

"Put it out of its misery, then," Prohaska said.

Its power was limited, Jacobs thought, but its perception was not. It knew these people—knew him—through and through. At times the depravity was so blatant it lost all effect, but for each of them there was a moment of dark revelation, of something reacting within them which appreciated the display. They were all contributing to the horror. He was breathing heavily.

A depression settled over Fowler. How could anything be worth the existence of so much horror? He turned away, choking. The implications were more than he could bear. There was no hope, no beauty, nothing in life worth having if behind all things lay a foundation of such hopelessness.

"It's a mindless master," Miss Unamuno said. Fowler nodded. Goya and Bosch had looked deep inside themselves, and seen only the tip of what the thing was showing them now.

Corpses having sex with infants. Infants giving birth to hags, and the hags devouring them, an ouroubouros out of hell. And the boar.

The van rocked as a wind blew across the levelled meadow. The boar was screaming soundlessly, its lips curled back displaying slaver-flecked gums and humanoid teeth. The tusks flashed. The eye was red as a dying sun, but cast no light on them or the trees. The hair was made of worms. Blood fountained from its mouth.

"Oh, Jesus, Jesus!" Miss Unamuno screamed. "Take us away from here!"

The driver was rigid in his seat, mouth hanging open. Fowler winced. With Miss Unamuno's cries, a tiny figure had formed in the cloud, as if seen from some infinite perspective. This display, he knew, was for him alone. It was an upside-down crucifixion, limned in bloody purple. The figure on the cross had the body of a pig and the head of Henry Taggart. The head fell away and dissolved. Blood poured from the neck in an incandescent ribbon into the trees. He shut his eyes.

"There's the first test," Burnford said. A truck behind them had opened a hatch in its side and a large, rectangular box had emerged. A pale-green line of light shot from it and pierced the cloud, making the figure writhe. "There are receptors up in the hills. We're going to analyze the spectrum and see what—"

"Are they hurting it?" Fowler asked.

"I doubt it," Burnford said. "Just for analysis."

As quickly as it began, the display vanished. The images tumbled like bricks of dream and the air over the hill stopped shimmering. Trumbauer held on to Miss Unamuno, who was sobbing. Fowler blinked.

The driver started the van's engine. All the other trucks roared to life together. In a line, they pulled out of the meadow onto the asphalt road and drove from the valley. Nobody in the van spoke. Burnford broke the silence when they went by the lookout point.

"It can't be the thing that took Lorobu," he said.

"Obviously," Jacobs said.

"But it must work the same way."

They passed six large semis hauling flatbed trailers, going into the valley. Fowler turned to look out the rear window. Something large and bulky was on each trailer, covered by roped canvas tarps. "What are those?" he asked.

"I'm not sure," Burnford said. "They haven't told me everything. I'd guess they're part of an experiment."

"To hurt it?" Prohaska asked.

"This time, I think so, yes."

CHAPTER FORTY-SIX

CORPORAL S.K. PERCHER'S HOME WAS NOW OCCUPIED BY THE northern quadrangle of Haverstock University, a small private school. The grass on the quad was sere between thin patches of snow. The trees were bent and distorted, bark wrinkled like plastic dipped in acetone.

Two hundred yards south, the silver dome of the university's small observatory glittered in the sun. Tim stood in the middle of the quad, with Thesiger a few steps away, and tried to concentrate.

"I'm taking away the shields now," Thesiger said. "Are you ready?"

Tim nodded. He was afraid, but Thesiger had told him it was best to be afraid. Thesiger had faith in him, that he was strong enough to withstand the experiences, that he could help solve the problem.

Thesiger raised his hand. "Now."

For a moment Tim felt dizzy. He had expected a flood of voices, like leaning into a stiff, bitter wind, but there was almost complete peace. Almost—there was an undertone, a hint of pain and terror, but not the blast he had expected.

"Well?" Thesiger asked.

Then they struck him. Beseeching, commanding, cursing, trying to tear at his mind. Tim clapped his hands to his ears. "They're with me," he said. "They're mad at me."

Thesiger put up the shield again. Tim opened his eyes and wobbled unsteadily on his feet.

"Are they close?"

Tim scrunched his face, trying to think. "I don't think so," he said. "It didn't hurt like when they were close."

"Then they're on their way to Dayton."

"You feeling anything?" Tim asked.

"Yes," Thesiger said. He pointed across the quad to the houses and apartment buildings outside the university grounds. "Shall we go over there?"

Tim shrugged his shoulders. "Are the dead people still there?"

"Not their bodies. We should see whether anything else is left of them, don't you think?"

Their ghosts, Tim thought. He straightened his shoulders and nodded. "Can we have lunch after that?"

"Certainly." Thesiger gestured to the four agents waiting on the edge of the quadrangle. As they all walked to the car, Thesiger pointed to the university observatory. "They had equipment working when it happened," he said. "They were measuring radiation from the sky, from the distant stars. TV screens and telescopes and antennae. So now we know what it's like—on the level of our universe."

"Oh," Tim said. Thesiger smiled and patted him on the shoulder.

"You're a brave lad, Timothy," the old man said. "I'm proud to have you helping me."

"Is it going to kill people in Dayton next?" Tim asked. Voltaire Simons opened the car door and shook his head.

"Not if we can help it, Tim. Mr. Thesiger and you are

the bloodhounds, but the hunter hasn't showed yet. Wait and see.''

Thesiger took Tim's hand. The shield was up again and Tim felt safe. But he was still scared. He had been scared now for a month, ever since Lorobu. It was hard to remember what it was like to not be scared. He looked forward to it being over just as he had once looked forward to Christmas.

Christmas was four days away.

CHAPTER FORTY-SEVEN

STILL SLEEPY, FOWLER WAS THE FIRST TO STEP OUT OF THE VAN, shielding his eyes against the bright late-morning light. Jacobs followed him, and then the rest.

Miss Unamuno was last. She frowned and put her foot on the chewed dirt of the meadow. Silvera and General Machen stood by a staff car at the beginning of the gravel road. "Let's go," Burnford said.

Machen was about fifty-five years old, Jacobs decided—a little younger than himself—with graying red hair and a scar across one lip which gave him a permanent, dolphinlike grin. He greeted them in a pleasant baritone. "Would you all follow me?"

Four corrugated metal plates had been thrown over the creek. Their feet made the iron ring dully as they crossed. Fowler hesitated, but Silvera prompted him forward. Jacobs walked beside Machen, trying to take his measure with occasional glances.

The road to the cabin was pitted as though great chunks of dirt and gravel had been dug out with shovels. Trees had been clawed bare, branches broken off, leaving pale white trunks. Some had been knocked over, blocking the path.

Where the priest had fallen, only a spray-painted white outline remained. The separate circle for the head was grotesque. Fowler turned away and looked at the cars. They had been flattened into lumpy sheets, like stepped-on cans. Piles of gravel and splintered wood were everywhere. The cabin was almost untouched. The only apparent damage was from a tree that had fallen across the rear roof, crunching a portion of the overhang.

"It's gone," Trumbauer said.

"No trace at all?" Silvera asked. Trumbauer shook his head. "How about you, Miss Unamuno?"

She shut her eyes and clenched her fists. She opened them and looked around, surprised. "Nothing! Where did it go?"

Silvera looked at Burnford and nodded. "It worked on this one."

"I'm amazed," Burnford said. "I wasn't sure any of the equations were right. Where is it now?"

"Where's what now?" Jacobs asked.

"You destroyed it? Or just made it go away?" Fowler asked. Prohaska stepped up on the porch.

"Apparently, it's gone for good," Machen said. "We dispersed it. The weapon is on its way to Siloam Springs, Ohio."

Jacobs looked at his list. "That's where Tech Sergeant Grimm lived. Why not Dayton?"

"There's no time. Dayton may be reached by tomorrow evening. We can't transport everything and set it up. Besides, the geography is no good. Too many people."

"What's the weapon?" Fowler asked. "Is that what we saw last night?"

Machen shook his head. "We're mum for now. In a couple of days, you should know as much as you want— more, probably. You're all under orders not to reveal anything you've seen until the whole project and all related items are declassified.''

Prohaska's face fell. "No story?''

"Not for at least twenty years," Machen said, smiling grimly. "We have a use for all of you, but right now you're just observers and advisors.''

"And you're keeping us together for security reasons," Fowler said. "I'm almost sorry I called you, George.''

"Don't be," Silvera said. "With the information we gathered here, and the information from Haverstock, we have a good idea what's been causing all these disasters.''

"And what's that?'' Prohaska asked.

Again, Machen shook his head. "No theories until Siloam Springs. And we aren't keeping you all together. The group will be split. Some of you are going to Dayton, some to Siloam Springs.''

"There's no trace at all," Miss Unamuno reiterated, turning around, hands seeming to grasp at the air. "The whole valley is empty. What did you do?'' Her face was drawn and bloodless. "No, this is more than curiosity,'' she said, voice trembling. "What happened here?''

Jacobs felt the edge of her fear and turned to Trumbauer. "Arnie, isn't there anything? A residue, a trail, something to show it's somewhere else, but not here?''

Trumbauer took Miss Unamuno's hand and tried to calm her. "Nothing, Franklin,'' he said, staring squint-eyed at Silvera and Machen. "It's as if it never existed.''

CHAPTER FORTY-EIGHT

JACOBS SAT APART FROM THE OTHERS ON THE AIRCRAFT, ELBOW on the armrest and chin in hand, musing. He had very little scientific expertise—only what he had gained in the service, decades ago—and the handicap frustrated him. He wasn't ignorant, but he had no way of interpreting Burnford's diagram or the equations on it. To make matters more difficult, he had only seen it for a few seconds.

Burnford had been exuberant on the return from the cabin. Fowler and Prohaska had toasted to the success of the mission—Fowler less enthusiastic than the reporter, but not unpleased. Behind him, Miss Unamuno and Trumbauer were reading or napping. The worry Miss Unamuno had felt was now communicated to Jacobs, but he wasn't certain why.

Burnford was on his way to Dayton with Fowler, Prohaska and Silvera. Williams had been reassigned—he was no longer on the project. Jacobs didn't know whether the physicist could have explained, or been allowed to explain more fully, but he would have given several fortunes to have certain haunting suspicions laid to rest.

Could a new secret weapon have been designed and put

to use in less than two weeks? He doubted it. Something already in the arsenal—but still secret—was a better answer. He racked his memory, trying to draw up some clue of what it could be.

Burnford had treated the elemental as a field of some sort. Jacobs had recognized the field equations from his brief stint as a radar technician. What, then, would disperse an electromagnetic field? (If, indeed, Burnford had been talking about electromagnetism.) Super magnets, bolts of static electricity? Had a huge Van de Graaff generator been used? He squeezed his temples and looked up to see General Machen standing beside him.

"Mind if I sit?" Machen asked.

"Not at all." Jacobs slid over.

"I'd like to apologize, and offer our thanks," Machen began, looking at the seat in front of him. "I'm not used to having civilian contractors on a project like this. Then again, I've never *been* on a project like this."

"We're hardly contractors," Jacobs said. "Just concerned citizens."

"Yes. I apologize for treating you like mushrooms—"

"Eh?"

"Keeping you in the dark and feeding you bullshit." Machen chuckled. "I'm not the Commander-in-Chief of this operation. I'd do things a little differently—not much, perhaps, but a little. And I'm thanking you for putting up with what appear to be blinders and heavy earmuffs."

"Yes," Jacobs said. "Well, we hardly have the complete picture, do we?"

"You've been a great help to us. I still find it hard accepting the fact that we're using psychics and experts in occult phenomena. I'm a practical man; I never have put much credence in the paranormal. Now it's everyday talk."

"Can you tell me when it became everyday talk as far as this project is concerned?"

"I can. About a week after Lorobu was destroyed. We

still keep alternate theories—we even talked about UFOs and space plagues when it became apparent that no secret weapons had been used, no CBW stockpiles had ruptured, and no subversive group could be blamed. It was too sophisticated, too *holistic*, if you see what I mean.''

"I'm not sure I do.''

"Too integrated and interrelated. When I was first called in, about four days after the incident, I began having nightmares. Haven't had them since I was a kid. Started taking sleeping pills for the first time in my life. I don't think I'd have had that reaction for anything political or technological. It had to be something else.''

"So you settled on the supernatural.''

"Should have heard the protests and seen the faces of the joint chiefs and everyone else involved.'' He shook his head, the permanent smile turning the gesture into mocking humor. "Oddly, the President was the hardest to convince.''

"And after you had the Haverstock University results, you called George Burnford in.''

"Fowler and the reporter were a bonus. Without them, we'd have to have tried our solution without a test.''

"So everyone now accepts the existence of demons. What about ghosts?''

"I'm reluctant to go into details.''

"Do you think the psychlone—'' He spelled it—"that's my name for whatever it was—do you think it's a demon, too?''

Machen shook his head, smiling on purpose this time. "No, Mr. Jacobs. May I call you Franklin?''

"Certainly.''

"No, we knew it had to be something more closely related to humanity. The list of names you handed over to us, the contacts with the inhabitants of the towns—that had to be more than coincidence.''

"And?''

"To confirm that, we're going to put you and your friends under the flightpath of the . . . psychlone. We have a house just outside Dayton which should be right under a straight-line path from Haverstock. I don't think we'll be in any danger but once we arrive, any of you can back out."

"You must have others helping you, then."

"Yes. One other. Two, if you count the only survivor from Lorobu."

Jacobs looked out the window at the bright, filamented clouds streaming past below. "When is it scheduled to pass over the house?"

"At eleven p.m. this evening. It will pass over Dayton ten hours later."

"Assuming it's traveling at—about two or three miles an hour?" Jacobs asked. Machen nodded. "And assuming it takes a straight-line path."

"We have reasons for assuming both. Other psychics have been contacted or have reported to us."

"But it only hits the target towns."

"Where the people on your list used to live."

"The POWs."

Machen's false smile faded. "Yes," he said stiffly.

"From World War Two. Hiroshima and Nagasaki."

"You're very knowledgeable, Franklin."

"Yes." He wasn't about to get Beckett in trouble. "I remember the papers a few months ago. It used to be classified information—"

"The complete list still is."

"The list Miss Unamuno received."

"No," Machen said. "Her list isn't complete. It's missing several hundred names."

"All prisoners of war, captured toward the end of the war. All killed during the atomic bombing of the Japanese cities."

"Believe it or not, some American POWs survived,"

Machen said. "They're on the project now, those that are still alive and healthy."

"If the psychlone isn't a demon, and seems to consist of human souls, how did it form?" Jacobs asked.

"We don't know."

Jacobs thought of Burnford's field equations again. "But you plan to treat it the same way you treated the elemental."

"We do," Machen said.

"So you assume it has many of the same characteristics."

"More than assume. We have data from the Haverstock observatory that confirms it. There are many points of similarity."

"And differences?"

"Some."

Jacobs frowned with concentration. He didn't want to voice half-considered ideas. "The weapon used on the elemental disrupts an electromagnetic field . . . disperses it."

"It's more complicated than that, but that's the idea, yes."

"Would an atom bomb have the same effect?"

Machen pursed his lips. "It might."

"How many people were directly under the explosions in Hiroshima and Nagasaki?"

"I'm not sure. Maybe fifteen or twenty thousand, all told."

Jacobs felt sick. The idea was clear now. "The human soul is probably not very different from the elemental in structure . . . basic structure. A field, partly oriented in our universe, immortal in a way—most natural processes cannot affect it, but can only affect its grip on a material body. When death releases the soul it slips away—"

"Franklin—"

"Please listen. This has been in my head for some time, but it hasn't come together until now. Am I right, that the fireball of an atomic explosion produces forces more severe than any known in nature?"

"Yes. I suppose astronomical events like supernovas are more severe, but on the whole, yes."

"Then thousands of people who died in the two atom-bombed cities may have vanished completely, forever. Not just dead in the natural sense, but wiped clean—their souls erased, dispersed. Or perhaps worse—for us—not destroyed completely. Just mangled. Portions of the souls gone, others surviving . . . incomplete. In eternal agony."

Machen's ruddy skin paled. "I don't think—" He stopped himself and stood up. "God would not allow such a thing," he said, his voice soft. "Mr. Jacobs, you are theorizing way over our heads."

"Does it scandalize you, General?" Jacobs said, his voice biting. "It horrifies me. The very possibility is more than I ever thought I'd face."

"You're saying we have the ability to destroy an immortal soul. That's unthinkable, impossible. It goes against the very Word, against the guarantees of religion."

"Perhaps it does. But if you can destroy a demon, why not a human soul?" His voice cracked. "Why not, General? In the core of a nuclear explosion. The perfect hell for dismantling the psyche, stretching it beyond any return. We can verify it."

Machen began to back away.

"Somebody in the psychlone has warned us—the POWs, perhaps. They gave us their names in geographic order, and now we have a defense. Their souls must not have been destroyed, or mangled . . . they weren't killed by the fireballs, but by the after-effects. Killed and taken captive by the dead, dismembered Japanese."

Machen shook his head.

"Is it true? They survived the fireball?"

"This is insane, Jacobs."

"I wish it were," Jacobs said. He was beginning to shiver. He fell back into his seat and shook his head.

CHAPTER FORTY-NINE

THE HOUSE WAS ON AN ISOLATED TRACT OF FARMLAND, SCAT-
tered around with trees, a gray old barn, and the rusted
hulks of an old harvester and a tractor. Tim stood by the
window of the upper room, under a peaked roof, looking
down on a cat stalking birds in the grassy yard. It was
ideal. He would love living in a place like this, even being
a farmer, though it was obvious the farm hadn't paid out
recently.

Thesiger was downstairs, talking with Simons and Davies. Even up here, Tim could feel the old man's presence.
It was like being surrounded by friends. Tim's maternal
grandfather had once described saints as "men who see
right through you, because they have more than one pair of
eyes, but they don't judge." That was Thesiger. Tim
didn't know if that meant Thesiger was a saint; perhaps it
didn't matter.

Two cars and a Jeep drove into the yard and parked by a
dry duckpond. Tim watched for a few minutes as three
civilians and four people in uniforms got out and talked.
They headed for the front door and he turned away to go
downstairs.

* * *

Jacobs surveyed the house critically. It was pleasant enough, but he didn't like something about it. He cocked an eyebrow at Trumbauer, but Trumbauer didn't catch the unasked question.

General Machen walked beside Miss Unamuno, carrying her baggage. Three soldiers with holstered pistols stayed by the cars; Jacobs and Trumbauer carried small suitcases.

A black man met them at the latched screen door, recognized Machen, and greeted them pleasantly, introducing himself as Volt Simons. They stepped into the entryway. Trumbauer jerked and looked into the hall leading to the kitchen. A thin, white-haired man with a hawkish face stood there, smiling at them. For a moment Jacobs thought he was looking at Bertrand Russell; then the illusion faded. He almost recognized the face. The man walked forward and offered his hand to Miss Unamuno, who was closest.

"I'm Edward Thesiger," he said. "You're Janet Unamuno—Miss Unamuno?"

She nodded, staring at him steadily.

Jacobs held out his hand. "I'm very pleased to meet you," he said. "I thought you were dead."

"No, just isolated for many years," Thesiger said. "I've had a chance to read some of your books, though."

"I'm honored."

Trumbauer stood awkwardly to one side. The look on his face as Thesiger shook hands with him was awestruck. He smiled and said nothing. Thesiger returned the smile and motioned them into the living room.

A boy stood at the foot of a flight of stairs. Thesiger introduced the new people and said, "This is my colleague, Timothy Townsend. Tim has met our adversary before and is proving quite useful."

They sat on the couch and chairs in the living room and Simons offered to bring in coffee and soft drinks. Jacobs asked for a ginger ale, if any was to be had.

Machen took a chair from the dining room and straddled it. "From here in, all we're going to do is sit and watch and take orders from you folks," he said. "We'll have trucks outside in a few hours, but they won't bother us here."

"Where is the rest of the team?" Thesiger asked.

"Heading for Dayton now."

"And when will it reach us?"

"We estimate eleven p.m."

"We are not the only team of psychics being utilized, I understand."

"No," Machen said. "We have four teams between here and Haverstock, and five more teams spread around the straight-line path. They're all in radio contact with us."

"The radio doesn't work when it's here," Tim said.

The general smiled. "We have other means of getting messages through."

"Mr. Thesiger is your center of operations?" Jacobs asked.

"He is."

"You're brighter than I gave you credit for."

Machen nodded. "None of you has a complete overview of Silent Night, any more than the soldier in the field sees a complete battle strategy."

Simons brought in a tray of glasses and Jacobs sipped his ginger ale appreciatively. "Why is Timothy here?"

"Because he wanted to be," Thesiger said. "He's a very capable young man."

"So he is," Jacobs said. "Shall we start planning for tonight?"

CHAPTER FIFTY

"WE'RE PUTTING TEN VOLUNTEERS INTO THE CENTER OF DAY-ton," Silvera said. "We have trucks and trailers ready. The trailers are rigged with padded cells and they'll be assigned one to a cell. Machines will record their reactions."

"They're guinea pigs," Fowler said.

"And they volunteered. Very brave of them, I'll admit. For the rest of us, there's a station being set up just outside the postulated attack zone. We'd like all of you to help us record and analyze the subjects' reactions." He paced back and forth across the small hotel room.

Burnford shook his head. "I'm not a doctor."

"No, but your expertise is just as important."

"When is the evacuation starting?" Fowler asked.

"Tonight at five o'clock. The target area is just outside a chemical plant. We can stage a mock release of poison-ous gases and clear a large section of the city for at least twenty-four hours. We'll be well outside the danger zone."

"You might as well tell the volunteers to commit sui-cide," Fowler said.

"Our program is well-planned," Silvera countered, looking at him sharply. "They won't be able to hurt themselves. We need the information badly or we wouldn't risk them."

Fowler was unconvinced. "Why do you need me? I can understand George—I can see he's central to some aspect of your project—but me?"

"You've experienced a similar attack. You can provide essential insight."

"And at any rate, you won't let me go anyplace for a few more days."

"You can understand that, I hope," Silvera said.

Fowler shrugged. "If it's a choice of sitting here for another week or doing something useful, I'll go with the team." He had to give them that impression now; he hoped he sounded sincere.

"Fine," Silvera said. "We'll drive to the outpost in an hour. Mr. Burnford?"

"I have a family. I don't think this is going to help any of us much. I'll have to think about it."

"Not in the target, remember. Only observing."

"We don't know how powerful the force is now. We won't know until after tonight. If it doesn't pick up . . . doesn't kill any more people, we might firmly have established its power. Then again, maybe not."

"You're coming with us?" Fowler asked.

Silvera nodded.

"We're all very brave and noble," Prohaska said. "Tell me if I'm stupid, but I want to be in there." He put his cigarette out in a glass ashtray.

"You're stupid," Fowler said.

"You don't have to go in with us, Mr. Fowler," Silvera reiterated.

"Listen—" Fowler started to say, but cut himself off. If he told them why he had to leave—to get back to Dot and keep his last worthwhile anchor from breaking loose—they would watch him more closely than they already were. His value to them was over. They couldn't seriously expect him to be of much use. Burnford, perhaps—or some of the others now waiting under the straight-line path. They were useful. He was just a security burden, best kept under close surveillance.

He had to talk to Dot.

"Just in case," Prohaska said, "I want an extra set of Pampers."

Burnford turned to Fowler and looked at him intently. "Larry has been having trouble with his girlfriend," he said. Fowler shook his head vigorously.

"I can handle it."

"I'm sure Mr. Fowler understands this is more important than any temporary domestic upset," Silvera said.

"Yes." Fowler nodded. Damn them all! He was a virtual prisoner and of little use to them. He felt like he was being taunted. The sick sensation in his stomach— worry about Dorothy and the decisions she would be making right now—made his throat dry and he coughed. "We'll be fine."

"You can make a phone call if you wish," Silvera said. "Might help cool things off until you can get back to her."

"I can't say anything meaningful with one of your soldiers listening in."

"Well, it has to be that way."

"Of course," Fowler said.

"When we set up our communications center, we'll route you through. That'll be this evening, unless something delays us."

CHAPTER FIFTY-ONE

STARTING AT FOUR P.M., DECEMBER 24, IN KILKENNIE, OHIO, fifteen fires broke out in ten minutes. Vandals were blamed. In one fire at a nursing home, seven patients were burned to death. Witnesses said the fires seemed to erupt by themselves.

A wheatfield outside of Kilkennie was scorched in six wide swaths, forming a giant asterisk in the snow-spackled earth.

Twenty miles farther along the path, whole hillsides were marked with crude designs: weeping eyes suspended above flames, hands with fingers missing, stick figures with twisted limbs.

Two deserted farmhouses creaked and shuddered in an unnatural wind. Elms—weakened by recent disease—toppled. Birds walked on the ground and would not fly, even when threatened. On the roads, automobile accidents increased. Minor incidents between motorists erupted into violence; three homicides occurred in four square miles within an hour.

Insects fell from the air, burnt to cinders.

The sky darkened. More snow was forecast for the evening.

In Haverstock, a soldier guarding the university grounds found a pay telephone inadvertently left connected. Worried by rumors, he called his father in Dayton. By seven o'clock, the government's small evacuation effort was a shambles. Phones were tied up across the city. Roads and highways were jammed. Airports were mobbed.

The word was out. What had happened in Lorobu and Haverstock was going to happen in Dayton, only worse.

CHAPTER FIFTY-TWO

THE CLOCK FINISHED CHIMING THE TENTH HOUR. JACOBS PUT away his book and sighed, turning to look at Trumbauer. Trumbauer was playing a game of chess with Tim; Thesiger looked on. Miss Unamuno was sitting by the window, looking at the black night and the flakes of snow faintly visible by the light in the room.

"Snow muffles sound," Jacobs said. "That's why it's so quiet outside."

"No wind," Tim said. "In Lorobu there was lots of wind."

Thesiger tapped the boy on the shoulder. "Pay attention to the game. This man will pick your brains if you're not careful."

"Really!" Trumbauer huffed.

Machen took a phone call in the kitchen. When he returned to the living room, he said, "It's getting worse." Jacobs nodded. They had heard about the panic three-quarters of an hour before. Now, with the fireplace blazing and such calm domesticity all around them, the reports seemed far away and unimportant. Jacobs noticed the sensation and worried about it. They were too calm, too steady.

Outside, a truck generator coughed and stopped. They had ignored the gentle hum until now. Tim looked up and said, "I don't want to play any more."

"What can we do to protect ourselves if something goes wrong?" Jacobs asked.

"Nothing will go wrong," Machen said, sounding too certain. "We've had no word of trouble—"

"Would we hear about minor things?" Thesiger asked. "Franklin is right. They might be normal occurrences for the most part, or too unusual to be reported by people not in the know, afraid they'll be called crazy. I can feel it. It's very strong now. More . . . willful."

"It may accelerate as it approaches its prey," Miss Unamuno said.

"The checkpoints report its progress is normal. Nothing unusual has happened."

"That we've *heard* about," Thesiger added. "Please, General, allow us our fear. It may save us if anything goes wrong."

But Machen shook his head stubbornly. Jacobs could recognize the symptoms—fear solidifying into trust and reliance on a grand plan. Finding comfort in the chain of command, in the known and projected rather than the unknown and unpredictable. Jacobs could almost relax and let the need take him over, too. In dangerous situations in the Navy, he had done that. He had survived. Others with the same attitude hadn't.

"Chain of command is essential in an operation like this," Machen said, staring at them one by one. His voice was subdued. The truck generator started again, louder this time, more abrasive.

"General, I think all electrical equipment should be turned off before the pass-over," Thesiger said.

"The trucks are filled with equipment. It would be awkward to shut them down now."

"This is more than a hunch," Thesiger said. "Mr.

Trumbauer feels it and so do I. It has changed. I'm not sure how, but my—''

''Yes,'' Trumbauer interrupted, rubbing his hands. ''My guide is jumpy, if that's the right word.'' He smiled weakly.

''Mine, too,'' Miss Unamuno said. ''The lights hurt my eyes. The noise hurts my ears.''

''Back to the cave,'' Machen said, almost fiercely. He pointed to Simons and Davies. ''Move the trucks beyond the barn and put them all on battery power. Is that okay?''

Thesiger thought for a moment, head cocked. ''Yes.''

''Let's turn off all house appliances and lights and get candles going. Can we run our tape recorders on batteries?''

''Yes,'' Thesiger said.

''And collect all weapons, knives and so on, as planned.'' Davies left to pass on the orders. ''Is it coming any faster?'' Machen asked. He was sweating, though he was across the room from the fire.

''Marginally,'' Trumbauer said, putting away the chess pieces. ''If I'm right.''

''You are,'' Miss Unamuno said.

Candles were brought out of the kitchen and placed on tables, the mantle, and shelves. Two propane lanterns were set up in the middle of the room. Tim sat on the floor near one, watching the glow through slitted eyes. Outside, it was even more quiet than before. Two men shouted at one another, their words inaudible. Tim flinched, but the voices broke into laughter. A third voice told them to shut up.

The snow fell soft and slow and large.

''Mine's gone,'' Miss Unamuno said, looking at Trumbauer. He nodded.

''What's gone?'' Machen asked.

''Our guides,'' Thesiger said. ''We'll have to work alone now. It's very close.''

''The angels abandon us,'' Simons said. Davies returned, closing the screen door softly behind.

Tim closed his eyes. Thesiger was still strong, but he could hear voices as if they were in another room, with all the doors closed. The old man put his hand on the boy's shoulder. "They're getting through, aren't they, Timothy?"

"Yes."

"Do they care about our presence?" Jacobs asked.

Thesiger said he didn't know. His voice was soft but clear, its high notes returning from the walls.

"I've gone into battle many times," Machen said. "Aachen, Inchon, during the Tet. Waiting is the worst time."

"Will we see anything?" Davies asked.

"We don't know," Miss Unamuno said. "We don't know much at all."

"Downwind from Trinity," Jacobs said.

Machen shook his head. "Mr. Jacobs has a theory about our problem."

"Trinity," Thesiger said. "The first atom bomb explosion . . . Alamagordo, New Mexico. 1945. And later— tests on animals where the researchers had nervous breakdowns. A whole village of goats and sheep subjected to a blast . . . I could feel them for weeks."

"Feel what?" Machern asked.

"The wanderers. Like little dust-devils, not natural at all. Not like the small, simple soul of an animal—yet not unlike. Wherever we have killed in the interests of nuclear weapons research, they have started."

"Is this all straight?" Machen asked. "You're not just bullshitting?"

Thesiger closed his eyes. "Please, Arnold, Miss Unamuno, withdraw and close tight. General, Mr. Simons, turn your recorders on."

"They're ready," Simons said.

"It isn't aware of us yet, but it talks to itself. They talk to themselves. The psychlone isn't integrated, not completely, but it behaves with one motive, one will."

"Where—" Machen began to ask, but Jacobs shushed him.

Thesiger lay back in the overstuffed chair, hands gripping the armrests. "Moving willfully. Now it knows where it is. It coerces the information. There is a portion not of the whole . . . in the mass, but not of it. The foreigners who were killed. Falling rubble killed them, clubs, naked fists. Burned people beat on them. Sticks and bricks and anything handy. Flash burns, under walls. All died, but none in the center of light, in the fireball. The captives know this country. Parts are still familiar. Across the countryside, following roads, railways, just like someone in a light plane without a compass. Unwilling. Many were pilots then, and they're pilots now. Forefront. Showing the way." He paused. Tim reached up and took one of his hands. The contact was almost electric.

"Before it happens, they try to warn. Name, rank, serial number. Friends will hear. Must hear. They guide it into the towns and cities they knew. They can't do otherwise. Those who die in the cities are sucked up, used, and when these targets are gone, they will provide others. The rage will force them." His voice changed subtly. "Thirty-five years to cross the sea, blind, this way and that. No marks on the sea, only boats and tiny islands. The currents cause them pain, but they must cross. Thirty-five years. Then up through Mexico, the pilots recognize the border, and in to the first town. *Shimpu.*"

"What?" Jacobs asked.

"Divine Wind," Davies said. "It's Japanese."

Thesiger became rigid. His arm muscles knotted, and Tim winced at the pressure on his hand. "Jesus," Trumbauer said, stepping back from the old man in the chair. Miss Unamuno opened her mouth in a silent wail.

"Look what they have done to me," Thesiger moaned. "This body, my servant, is ash and vapor, leaving only the unvoiced scream. They do not even know me! My pain

is nothing to them. My end is not important. My children are flying rags and dust. My spirit's torment is unimagined. As I am damned, so shall they be. The *Shimpu* shall be felt in their land, and they shall wither, and when all is done, I shall have them.''

Tim jerked loose and backed away. Jacobs took the boy in his arms and held him. Thesiger stood up like something on wires, jerking this way and that. Jacobs suddenly realized how thin the man was, how frail. His white hair streamed as if a wind was radiating from his body. ''Incomplete. Shattered. Even together, they aren't whole. The upper ranks are shorn, the lower splintered and cracked. Only the pain, not the dignity. No understanding is left. It is here with nothing but vengeance and no mind. The memory is in fragments, it remembers only the last moments. The buzzing of a mosquito, high overhead, a single aircraft. The light. Bones show like X rays and then flesh is gone and then bones are gone and shadows remain against the walls. And then the walls are gone. A man on a horse, pounded into a crack in the ground like a stake hit by a hammer. The blood fountains and glows in midair and is gone. Children play on a roof and a mile away their toys come to earth. In the castle, the walls are topped with broken glass. The glass catches the light of hell and rays it into the yard. The walls seem to have their own sunrise, on all sides, and the air glows purple above. The men in the yard are smashed by the fists of air. The walls come down. In the purple cloud, faces fly. All the guardians withdraw, all the angels and ancestors and *kami* leave. Those who die are on their own. They are sucked into the fireball and dismembered, flies with wings plucked, already dead and now killed again. In the middle, a new death is spawned. Days later, the two cities join. They whirl and examine. So many have died, but this cloud of souls is familiar, fragmented. Together they will seek.''

Miss Unamuno was sobbing silently. Machen was still

as stone except for one hand, which was shaking. Trumbauer leaned against a wall, nodding his head. "That's it," he said. "That's it."

Then Thesiger slumped. Jacobs smelled burnt metal.

There Feel Tim?

The strength was gone. Tim could feel the sudden sweep of probing fingers, hands, eyes. They were all directly above. They knew he was in the house. He had to leave. Outside, soldiers were shouting.

While Jacobs and Machen went to help Thesiger, Tim stood beside the door. It was very dark outside, but if they knew he was in the house, then he had to go somewhere else. Maybe Thesiger had taught him something. Maybe he could have his own shield now.

A soldier came in through the door and Tim slipped around him, then outside. No one noticed.

"He's still alive," Machen said, holding Thesiger's wrist. "Simons, get the medical team in here. Davies, water and a wet towel." Jacobs looked down on the old man. He looked very fragile, like the body of an incorruptible saint, preserved in the earth for years.

Then Jacobs felt the pressure himself. It was like a prickly blanket, demanding some foul action. He tried to subdue it.

Tim stood on the porch, watching the soldiers across the grass, watching the snow fall. The big flakes clung to his skin and melted. His feet crunched the frozen grass. His nose tickled and smelled the cold. He looked up.

Through and around the clouds, faces moved. His father and mother were there, but he couldn't see them clearly.

He passed the harvester on the way to the barn. In the barn, the empty stalls and concrete floor were vague squares of light and dark. Sparkles moved in the dark. A circle of hands formed above the center aisle, glowing green. These were the fringes. There were no faces here. He could hide and perhaps not be noticed.

He tried out the shield—
Join
And hid in a stall, shivering.

The wind rose outside. In the house, the candles dimmed.
Jacobs held a towel on Thesiger's forehead while the
doctor checked blood pressure, pulse, and reflexes.

Simons suddenly lifted his head and asked, "Where's
the boy?" He looked in the kitchen and called up the
stairs. "Did anyone see him?" They all shook their heads.
"Damn!" He ran across the front porch, calling for Tim.

Jacobs stood. "Arnold, can you feel anything?"

"I'm . . ." Trumbauer shook his head. "I'm shut. I
don't dare open up now." In the yard, a man screamed.

"Not even a crack?"

Trumbauer was shaking. Jacobs turned to the woman.
"And you?"

"It's here. Not completely. An arm, a fringe, a tentacle.
I'm closed but I know that."

"Is Thesiger dying?"

"No," Trumbauer said. "We would see a change."

"I'm going to help look for the boy," Jacobs said.

Tim huddled closer into the corner. It wasn't working.
The faces were in the air over the center aisle now, circles
of faces, wheels without hubs.

"You already got my town," he said aloud. "Go away!"
Unto the generations
Then Tim knew it was over for him. In his talks with
Thesiger, there had always been left open the possibility
that something would fail and he would be where he was
now. The old man had never deluded him about it. Even in
Salt Lake City, when he had wanted to return to Lorobu,
he had considered meeting the faces and voices again, up
close, and dying. He looked down and saw the blood
glowing on his hands. The inner glow was red, but the

outer halo was becoming green. He was going to be Carrying the Fire soon. He could feel the voices gathering around the barn.

He bolted from the stall and ran for the ladder on the far end. Maybe the others would get here and stop him, lock him up. If they didn't, it would happen all over again. The memories were coming back sharp now and anything was better. He grabbed the ladder with his hands and wondered they didn't leave stains on the rungs. Somewhere, he knew, his parents would exult for him, but in the open, where the others could see, they told him to

Join

He reached the top and crawled over the lip of the bare loft. Piles of burnt beef were laid along the floor—no, that couldn't be right. They weren't beef.

He shut his eyes and screamed. "I'm not a grownup! I don't know anything about this! Leave me alone, please, leave me be!"

Join

His parents were weeping. He could feel them. The others were so full now, so busy handling the captives, that some could weep and not be kept in line. But their strength was too much even still. Beyond the weeping, none could deviate.

Hands tried to grip him but he broke loose. In one corner of the stall, he heard derisive voices and saw Cynthia and Michael, naked, standing as though for a portrait, unmercifully illuminated. This angered him so much he howled. "Let them alone! Leave all of us alone!"

For a moment, something happened, a reprieve. The faces vanished. He almost fell over. The wind outside was still strong, but the concentration was not on him. The hands were gone but they would be back. He only had a few seconds.

In the house, a long, long time ago, they had gotten to him and he had picked up the knives like all the others.

That could never happen again. It was a very grown-up
decision to make. "I am, right now, grown up," he told
himself. "I have control and I'm not a little kid."

The loft was twenty feet above the concrete.

It was a very big responsibility. Maybe God would
understand.

He leaned into the air and felt his feet rise free. In the
barn door, Simons ran with arms held out, but he was too
late.

Thesiger jerked up. Trumbauer and the doctor helped
him sit with his back against the chair. Jacobs opened the
front door and came inside, letting the wind howl through
the living room.

"Have you got a pistol?" the old man asked Machen.

"No," Machen said.

"Then a knife."

"No."

"Doctor—do you have poison?"

The doctor shook his head. "I can't administer anything—
not like that. Why? You want us to—"

"The boy is out. All the guardians are gone, all the
angels gone."

"Please settle back, sir. I have something here . . ."

"No sedative. I must not sleep. I promised to protect
him."

"Tim's dead," Jacobs said.

The doctor prepared his syringe. Thesiger looked at
Machen. "You have all you need," he said, "and God
forgive us all." He closed his eyes. On the floor next to
him, the doctor's machines began to beep.

CHAPTER FIFTY-THREE

THE CONVOY OF TRUCKS HAD BEEN STALLED FOR THE NIGHT five miles outside Dayton. A steady stream of automobiles blocked both inbound and outbound lanes, ignoring direction signs. Wrecks littered the sides of the roads. National Guardsmen were being airlifted into the center of town from Wright-Patterson Air Force Base, but they weren't connected with Silent Night. A special helicopter was coming, Colonel Silvera said.

A small truckstop cafe and service station squatted empty less than a hundred yards from where the convoy had pulled off the road. Fowler examined it closely, and found what he was looking for—a pay phone. He climbed down from the van, not looking at Prohaska or Burnford, and approached Silvera. The Colonel was talking to a cluster of drivers. Fowler waited until he was noticed, then spoke up.

"I have to make another call or my fiancée is going to be worried," he said. "I told her I'd check in frequently."

Silvera sighed. "Jackson, are the field telephones still out?"

"Yessir. All communications are tied up."

"There's a pay phone booth at that diner," Fowler suggested.

"Please be circumspect, Mr. Fowler. Jackson, go with him and see he doesn't get hurt."

"I'll need change, lots of it," Fowler said. "I only have a dollar and a half. It's to California."

Silvera jingled his pockets and found another dollar in change. Jackson came up with fifty cents. "It'll have to be brief," Silvera said. Fowler nodded.

The Major followed him across the grassy knoll to the diner and stood outside the phone booth as Fowler dialed and pushed in quarters. The phone rang five times before it was answered.

"McKinley residence, Thomas DeCleese speaking."

"Tom, this is Larry Fowler. Is Dot there?"

"No, Larry. I'm caretaking. She's gone off to Ohio. Said she was going to find you. Where are you?"

"Where was she going?"

"Dayton. She's been half-crazy the past few days, re-gretting things right and left. You two must have had some spat."

"Tom, how did she know about Dayton?"

"Last night, in the news about the panic. She tried to call somebody . . . Sheila, I think—"

"Yeah, Sheila Burnford."

"And she said she thought you and her husband would be working together. That made Dorothy suspicious. I don't follow her chain of reasoning, but she says you have to be in Dayton."

"Did she say where in Dayton?"

"She sure did. She has a friend who lives near the art museum there—here's the note. Louise Muhler, M-U-H-L-E-R. And a phone number." Fowler jotted the number down.

"God bless female intuition," he said.

"You two must have had quite a spat."

"I don't know what we had, Tom. This is all crazy."

"What's going on with this country, Larry? I thought you two were good for each other. Now everyone's flying all over the place, and people are panicking. She said something about Lorobu. This have anything to do with Lorobu?"

"She's a very smart woman, Tom. I can't say any more—have to call this number." He glanced at the Major, who stood outside the booth with his coat collar raised against the cold. "Thanks for everything."

"You treat her right, you hear?" Tom said.

"I hear. Good-bye, Tom." He put the receiver on the hook and felt a rush of exultation. Something had cracked through her crazy reaction. All the same, he would downplay what was happening. He hoped and prayed there was a line clear to Dayton. "Major, I have to make another call. I've got enough change, I think."

Jackson nodded. "We have time. Just be mindful of security, Mr. Fowler. That's why we're in this mess."

Fowler looked at his watch. The event was due at nine in the morning and it was now seven-thirty. He had to get her out of Dayton, or at least out of the area where the concentration was expected. He dialed the new number. A woman answered, quiet and tense.

"I have to speak to Dorothy McKinley."

"Who are you?"

"Larry Fowler."

"She's been waiting—"

Dorothy grabbed the phone and he heard her sudden rush of nervous laughter. "My God, Larry, I've been going out of my mind! I didn't know how I was going to find you once I got here, and now everybody's leaving. The airports were jammed when my plane came in last night. Where are you? When can you be here?"

"I can't talk, Dot."

"The government has you?"

"Yes."

Her voice tightened. "You're helping them on something, aren't you? Something to do with the cabin and Lorobu."

"Yes."

"Larry, I can't take that now any more than I could."

"I can't either, honey."

"They're holding you against your will?"

"Something like that."

"Goddamn them. I had to make up my mind and I couldn't think about just giving up on you, you know, just going away because you were weird."

"I don't want you to go away."

The Major glanced at him apprehensively. Fowler held up his hand and shook his head. "Dot, I can't talk."

"Can you get away?"

"I can try."

"Escape?"

"I suppose that's what it will take."

"Christ, I feel like a fucking spy. Larry, are you in any trouble or danger?"

"No."

"Am . . . are *we?*"

"I don't know."

"I'm just a poor little rich girl. I can't take this. Let me think. If you're with the government, they probably flew you in to a military base."

Jackson stuck his head into the booth, putting his hand on the mouth-piece. "Come on, Mr. Fowler. That's enough."

"Just a few seconds," Fowler said. "This is very important. We had a fight. I have to settle things, settle her mind, or she'll cause all sorts of trouble. For you, for Silent Night. She knows congressmen and stuff."

Jackson shrugged and backed off, but left the booth door open all the way.

"They flew you in to Wright-Patterson." Dorothy said. "Louise tells me that's the Air Force Base here. Are you there?"

"No." He lowered his voice. "Four."

"What?"

"Four."

Dorothy muffled the phone and talked with Louise. "Louise says you must be on Highway Four. Is she right?"

"Yes."

"Can you get to the intersection of Valley Street and Four?"

He tried to remember the streets they had passed. "Yes," he said. "I can."

"Then I'll be there to pick you up. Is that all right? In a blue Rabbit—a VW."

"Yes."

"Louise wants to know if it's safe where we are."

"I don't know. I don't think so."

"I've got to go. I'll meet you there. Louise will be with me. She knows some back roads that shouldn't be too crowded. In an hour?"

"Fine. I love you."

"Oh, Larry . . . I'm glad you're where I thought you'd be. Thank God for everything . . . almost everything."

He hung up and stepped out of the booth. "She's still mad at me," he told Jackson, "but I don't think she'll cause any trouble. I have to use the restroom. I'll be back at the van in a few minutes."

Jackson looked at him sharply.

"Jesus Christ, Major, I'm not going to do anything stupid. Where the hell would I go around here? I know next to nothing about Dayton."

The Major nodded. He had been given no specifics about the civilians they were escorting; it was reasonable to assume they were reliable, or else they wouldn't be on the project in the first place. He turned and walked back to the convoy.

Behind the diner, out of view of the highway and the trucks, was a thick patch of trees and brush. The trees were skeletal, but the brush was still fairly dense. He could run up the low hill and, with some luck, not be noticed for a few minutes. He *did* have to urinate, but it would have to wait.

Behind the diner, by the men's room door, he wondered what the hell he was doing. He had never been so foolish and irresponsible in his life. Then again, he had never been held against his will before. He had always disliked government security. In his youth, he had had leanings toward libertarianism. Now, spurred by Dorothy, it was all welling up and he had to leave.

He made a dash for the brush. From behind a tree, he looked at the convoy. No one was pursuing—he hadn't been spotted. The intersection was about half a mile east.

As he walked, he wondered what penalties he'd be subject to. So far as he knew, martial law hadn't been declared in Dayton. As long as he kept details about Silent Night to himself—and he didn't know that much in the first place—he couldn't see any serious legal problems. If he kept quiet, he fulfilled the provisions of the paper he had signed. The ethical question was something else again. If the government really did know what was happening, and how to solve the problem, wasn't he obligated, as a citizen, to help them any way he could?

There was the crux. He could think of no possible use for his expertise. He knew next to nothing about psychic phenomena, and his experience at the cabin had been limited. Clearly, the psychlone was not an elemental. He couldn't shake the suspicion that his usefulness on the project was nil, that he was being held only for security reasons.

*   *   *

The intersection of Highway 4 and Valley Street was as much a mess as any other stretch of the road, but Valley Street itself was reasonably clear.

He suddenly felt very, very lost. If something went wrong, he was in deep trouble. His position was untenable.

"Stop it," he told himself. He sat on the cold ground to wait. He was partly hidden by a concrete wall, but there was no way to avoid being seen by serious searchers. He hoped they'd be too busy with other matters to give chase.

The ribbon of cars seemed to stretch on forever. Overhead, a helicopter with Air Force markings whickered noisily toward the convoy.

"Best of luck," he said.

CHAPTER FIFTY-FOUR

AIR PRESSURE CHANGED ACROSS A SQUARE MILE OF THE CITY
and windows blew outward with sounds like rifle fire. The
forces rolled across the house tops, caving in shingles and
beams.

The cloud spread out, a pearly umbrella which gave the
sun a faint blue halo. The cloud descended, and shadows
marched down the streets, melting the asphalt behind them.

CHAPTER FIFTY-FIVE

"IT'S IN DAYTON NOW," MACHEN SAID, LISTENING TO THE phone report. Jacobs nodded, too numb to respond with words. They had been awake all night. "Apparently it's in the evacuated area, just as we predicted. But its influence is spreading beyond."

Trumbauer and Miss Unamuno sat on the couch, holding each other lightly. "More power, more will," Trumbauer said.

Jacobs picked up his steno pad and tried to record some of last night's impressions. The psychics had had a rough time of it. Trumbauer and Miss Unamuno had become feverish, then incoherent—even though both stoutly maintained they were "closed tight as clams."

Thesiger's body was in an Army truck, alongside Tim's. Jacobs wished them luck. His heart seemed to flood when he thought of Thesiger's last moments. Even if he was given a chance, he doubted if he could write about what had happened.

Helicopters were coming for them. They would be transferred to Siloam Springs for this evening's event. The equipment, Machen said, was already in place.

Jacobs looked out the window into the yard. The trucks were packed and ready to leave. The barn was clear in the white light of the overcast sky. The wind was cold and the snow was staying on the ground.

"They're starting fires," Machen said.

CHAPTER FIFTY-SIX

FOWLER SMELLED THE SMOKE, BUT HE HAD SEEN IT SEVERAL minutes earlier. It was thick and oily, lying close to the ground, climbing over the buildings and flowing onto the highways. In minutes, the sun glowed orange through it, then deepened into red. He had never seen anything like it, even in the middle of a brush fire. The odor was faintly nauseating. It was like a pork roast, but subtly, horribly different.

The smoke was purple. A pall rose over the city, white and red. Then he could see the flames. They towered much higher than ordinary flames should.

The psychlone was changing its pattern. The central pillar of smoke was moving back and forth like something alive. It seemed to be moulding itself to a particular shape, yet the winds were steadily westward.

It looked as if a bomb had been dropped on the city. He stood and brushed his pants off. If the smell was what he thought it was, thousands of people were burning to death in the city. But that hardly seemed likely. By now, most of the downtown area would be clear. Silvera had said everyone in the area of concentration, except for the experimental subjects, would be evacuated by ten last night.

So it was most likely an illusion. The psychlone was creating a psychological atmosphere of terror and destruction, just as the elemental had at the cabin.

Join

He shook his head. The voice was dull but insistent. He didn't know what it meant. Without thinking, he started walking away from the highway toward Valley Street. He'd meet Dorothy before she could get to 4.

At the first crash, he turned around. One by one, the cars were jamming into each other and angry motorists were climbing out. Overhead, the helicopter—now carrying Burnford, Prohaska and the others—hesitated, hovered, then flew on. He almost regretted leaving them—but if something was happening even this far out, how could the areas in Dayton be considered safe?

The smoke was thick and cloying. He watched its rolling progress along the freeway. The level was rising and now the sky was almost black. A dull red sun peered through weakly and a pall of purple ash fell like snow in Hell.

Feel Join

The crashes were supplemented by screams. For a moment he thought they were animals, then he realized it was people screaming. He clenched his fists and ran stiff-armed. Valley Street was less crowded, but clusters of people still wandered away from their cars, stopping occasionally to stare up, mouths agape.

Desolation

It was more an image than a word; an image, and a command. He remembered the elemental's attempts to influence him, to influence Jordan and Henry. That must not happen again.

He followed Valley Street under the darkness. Car

headlamps shone faintly through the haze. He began to wander from car to car, peering through the windows, staying away as people leveled pistols and knives at him. Their faces were fearful, malevolent. They didn't seem to be killing each other, just milling around or staying in their stopped cars, some groups fighting and screaming, but none trying to kill—yet. On the highway things might be different, he thought. Avoid the highway. More people concentrated there, more flash powder to ignite.

In the murk ahead there was a resounding *whang* and the sound of tearing metal and shattering glass. Cars bounded off the road, narrowly missing him. One rolled over and caught on fire, its rear exploding and throwing hot shrapnel. A piece nicked his arm. He was tossed on his butt by the force of the blast. There was nothing he could do.

Nothing he wanted to do.

Let them burn

Most of the cars were off the road now. People were shambling down the center of the street, four and five abreast, clutching their coats and skirts about them, leaden-eyed, faces smudged. They looked like they were in line for Charon's boat ride. He smiled at that. Such comparisons proved he was sane. They warded off his urge to go down among them and . . .

Fowler shook his head. "Look for Dorothy. She'll get us away from here. Look for Dorothy."

It had been over an hour. The smell was growing more intense, maddeningly sharp and cloying. It was a smell of burnt metal and citrus fruit—oranges or tangerines. It made him want to retch. It wasn't unlike the smell of the elemental, but it wasn't the same, either.

For a brief moment—it had to be brief, but it seemed to last for hours—he thought he saw people walking on the air overhead. Their clothes and flesh hung from them. Their bones stuck out. Some were moving without legs, others crawling with barely a body. He shut his eyes and the vision disappeared in a whirl of—green hands? Yes. Green. Glowing. Dissipating wheels.

An eternity later—though his watch said it was only ten o'clock—he came across a tangled wreckage of cars. He frantically searched through them, but none of the bodies within were Dorothy. Then he looked up and saw another car. It had run off the road, perhaps trying to avoid the wreckage. It was wrapped around a tree, steam still escaping in spurts from the radiator, one half-deflated tire hanging from an upthrust axle.

The mangled car was blue. It was all he could do to approach the solitary pile.

There were two people in the car. One—Dorothy's friend, he guessed—had gone through the windshield and then fallen back. Dorothy lay half out of one door.

He bent down to look at her face closely. Her scalp was cut and blood soaked through the clothes around her stomach. Fowler reached for her wrist.

Her eyes opened slowly, then widened. "Larry," she said. Blood dribbled out of her mouth.

"Shh," Fowler said softly. "You're hurt. Don't move."

"We have to get out of here," Dorothy said.

"I don't know how I'm going to move you, honey."

"I don't feel anything. Move me now."

"You don't understand—"

"Larry." Her tone was steady. "I can feel them up there."

"If I move you now, I'll hurt you more."

"I can't die here," she said. He tried to wipe away the blood around her mouth with one hand, but there was too much. She began to cry. "Larry, Larry, *they'll* get me. I can't die here."

"You're not dying, honey."

"I'd be dead already, but I can't die here."

"Shh," he said, helpless. She tried to say something but coughed.

She moaned after the fit was over. "Get me away," she said again, almost inaudibly. She stopped breathing, but her body didn't relax.

He held her for what seemed an endless time, then let her fall back. He didn't remember picking her up to hug her, but he had, and there was blood all over his clothing. He didn't know what to do. Nothing mattered now. Everything was over. He had forsaken any hope of . . . anything.

He walked a few yards away from the wreck and sat. His eyes stung, but not with tears. He was too numb.

Feel

"I know, damn you," he said, choking on the smoke.

Know

Whatever the psychlone was, it was having its revenge now. Great waves of simple, derisive messages flowed from the city, exulting. Animal exultation, lion over its kill, wasp over the paralyzed spider. Merciless. Dead. Beyond hatred.

There was blood on his hand. He wiped it on the grass. There was nothing left to do but try to sleep until it was all over. He felt very tired. Of course, the dreams wouldn't be pleasant. . . .

Dorothy opened her eyes. Fowler took one last look at her, saw her eyes were open, and stood. He would have to close them. That was the thing to do.

Her hand moved. The arm came down like a mechanical limb, searching. It found a piece of window glass and slowly, easily tore it from its frame. Her face was expressionless, eyes focused intently on Fowler. The other body jerked against the restraining seat belt.

For a moment, he felt a surge of crazy hope. Then he knew.

Dorothy climbed from the wreck, her mouth working. She dragged one leg as she crawled.

Fowler almost welcomed her. There was no horror left in him. The glass glittered orange in the smoky pall, then fell.

On the highway, the noises faded. The smell of burnt metal and smoke merged, danced, and became dusty, like a forgotten attic.

CHAPTER FIFTY-SEVEN

MOUNT METCALF LOOKED OVER THE SMALL TOWN OF SILOAM Springs. A fire trail had been expanded and compressed by heavy equipment the day before. On a natural plateau three hundred feet above the town, six olive-green trucks were parked, the bulky loads on their trailers covered by tarpaulins and guarded by thirty heavily armed Marines. At a distance of twenty-five feet surveyors' stakes connected by yellow ribbon indicated a perimeter beyond which no one but specially dressed project members could pass.

On the opposite end of the plateau, a command truck had been parked. A cable snaked down the trail to units at the base of Mount Metcalfe. Beamed transmissions were unreliable for several reasons—interference from the psychlone, and whatever effect such transmissions might have upon it. George Burnford stood by the truck, eating from a tin plate of reconstituted eggs. His eyes were bloodshot and his arm was in a sling. The helicopter had made a rough landing in Dayton and he had sprained his shoulder. When he was through, he put the plate down on a wooden folding table and leaned into the doorway of the mobile

command room. Machen and an aide were poring over
maps and charts.

"How long?" he asked.

"Four hours," Machen said.

"Too long. I'll be asleep by then."

"I doubt it."

"Could you hand me my notebooks and the calculator?" Burnford asked. Machen's aide picked up the plastic
folders and the slim case and passed them down to him.
Burnford put the material on the wooden table, pocketed
the calculator, and walked to the edge of the plateau.
Siloam Springs was empty. The evacuation had gone more
smoothly here. The town only had a population of seven
hundred and eighty.

"So many small towns," he said. How many American
casualties in World War II had come from small towns? It
didn't much matter now. The psychlone didn't discrimi-
nate. It affected whatever it could and then went on its
way. If they didn't stop it here, its next target would be
either Akron or Cleveland, and then Pittsburgh. If the
tapes of Thesiger's last statements gave any real clue to the
psychlone's nature, it would finish its tour of the POW
home towns, then branch out to take in the homes of its
new victims.

It had to stop here. His work had to be accurate. Burnford
wasn't the only physicist working on Silent Night—for
which he was grateful—but he was the only one who
would be on the mountain, observing.

He returned to the wooden table and sat on a folding
chair. Carefully, following a ritual, he laid down a mechanical pencil, opened his scratchpad, and removed the
calculator from its case. It was a new model with no
moving parts—no buttons or mechanical on-off switch. It
was about the size of his hand and barely a centimeter
thick. The liquid-crystal display consisted of black numer-
als and characters against an eye-saving yellow background.

He considered it one of his more useful toys—it had the calculating power of a small computer.

He lined up all his tools, then opened the large black notebook where his final figures were kept. A few hours earlier, he had written down key statements from Jacobs and Thesiger and was now preparing to see what they implied.

First: the elemental in California had responded to the solution. If the psychlone was related—and all evidence indicated it was generically similar—the solution would work on it, too.

Second: if, as Thesiger had apparently confirmed, the psychlone had been created in the fireball of a nuclear explosion, then the environment of the solution would come very close to replicating those conditions. Perhaps the process that had created it would eventually lead to its total destruction. He made a nervous checkmark next to his notes at that point.

For a few minutes, he lost himself in a side branch of speculation. He reconstructed a few of the equations describing conditions in the early moments of the universe, before the appearance of matter. Making comparisons, he saw that no complex of fields like the elemental or the psychlone could have survived in those conditions. Or— and he reworked part of the key framework—no such complex could survive independently. If the early universe had been pervaded by such a field, a single entity could have survived. After the formation of matter, it would have broken up. Taking the human soul as a similar field—

The calculator beeped. He jerked and looked down at the display. When it was turned on—activated by a pressure-sensitive switch—it beeped. Each subsequent entry also caused it to beep. It automatically shut itself off after three minutes if no entries were made. Apparently he had bumped against it with his insensitive elbow and sling. The display read: *2.7182818*. He frowned. To get that, he would have to have pressed the e^x button—the natural number e to a certain exponent, namely, e^1—to bring the number itself on the display. That was two distinct entries, very hard to get by accident. He cleared the calculator and pressed the on-off switch.

A helicopter bass-drummed the air as it flew over the mountain. Burnford looked up, shaded his eyes, and saw it hovering before coming down on the plateau. Machen came out of the command truck and walked to the make-shift landing area. Burnford returned to his notebooks.

From there on, the details became very technical. Despite the fact that everything seemed to work, his assumptions were shaky. He was on the fringes of accepted physics, leaning precariously over an abyss of unconfirmed theory. Whatever the field of the elemental had been, it had violated several near-sacred tenets. He rubbed his eyes and yawned to bring moisture to them. The air was cold but still. In his jacket, the cold didn't bother him, but it was dry and he had always had eye trouble in dry weather.

The calculator beeped. This time he knew he hadn't pressed it. As he watched, a number marched across the display, digit by digit: *2.7182818.*

"Something's wrong with the damn thing," he said, picking it up and shaking it. He set it down and turned it off again. Just as quickly, it beeped on, and beeped for each entry in a new set.

Digit by digit: *3.1415927.* Pi, another number easily available on the calculator—there was a button for it—but not digit-by-digit. The calculator was generating non-random numbers by itself.

Then the display cleared. He moved his seat back quickly and stood up, wincing at the pain in his shoulder.

Digit-by-digit: *12* (clear display) *6.*

Twelve and six. He reached down gingerly and pressed it off. It beeped on again. Twelve (clear) six, (clear), twelve (clear) six, (clear). "Goddamn!" he said. He reached out to shut it off again, then hesitated. Twelve and six, twelve and six . . . e and pi.

If communicating across interstellar space, two species would begin by recognizing each other as intelligent. They would send signals which would not be replicated by the whims of nature—constants of mathematics, perhaps. His heel caught one leg of the chair and pulled it over.

Following the first signal, some code would have to be arranged. He almost stumbled and fell backward. He was now about two yards from the table and couldn't see the display clearly. Twelve and six.

The helicopter blew clods of dirt and water from snow puddles as it landed. Burnford watched it, hand thrust hard in his jacket pocket. Jacobs and the two remaining psychics—he couldn't remember their names now—climbed down. It was obvious they weren't allowing Prohaska on the mountain during the enactment of the solution. This was the last flight. Two men he had never seen before left the aircraft and the group walked to the command truck. Jacobs greeted Burnford with a nod and his usual intense gaze. Machen accompanied the two strangers and climbed into the back of the truck with them. Almost surreptitiously, he pulled the door shut behind, telling Burnford, "Keep our colleagues entertained for a few minutes, will you?"

"Your arm," Jacobs said.

"I injured it in Dayton. A rough helicopter landing. The pilot was affected—not badly, thank God for us. I'm sorry if I'm a bit distracted. I've been working on—"

"Who's here?" Miss Unamuno said, looking around, her nose wrinkled.

"Looks like they're preparing to set up a circus," Trumbauer said, "as it were. So many trucks and tarps."

"All top secret," Burnford said. "Don't try to get near them. The Marines are fluttery enough as is."

"Is somebody here?" Miss Unamuno asked Trumbauer.

"I don't know."

"Very weak."

"What's the matter?" Jacobs asked.

"I'm not sure," Miss Unamuno said. "Mr. Burnford, is your side hurt?"

"No, just the arm."

"Somebody has a cut in the side. Very serious—of course it's nobody here. But—" She stiffened. The calculator was beeping again.

"Something's wrong with it," Burnford said.

"For God's sake." Jacobs picked it up and examined it. The beeping stopped, leaving a number on the display. "I thought these things were foolproof."

"It worked fine until just a few minutes ago."

Trumbauer tapped Jacobs on the shoulder. "Franklin, our guides won't be back for some time. But I think someone needs to talk."

"What's all this mysterious shit?" Burnford said, a bit too loudly. "You're right about the circus."

Miss Unamuno shivered. "Are we going to stay out here all night?"

"They'll have a tent up in an hour," Burnford said. "They're not very organized yet."

Jacobs put the calculator down. It beeped four times. "It's flashing numbers now," he said. "Twelve and six."

"It's been doing that. Must be the keys."

"Twelve and six," Miss Unamuno said.

"L and F," Trumbauer added.

"What?" Burnford asked.

"L is the twelfth letter in the alphabet, F is the sixth. L and F."

"It's that man from the cabin," Miss Unamuno said. "Fowler."

"He's not here," Burnford said. "We don't know where he is."

"He's dead," Trumbauer said.

Burnford gaped at them. Jacobs nodded. "Your calculator's trying to tell us something, Mr. Burnford. Before the others get out here and spoil the atmosphere, let's see what it has to say. Perhaps Miss Unamuno should act as sponsor . . . antenna. Whatever."

The woman nodded and put both hands on the table. "We understand," she said. "Lawrence? Larry. Larry Fowler. Go ahead."

"Better write these down," Jacobs said. "May I borrow a piece of paper?" Compared to what had happened the past few days, this seemed almost normal to him. It was more ingenious than the usual seances, but then Fowler—if it was Fowler—was choosing a medium familiar to him.

"Five, nineteen, three, one, sixteen, five," Miss Unamuno read off. The beeping and flash of numbers sent chills from Burnford's scalp to the tip of his spine. He felt like all his hair was standing on end. Not even the encounters with the elemental and the wash of the psychlone had affected him so deeply.

" 'Escape,' " Jacobs decoded. "Who, us?" he asked the empty air.

"Jesus," Burnford breathed.

"Fourteen, fifteen."

" 'No,' " Jacobs said, recording the answer with Burnford's mechanical pencil.

"Twelve, six, five nineteen, three, one, sixteen, five, four."

" 'L F escape . . . D. L F escaped.' From what?"

The beeping halted for several seconds. "From the psychlone?" Jacobs prompted.

"Twenty-five, five, nineteen."

" 'Yes,' " Jacobs said.

"Four, five, one, four."

"You are," Jacobs said without decoding.

"What? Are what?" Burnford asked, his voice shrill.

"He's asked if he's dead. It appears he is, and that he's escaped from the psychlone. How did you escape?"

"Six, twenty-one, twelve, twelve."

" 'Full.' What's that mean?"

"That it's full?" Burnford ventured. He cocked his head and looked at the calculator.

"Twenty-five, five, nineteen."

" 'Yes,' " the physicist translated. He wiped a tear from one eye. "Pardon me. This has . . . this has never happened before. I'm not up to it right now. I didn't even know he . . . you . . . I didn't know he was dead."

"What do you mean, full?" Trumbauer asked. Miss Unamuno spoke the numbers and Jacobs decoded quickly, catching the knack.

" 'No more.' "

Another sequence.

" 'Cant hold all.' "

"Is it giving up?" Trumbauer asked.

" 'No.' "

"It's still coming for this town, then?" Jacobs asked.

" 'Yes.' "

"On schedule?"

" 'Yes.' "

"Where are you?" Burnford asked. The next sequence was longer than usual and Jacobs had to spend more time decoding. He read the reply with a smile.

" 'Good old scient.' Scientist, I think that is. 'Dont know.' And a pause, I assume a break in the sentence. 'Here I am.' "

"What do you see?" Burnford continued, his face flushing with excitement. He was walking back and forth on the dirt, almost dancing.

" 'Every.' Pause. 'Clarified, empty, shell.' Now I'd like to ask—how do you feel?"

" 'Like salt in water,' " came the reply. " 'Not much time. Storms and sickness.' "

"Larry, my God, Larry," Burnford said. "What'll I tell that woman, Dorothy?"

" 'Here. Salt in water. Downstream.' "

"Heaven and hell?" Burnford asked impulsively.

" 'Wine,' " Jacobs translated. " 'Spirit wine. L F leaves. Storms.' "

"So many questions," Miss Unamuno said, touching Burnford's arm. "We all have them. Let it go now."

"It?"

Jacobs addressed the empty air as the sun touched the horizon. "Go very far, very fast," he said. "I think tonight we will learn new guilt. It will be very dangerous. Godspeed."

The calculator shut itself off. They stood in silence for a moment, then Jacobs said, "Let's prompt them about that tent. We'll all freeze in an hour if we don't have something, and it stands to reason they won't let us in their exclusive club." He pointed at the communications truck.

CHAPTER FIFTY-EIGHT

"I ALMOST FORGOT," BURNFORD SAID, SIPPING A PLASTIC CUP full of bitter coffee. "It's Christmas."

"The eve of Christmas day," Miss Unamuno said. Outside, workmen were racketing back and forth across the plateau with generators, electric tools, hammers and curses. The small tent offered scant protection against the cold, but now everything was off-limits for them. Machen opened the flap and stepped inside.

"It's coming," he said. "The reports are coming in on schedule. Everything's doing fine outside. I have a message for you, Mr. Jacobs." He handed Jacobs a note. "Received ten minutes ago."

He unfolded the note and looked it over. "It's from Colonel Silvera," he said. "The ground base has received a call from the President."

"Until now, we weren't sure he knew," Machen said.

"The President wants us to observe and record all we can, as civilians, for posterity. Even though it may be a century before it's released."

Machen grinned. "Isn't that something? You have a

free ticket this evening. Look, see, but don't talk right away.''

Jacobs nodded. He wasn't enthusiastic. He looked up at Machen, who seemed to be going through pre-battle exhilaration, and said, "Tell him thank you. After tonight, we may have a lot to talk about."

"Of course," Machen said.

The generators started outside. Three truck-trailer rigs carried six massive generators, all tied to transformers on another bed, all raising a hell of a racket. "That's it," the General said. "We'll have to risk the electrical attraction tonight."

"What are they using, now that we're privileged?" Jacobs asked.

"Mr. Burnford might be able to guess. We're using it because of his work."

"I think it's a PBW," he said. "A particle-beam weapon. But I'm not sure what kind. I made several recommendations."

"I see," Jacobs said. "And it will re-create the conditions in the atom bomb blasts?"

"Some conditions," Burnford said.

"What's a particle-beam weapon?" Miss Unamuno asked.

"Depends on what you want it to do," Burnford said. "If General Machen wants to explain . . ."

"I can't, and wouldn't if I could," Machen said.

"It's a particle accelerator," Burnford said. "If you want to penetrate a target, you use leptons—an electron is a good example. A TV set creates an electron beam, but it never leaves the tube. Adapted properly, an electron beam can slice things up pretty well. If you want a non-penetrating beam, hadrons can be used. Protons are hadrons. Non-penetrating beams heat up the surface of an object. There was talk a few years ago that the Russians had PBWs. I was skeptical then, and I am now. I don't think they're practical weapons."

"Not yet," Machen said. "This is an experimental model. It's not much good for shooting down aircraft or missiles."

"The best place for a PBW would be a satellite in space. You don't have to worry about atmospheric interference then. I imagine we could orbit that thing," he indicated the tarps on the truck-trailer rigs, "but it would be bulky as hell and probably not reliable enough for a major program. So I suspect we're the only ones who have found a use for it."

"It's still top-secret," Machen said.

"That means you have high hopes for its future," Burnford said, smiling grimly.

"Coming up on time," Machen said, consulting his watch. "From here in, it's out of our hands. Orders have been given and will be followed. I'm as much an observer as you. Shall we go observe?"

The last tarp had been pulled away, revealing an ugly, black object shaped something like a soda-bottle cannon from the Civil War. It was mounted on a three-axis drum. Around its butt was a maze of wiring, gray slabs of metal, bronze-colored tubing and fist-thick cables. The vibration of the generators was shaking the ground. Diesel smoke poured east across the star-filled night sky.

"It's right out of Jules Verne," Miss Unamuno said. It did remind Jacobs of something Captain Nemo might have had socked away on his island. But there was no trace of Victorian whimsy about it. Along the barrel, spikes of metal rose from a bulbous midriff. Just in front of it, a white-enamel U, like a giant tuning fork, was cocked at a forty-five-degree angle away from the barrel. Behind it, four doughnuts at least six feet across were stacked atop one another, separated by ceramic blocks and connected to the barrel by chrome-shiny tubes.

To the west, Siloam Springs was illuminated only by

streetlamps. The grid of streets and houses was clean and simple. It was only eight o'clock, and nothing moved in the town.

Jacobs wondered if the psychlone could perceive a trap. Would its captives feel obliged to warn it? He grimaced and rubbed the back of his neck with one thick-fingered hand. It was just a nightmare, perhaps. The garden would be awaiting him when he woke up. Millicent would chide him about eating cheese with wine late at night.

Trumbauer and Miss Unamuno stared across the panorama, faces blank. Without their guides they were almost defenseless. Their range was shortened, their acuity lessened. Yet they had volunteered to come up on the mountain, facing perhaps a greater danger than any of them. They were like lightning rods, highly visible in the psychic landscape.

The white-coated technicians around the PBW called out equipment checks. The lights strung on poles around the perimeter dimmed, brightened, and then were shut off on order of a distant, authoritative voice. Four men on the edge of the plateau examined the sky with binoculars and equipment Jacobs didn't recognize.

"Levels are up," one called back.

"Let's set it for a sixty-by-twenty sweep for ten seconds," said a technician standing by the PBW's control panel, a box mounted on the side of the trailer. "Broad-range penetration and light scattering effects. We want to punch three clear holes and let them snake around to stir it up, then go for the final solution."

The wind was rising. Burnford held his hand out to Miss Unamuno. "I don't need comforting," she said stiffly.

"I think I do," the physicist said. "Some of my friends are out there. I knew three of the researchers in Haverstock."

Jacobs wondered if Thesiger and the boy were out there,

too. He hoped not. Thesiger should have had the expertise to guide them clear.

The lights in the town went out.

"It's in range," someone called.

"We have full storage."

"Levels higher."

Jacobs could see the horizon stars wobbling, twinkling. New stars seemed to be added, then vanished.

"All sensors in the town are down."

"The front is approaching. Slope and plateau sensors show high activity."

In the center of town, a tiny green glow moved from building to building. More appeared, dancing like will-o'-the-wisps, or like lanterns carried by a crowd. In their wake, red glows flared into fires. Circles of black smoke whirled above the fires. It was a calm, subdued display, almost dignified. The fires grew, leaping in fingers from building to building. The sky above glistened with an oily purple sheen, as if a jellyfish had settled over them.

Trumbauer groaned. "It's bigger," he said. "The edges are dissolving, but the center is more powerful than ever."

Purple smoke began to pour from the center of town, snaking down the streets, rolling over the rooftops in viscous waves. The smell of burning flesh reached the plateau.

The wind whipped their coats and pants.

"Clear some tunnels," a technician yelled.

The generators screamed and the PBW trailer bounced furiously. The mounting was as steady as rock, however. The ponderous barrel rotated slowly, then stopped.

The lights in the town came back on. The green glows vanished and the fires winked out. Jacobs squinted to see what was happening.

"Hold the sequence," Machen shouted. The air was clear and the wind had stopped. Trumbauer and Miss Unamuno whispered to each other, then turned to Jacobs.

"They haven't done anything yet, have they?" Miss Unamuno asked. Jacobs looked to Machen, who shook his head. "It seems to be gone," Trumbauer said. "We can't sense anything."

"Shit," Machen said. "It can't just go away like *that*." He snapped his fingers. "Can it?"

"Why not?" Jacobs said. "It may have moved in some fashion we don't know about. Maybe it sensed a trap."

"How can we be sure?"

Trumbauer shrugged his shoulders. "Is your equipment in the town working?"

Machen consulted with a technician. "It's still out," he said. "God damn, we've missed it!"

"Not necessarily," Trumbauer said. "Franklin, to be sure, I'll have to go into the town."

Jacobs made no move to show a sign of either agreement or disagreement. The thought terrified him.

"I can't go," Miss Unamuno said.

"Franklin?" Trumbauer looked at him pleadingly.

"I'll have two soldiers go with you," Machen said.

"Fine, but . . . Franklin, I'll need someone I know, someone strong. To do what Thesiger did for the boy, if we're caught. Both of us. Together."

Franklin nodded. All feeling had left his hands and feet.

Machen called for two soldiers and a Jeep. The vehicle rolled up behind them and a white-coated technician got out, making way for a man and a woman in kelly green. They took the front two seats, placing a walkie-talkie between them. Trumbauer gripped Franklin's shoulder. They climbed in behind.

"Where will you need to go?" Machen asked.

"Into the town, into the center," Trumbauer said.

"Take them there," Machen said. "I want a steady report."

"Yessir," the woman said. She put the Jeep in gear and

backed it up, then turned it around and drove onto the fire trail. They bounced in and out of the heavy trailer ruts, the Jeep's lights bobbing against rocks and grass and tree trunks.

"My name's Sally," the woman said. "This is Nathan." The man nodded. "Any idea what we can expect down there?"

"No, regrettably," Trumbauer said. The fire trail joined a paved road and they drove toward the brightly lighted outskirts of Siloam Springs. Jacobs looked at the woman's short-cut hair, bunched up under the green cap. She was stocky, with large eyes and a touch of down on her upper lip. She wore glasses. Nathan was thin and tall and quiet, keeping his attention on the town. He carried an automatic rifle.

The Jeep crossed over railroad tracks and between rows of warehouses—much like the ones in Lorobu, Jacobs thought. A colonnade of silos and a grain elevator were topped by red aircraft warning lights on their left. The lights blinked in the steady night air. "How much farther, sir?" the woman asked.

"To the center—there was a post office, I think," Trumbauer said.

"Anything yet?" Jacobs asked. He shook his head.

A row of houses showed signs of the fires they had seen from the plateau. Smoke stains blackened the upper frames of windows and doors. Trumbauer frowned, then told the woman to halt the Jeep.

They were on a tree-lined street between two small stretches of park. A brick library stood just behind them, frosted-glass pole lamps flanking two concrete lions on the steps. Jacobs pulled his jacket up closer around his neck.

"Party One to Silent Night. We're in Nielsen Park," the man reported on the walkie-talkie. "Nothing sighted yet. Out."

"Sally, stop by that house with the towers, on the right," Trumbauer said. He looked at Jacobs. "I'm beginning to hear something. It sounds like people walking."

"I don't hear anything," Jacobs said. Trumbauer smiled at him, cocking his head. The Jeep stopped smoothly and the woman turned to look at them.

"What is it?"

"I'm not sure," Trumbauer said. "But tell the General I don't believe the town is empty. I think we're the ones being tricked, as it were—"

His head jerked back and he nearly fell out of his seat. Jacobs grabbed for him and pulled him back. "Arnie!"

"Tell Machen!" Trumbauer shouted, swiping at his hair. "Franklin, am I on fire? Help me put—"

"You're fine, there's nothing in your hair," Jacobs said. But Trumbauer slumped against his shoulder, eyes drawn up until only the whites showed. Saliva dribbled from one corner of his mouth. "Arnold, come on . . ." Jacobs shook him until his head lolled back. Trumbauer blinked once.

"I'm closing up, Franklin. I can't take it." He went limp and curled into a fetal ball.

Nathan had finished reporting their situation to Machen. "What's happening?" he asked Jacobs. The soldier's eyes were narrow, as if he was prepared to flinch from a blow.

"Get us out of here. Do they know up on the hill?"

"They know," Sally said, spinning the Jeep around. Jacobs held on to Trumbauer and tried to keep his head down.

The glass globes on the library lamps exploded. The library windows blew out and flames shot through them, making nearby trees flare like matches. The Jeep careened to avoid a car burning furiously by the roadside.

"Jesus!" Nathan shouted, covering his face. A funnel of green and purple was forming over the center of Siloam

Springs. It was oddly dimpled and glowed as if a neon light had been turned on in its middle. It descended.

Jacobs felt his ears pop. All around, buildings were shivering, throwing off shingles and bits of timber. Bricks fell ahead of them and Sally expertly swerved.

The funnel's base spread out into a viscous purple mass, pouring outward like a wave. Jacobs glanced back, then turned away—

As the sudden glare baked his neck. Like a distant reflection, across thousands of miles and more than three decades, the sky over Siloam Springs became bright as day. Sally looked in the rear-view mirror and was dazzled. Around the street, all the buildings flared and caved in. Jacobs' white jacket reflected the heat, but Trumbauer was wearing black and his jacket caught on fire. Jacobs tried to slap it out as the Jeep twisted back and forth on the road. It keeled over, was caught in a blast of hot air, and flipped up over them, spilling them onto the street. It flew off like a leaf in wind. Jacobs held on to Trumbauer as they were pushed over the asphalt, which heaved and cracked behind them.

He lay on his stomach, hand still clutching his friend's smoking coat. He looked up and saw a wall of dense smoke, occasionally pierced by the glare of fires.

Then he saw them. Coming through the smoke, rising up from the road like two-dimensional figures in a shooting gallery, assuming three-dimensional form, stumbling, crawling, lurching, their skin like black wool, falling away, their eyes empty. Sexless, ageless, equalized. Baked plasma dripping clear from their skin. They marched, and behind them the road steamed.

Jacobs tried to stand, fell to his knee, then tried again and pulled Trumbauer on to his shoulder. Nathan and Sally were nowhere to be seen, but in the chaos he could hear the sound of automatic weapon fire. Carrying Trumbauer,

Jacobs pushed between the smoky, hazy figures, smelling them, hearing them chant. His neck itched distantly. There were blisters on the back of his hands. Trumbauer was like a rag.

Circles of green hands and faces spun in the smoke.

The ground split and Jacobs leaped across. From the crack, a bloody horse tried to rise, but there was no order in its bones. Its rider was spread across its back like butter.

A broken fire hydrant spewed water across the road, and, insanely, bodies floated in the river, bobbing, swollen, anonymous faces upturned, black hands beseeching.

Jacobs tried to run but Trumbauer weighed too much. He sloshed across the shallow stream of hydrant water.

And then, ahead, he saw a figure in khaki, waving them on. Squinting against the smoke, Jacobs followed. The silos and elevator were mangled skeletons of steel. The road beyond was intact. Unburned grass grew between the railroad tracks. The purple smoke was thinning.

He looked up, rubbed his eyes with one hand, and saw the hill, the lights circling the weapon, tiny figures running. He saw the barrel lift. Nothing seemed to issue from its tip, but streamers of violet radiated outward from the plateau. For an instant, the streamers were steady like searchlight beams. Then they began to bend and twist into helices. Lightning flared over Siloam Springs, playing through the clouds of smoke, some of the bolts bending back upon themselves in mid-air. The purpleness at the center of the town seethed and bubbled. Jacobs was reminded of the blebs in a living cell about to divide.

The air filled with a metallic buzz. From loudspeakers on the hill he heard a tinny shout, "Penetration!" The violet beams dissipated. An amber glow rippled like a circular blanket above the town. Pseudopods of blood red writhed on its edges. One arm extended toward the hill, dimming as it passed outside the influence of the beams. Then it fell back.

On the hill, men were dancing, on fire, like clowns in hell.

"Solution!" the loudspeakers rang.

The noise was sub-sonic. It reverberated through Jacobs' body, making him feel like a bell.

Miss Unamuno helped hand out the fire extinguishers and personally foamed down two technicians. She glanced wild-eyed at the weapon. The doughnuts stacked behind the barrel crackled and snapped.

The spikes on the bulbous midriff leaned forward.

And one by one, the generators shorted and caught fire. One tore loose from its mount and pin-wheeled across the ground, breaking through the ribbon perimeter and gouging a furrow in the dirt before coming to a smoking rest.

Above Siloam Springs, the night returned.

Burnford stopped groaning and lay still on the ground. He sat up and wiped tears from his eyes, feeling his face with his fingers. Miss Unamuno stood behind him, sighing with a shudder.

The second shock-wave—if that was what it was—hit without warning. Trumbauer was lifted from Jacobs' back and he felt himself falling dreamily to the ground. His head was filled with faces, some horribly disfigured, others whole, beseeching . . . and fading.

The screams lingered, but only Miss Unamuno heard them, and heard them fade, too.

It was over. Men swarmed across the generators, spraying them with water and foam. Steam hissed into the air. General Machen got to his feet unsteadily.

"They're gone," Miss Unamuno said.

"Where?" Burnford asked.

"No trace. I could feel it—and so could they. The end of all things, all perceiving."

From the edge of the plateau, one of the four technicians who had caught fire, his robe blackened and hair singed but otherwise unhurt, called out, "Solution! All sensors nominal!"

Jacobs found Trumbauer still alive, not even badly injured. He picked him up in his arms. Footsteps came up behind him. It was Sally, clutching the walkie-talkie, her eyes almost swollen shut. A few yards to one side, Nathan limped across a field.

Jacobs turned back to Siloam Springs. The air was black except for the light of scattered fires. He looked down on Trumbauer, still unconscious but breathing easier.

"Now we have the power," Jacobs whispered.

CHAPTER FIFTY-NINE

MILLICENT JACOBS BROUGHT HER HUSBAND'S BREAKFAST TO
the small house behind the garden. He was sitting by the
typewriter, biting his thumbnail. She set the tray down on
top of a bookcase, balancing it precariously. Every other
surface was covered with books and papers.

"How's it going?" she asked.

"You don't want to know."

"Trouble?"

"I can't write. It's too cold out here."

"I think it's fine."

"Yes, well, every time you open the door it gets too
cold."

"This is the first time I've been here since you started
this morning," she said patiently.

Jacobs sighed and backed his chair away from the typewriter. "I can't write anything to publish because I can't
say anything important. They won't let me."

"My husband, the man of mystery."

"I could get put in jail if I even told you."

"I'm not sure I want to be told, anyway," Millicent
said, looking blankly at the dusty window across the room.

She had never known her husband so deeply upset, irritated, jumpy.

"No, maybe not. But I have to write it down, even if nobody reads it. I wrote the President a letter, but I wonder. . . . It's very crackpot stuff, you know. I've tried talking to others. They won't listen to me. That scientist, Burnford, he's moved away and I don't know where. Prohaska isn't working for his station any more. They say he's on extended leave, writing a book about logging."

Millicent put her hand on his shoulder. "Arnold listens," she said.

"He knows what happened as well as I. I don't need to tell him."

"Then . . . tell me. If it's so important, tell me."

"I can't," he said, staring at the typewriter. As soon as she had come in he had put a piece of cardboard over the page, obscuring what he was writing. "I can't tell anybody, and it's eating me alive."

Millicent's face hardened. "What does this have to do with patriotism? What do they—"

"Listen," Jacobs said softly, "I'll eat breakfast. Then I'll write what I have to write. But you can't be here."

"All right," Millicent said, trying to sound neutral. "Perhaps later we can go to a movie."

"Yes."

She left and closed the door behind her.

"No more movies," Jacobs said quietly. He took his hand away from the page. "Dear Mr. President," he read silently, lips mouthing the words to feel their sound and sense. This was the fourth draft.

"Dear Mr. President. Thirty years ago—more than thirty—" He scratched out the sentence. "At the end of the Second World War, we used a weapon of awesome power in an attempt to save human lives. We have lived under the shadow of even stronger weapons ever since . . ."

He shook his head and scratched out the passage, then ripped the paper from the machine.

"Dear Mr. President," he began again. "Once more, we have used the power of science to end a struggle and try to save human lives . . ."

Again he ripped the paper from the typewriter. It had to be succinct and clear. That was why he was afraid nobody would listen—expressed clearly, it was outrageous. He could hardly believe it himself. He pounded one fist on the edge of the machine, making it rattle. To hell with who read it and who didn't.

"We have been given the keys to our cage," he wrote, "one by one, across tens of thousands of years. A key to the bars of cold and raw meat; a key to open the doors of understanding—thousands of keys for that, and more doors still to be opened. You, Lord, have given us more and more freedom—freedom over procreation, freedom from many diseases, freedom from dark and some old fears, as if You thought we were growing up, getting more mature. Each time we had a new key, we thought it was the last door, the final conquest—freedom, now, to shape our bodies and those of our children, to leave the Earth, freedom even to choose whether or not we should live or die. But there always seemed a barrier to truly botching everything, a final safeguard—I know I felt secure thinking that. Thinking there was a final protection, that beyond death we might have more chances, more trials. It seemed an indestructible guarantee. You would always hold that finality back from us."

He paused, fingers barely tapping the keys.

"Thank You, Lord, for believing we have grown up." He read over what he had written and shook his head. "Thank You for giving us this final key. You must think we are ready for it, terribly mature, terribly ready to accept all responsibility. Thank You for giving us the final powers of a god. For that final freedom to choose."

It must be the curse of the totally free, he thought, that they would never sleep soundly, never close their eyes without deep and abiding fear.

How long had it been since Arnold had told him, two days? Arnold had felt the little whirlwinds; out in the desert, in Nevada and Arizona, they were testing that terrible machine, first on animals. The wounded and desiccated souls of goats, sheep, dogs, baboons. The strange, metallic-tasting particle-scatter of total death. Arnold had felt it happening.

Soon enough, it would spread.